The Animals After Midnight

Books by Jeff Johnson

Lucky Supreme: A Darby Holland Crime Novel (#1) (2017)
A Long Crazy Burn: A Darby Holland Crime Novel (#2)
(2017)
Dead Bomb Bingo Ray: A Novel (2017)
Knottspeed: A Love Story (2017)
Everything Under the Moon: A Novel (2016)
Tattoo Machine: Tall Tales, True Stories, and My Life in
Ink (2010)

THE ANIMALS AFTER MIDNIGHT

A DARBY HOLLAND CRIME NOVEL
#3

JEFF JOHNSON

Arcade Publishing • New York

Arcade Publishing books may be purchased in bulk at special discounts for sales promotion, corporate gifts, fund-raising, or educational purposes. Special editions can also be created to specifications. For details, contact the Special Sales Department, Arcade Publishing, 307 West 36th Street, 11th Floor, New York, NY 10018 or arcade@skyhorsepublishing.com.

Arcade Publishing® is a registered trademark of Skyhorse Publishing, Inc.®, a Delaware corporation.

Visit our website at www.arcadepub.com.

10 9 8 7 6 5 4 3 2 1

Library of Congress Cataloging-in-Publication Data is available on file.

Cover design by Gigi Little
Cover photo credit: Morguefile

Print ISBN: 978-162872-975-7
Ebook ISBN: 978-162872-979-5

Printed in the United States of America

The Animals After Midnight

The night the frenzy under the surface reached a rolling boil, I could see my breath in the neon spilling from the windows. The steam made the glow pretty in a sulfurous way. Something had come to town, and I could feel it in the tremors of the wet sidewalk and hear it in the hiss of tires, feel it watching from the orange halos of all the electric lights.

Around 3:00 a.m., after the bars close and Portland's Old Town powers down, that was when I could sense it most. Change. The bad kind. The spirit of the city was a hobo's garden, almost gone every second it was there, and Ming's Shoe and Boot Repair was a holdout in the middle of it all, a relic like myself, too stubborn to move and too blind to understand it should change, so not long for a new world that kept getting newer. The old neon boot icon was set to slow blink and so was I. It was Wednesday. No matter how hard I tried, I wound up drinking in the alcove in front of it two or three times a week. Recently, more often.

A giant figure stepped out of the rain and loomed over me. Television huge. Dark blue suit. Expensive hair and spendy shoes. The dead eyes of a professional beating machine. He didn't frown in disappointment or smile in wry disgust. I was a creature from days past; bomber jacket and jeans, combat boots, plastic bottle of vodka, lounging in a doorway. Part of the old Old Town, and he looked at me the way you look at apes in the zoo, expectantly, waiting for me to freak out or do something funny. When I didn't do anything, he held out the greasy paper bag he was carrying.

"What is that?" I asked.

"Teriyaki doll head for all you care," Santiago growled. He knelt next to me, but he didn't sit. The Mexican Conan was too dapper to touch the tiles. I passed him the vodka and he took a little nip, blew out the fumes, and his face finally wrinkled in disgust. "You own a bar full of top-shelf booze and you drink discount snake juice."

I took the sandwich he'd brought out of the bag and started in on it. Pulled pork, balsamic arugula, pine nuts, and Turkish fig aioli. It was from the appetizer menu at Alcott Frond, the bistro that had risen from the cadaver of "mitri's izza."

"I was thinking about Yellowstone," I managed, my mouth full.

"You were?" Santiago considered, then took another nip of vodka. He set the bottle down next to me and dusted his hands. "Never been there. Went to the Tetons once."

"Yeah?" I crammed the second half of the sandwich in my mouth, chewed a few times, and swallowed. "Good times?"

"Went with a woman."

We watched a car go by. I wiped my hands on my pants. Santiago took his cigarettes out and offered me one. I accepted. We fired them up and smoked, and he seemed to admire the view. There was a trash can right across from us, beyond that a new cubist Lego Modern apartment hive.

"Good turnout tonight," Santiago commented after a little while. He knew I didn't care, and I knew he was going to tell me anyway. Our relationship was unlike any I'd ever had before. Santiago Espinoza had been an ex-con working for a real estate developer when I first met him. For a variety of reasons, I'd drugged his boss and sent him off to die in Russia after I ripped him off. Then, after beating the shit out of him, largely by cheating in that fight, I offered Santiago a job. His dream job, as it turned out. He'd prospered wildly in the last year and for some reason he still felt I was responsible for it, even though he'd done all the hard work himself. I'd told him the truth, time and time again, that I'd needed him just like his last boss, that he was doing me the favor and not the other way around, but Santiago never bought it. That's why he brought me sandwiches at 3:00 a.m.

"Kid puked in front of the Lucky," I said. The Lucky Supreme, my tattoo shop. "Flaco hit it with some Windex. Rain got the rest." Flaco, from the taco kiosk next to the shop, was not a world class problem-solver.

"Need a ride?" Santiago straightened his suit coat.

"Nah. Catch a cab over on Burnside. I'm not done hanging out yet."

Half an hour later, I got up and shook out the cold, tossed my empty in a garbage can, and headed for a cab, sticking to the awnings and getting wet anyway. Store decorations were pumpkin heavy, with a multicolored Indian corn sprinkled in the mix. I stopped and looked through the dark window of an overpriced café and stared at an ear of it. The Cadillac of corn.

On Burnside, I stood on the corner down from Voodoo Donut, a purely bizarre place the new version of the city couldn't kill, and got scooped up by one of the cabs that circled it at all hours. The driver was a white kid. Portland is a white, white city. He sported a stylish blend of heavy metal and new hippie. Guy was a talker, too. I gave him my address.

"Just off work? You a bartender?" He seemed a tiny bit excited. Strong coffee or a slow night.

"Nah."

"Partying?"

"Kinda trapped in a never-ending party, so no. Not really."

"Huh." He glanced in the rearview. "You from here? Swear I know you from somewhere."

A year ago my face had been all over the papers. Massive federal manhunt after a bomb went off downtown and blew the shit out of most of a city block. I hid out in a bartender's house, eating sardines and stale cake while I recovered from a near-death beating that left me in a dumpster and resulted in the cool-guy scar on my face.

"I get around."

"Me too." The kid shook his head at the grooviness of it all. "Life behind the wheel, man. You all set for Halloween?"

"Need to get some decorations for the house. Maybe

some of that corn I keep seeing. My chick is in Seattle, so I might drive all the way the fuck up there again. Dunno. The whole party thing just pisses me off anymore."

"Always the strip clubs, baby. This is Portland. One on every corner."

"Dude. Do not get me started."

"So lemme get this." He glanced in the rearview again. "Dicey long-distance woman scenario, not interested in parties and the club scene. Cruising Old Town at what, like, four in the morning?" He snapped his fingers. "You're a Method actor!"

I laughed. "Busted."

"Checkmate." He giggled. "It's like I have telepathy."

I tipped him an extra few bucks when we pulled up in front of my place, and after he jetted away down my tree-lined street, I stood in the rain and stared at my house, testing the feel of it. It was an old Victorian duplex with me on the first floor, a big porch, and the Oregon standard rhododendrons on either side of the stairs. Dark windows.

Haunted.

The place had taken on a different kind of vibe in the last month or so. It wasn't that my girlfriend, Suzanne, had taken a job in Seattle and moved out of the daily picture, leaving a void where her soft morning singing and moods bright and terrible had been. It wasn't the change in the weather, having the sky turn into a featureless gray cave roof. It wasn't that I was dragging the ghost of change and judgment out of the bones of Old Town every night. It wasn't even a combination of all that. There was something new and wrong about my house, like radiation, there but invisible, and looking at the dark shape of it made me want to go back to the shoe and boot alcove.

"Hello," I said to nothing.

It was impossible to prove, too. As I went up the stairs and fished the keys out of my pocket, I mentally drifted over the faces of all the people I'd pissed off in my month-long bout of paranoia. Pretty much everyone. I silently unlocked the door and slowly, slowly opened it.

Dark. Warm. Quiet. It smelled like Dollar Store furniture polish, coffee, and books. No broken windows or I would feel the difference in the air. I reached in and turned on the light. Chops and Buttons, my two cats, were asleep on the couch. They woke up and blinked at me. Chops yawned before he closed his eyes again. Nothing from Buttons.

I locked the door behind me and took off my wet jacket and boots, left them by the door. As I went through the place I turned on the lights. Dining room with a big table, where for years I never sat, then ate at morning and night with Suzanne, then stopped using again after she left. Kitchen. Very tidy, almost like no one ever cooked there anymore. A bathroom off to one side that smelled like masculine Dial antimicrobial soap and wet towel instead of ten kinds of tall woman. And the bedroom, lavish in an old antique way, filled with furniture I'd finally gotten around to restoring courtesy of Suzanne's subtle scorn. It was a bedroom that belonged in a showroom, or the bedroom of a guy who slept on the couch in his wet clothes.

Empty. No phantoms, cops, women, killers, art dealers,

rivals, former employees, drug dealers, feds, or girlfriends. I went back into the kitchen and poured myself a nightcap and carried it out to the couch, turning all lights off as I went. Sitting in the dark made me feel grounded. If there was a presence in my house, it put us on the same creepy playing field. I eventually lit a cigarette and sipped the absurdly expensive scotch I'd transitioned to and listened to the familiar soundtrack of "old house at night." When the glass was finally empty, I turned on my cell phone. Sixteen missed calls since I left the shop, at precise thirty-minute intervals, all from Delia.

Delia was the largest of my current problems. Certainly the most colorful. Definitely the loudest. My sidekick, my most trusted confidant, my best employee, was leaving Portland. Leaving the Lucky and the glory of Old Town. She was emerging as an artist of merit in other mediums and haring off to Austin. Before she left, she was dead set on marrying the idiot douchebag she'd been supporting for the last year, the semi-cretin lead spaz of the punk band Empire of Shit, the infamous Hank Dildo.

The marriage part of her transformation was beyond implausible. Delia was a genius. She was the best artist I'd ever worked with, hands down, but it was more than that. What was hard for the rest of us, she stepped over effortlessly. Delia was a tiny, titless, mouthy fireball and in every way that counted she was the biggest woman I'd ever known. It was terrible of me, and my troublesome girlfriend, Suzanne, would laugh bitterly if I said it out loud, but it seemed irresponsible for someone with so much going for her to marry a musician. Especially one like Hank.

Hank, for instance, liked spray paint. As a refreshing intoxicant. I thought it was all for show in the beginning, the kind of facade one would expect from the front man of a mad punk band like Empire of Shit, but now I suspected otherwise. Hank liked other drugs in a generalized way, but thankfully punk music on his level didn't net the kind of funds required to become a proper junkie. Not yet. Probably. Hank didn't strike me as especially clean, either. He most definitely wasn't a romantic. But the worst part was that the bastard was so charming I was having trouble hating him. He lit up the room, like Jude Law's bipolar little brother.

Delia. Suzanne. The creamy transformation of the City of Roses. I missed all kinds of things that weren't quite gone yet. I got up and drifted silently back into the kitchen, sloshed a little more scotch in my glass. Then I looked out the window at the neighbor's backyard. There was a forlorn old Big Wheel, upside-down and worn and broken, just visible in the dim light from their back porch bulb. The grass was dead, and staring out at the Big Wheel a few nights ago had given me an idea. The tracks around the thing, specifically. I set my drink down on the counter and went silently to the front window, peeked out at the street. All quiet. No new cars, no pedestrians, steady rain. I opened the front door just wide enough to slip through and went out low and fast.

Willing myself to be a half-drunk shadow, I vaulted the porch railing and dropped barefoot into the wet yard on the side of the house, then stole toward the backyard. At the edge of the house, I cautiously peered around the side.

Empty. The back of my shirt was soaked and the wind hit me as I rounded the corner and slunk up to my bedroom window. I'd pulled all the grass out below it in a frenzy a few nights ago. The bare spot was roughly the size of a welcome mat. It was too dark to see clearly, so I dug my phone out and flipped it open, turned the tiny blue screen toward the patch of wet earth.

Boot prints. The rest of my warmth gusted out of my rib cage.

Someone had been looking through my bedroom window, and from the freshness of the prints, they'd been there moments ago, when I'd turned on the bedroom light and stood there, staring at Suzanne's pillow.

My phantom was real.

Everything about the new and improved Lucky Supreme, that pinnacle of neon whorls and gold leaf, old-fashioned barber chairs with polished chrome and speckled star field vinyl upholstery, the refurbished '50s jukebox with bubbly lights and Cash Only, it was all my idea. My doing. I was rich, after all, and we'd been rebuilding from scratch. There was some resistance at first. Delia had nitpicked and micromanaged everything, at every step, attempting to distort my vision through willpower, tantrums, and cold, bony shoulders, and some of her had ultimately crept into the place. But in the end, the blame for transforming a venerable tattoo shop in Old Town into a swank bordello tangled with a phony yuppie stereotype was my bad.

I surveyed the assembled crew with a stern expression. I have a big scar on my face, so my stern is positively gnarly. Nine thirty a.m., Code Omega Red, emergency meeting. I was in no way trying to inspire confidence, which was what I usually had to do. This time I was sharing an unhealthy dose of terror. What I had before me in the dark tattoo shop was not promising.

"I think I speak for all of us," Delia began, stepping forward. Behind her, the three guys frantically made "no, no" gestures. Delia was wearing an ancient Burger King kid's tee and fire-engine-red overalls. "Now, I don't know the Webster's Dictionary definition of anything, not by heart, but 'fruitcake' means so many things that resonate with—"

"Dude, it wasn't the bathroom window, right?" Chase interrupted. Chase was new. He had replaced my trusty former employee, Nigel. The period of time it had taken to transform the Lucky from a burned-out husk into the stale, soulless farce we stood in had given poor Nigel just enough time to get into the kind of trouble he couldn't get back out of. A few weeks before the grand reopening, the two feds who'd been dogging me for three years busted him for moving gun parts, pills, and more, and the upshot was that he'd be cooling his jets inside until 2029. We sent letters and cookies, and I did a little more on the side. Chase Manhattan, who had perhaps the dumbest tattoo handle of all time, was also an old pal of mine. I trusted him to a point, and that's rare enough. "I mean, you did check outside the bathroom, right? Darby?" Then he looked pained and shut up.

The other two guys, Stewart Something-Or-Other and Billy or Danny Who-Cares, didn't say anything. I made them nervous quite easily, especially when I was trying to.

"Let me try this one more time," I said evenly. I detached from the counter and started pacing. "Now, who here doubts I'm paranoid?" I stopped and stared. It was a confusing question, designed to shut them down. Delia bravely raised her hand and drew a breath to deny doing so. I stopped her with a glare. Chase shrugged, rolling with the moment, a very lost surfer. The two new guys looked at Delia, began to raise their hands in complicity, then stopped, then started again, clearly agonizing. "This isn't a trick question." They raised their hands.

"Or is it?" Delia simpered. Both guys lowered their hands and clasped them behind their backs, looked down. I rolled my eyes.

"Now, as a super-paranoid motherfucker, I notice all kinds of shit most people wouldn't. Sometimes it makes no sense. This time it does. Someone is stalking me. For a month now, maybe longer. This is now an established fact. But why the fuck would I tell you guys? That's what you're asking yourself, right?"

Delia sneered at me. Chase had no reaction at all, just looked on, smiling, waiting for me to get to the point. The new guys both looked surprised, as if this had just occurred to them.

"I'm telling you this because I expect you to behave like someone is following *you*."

"Ah!" Chase's face lit up, like the idea was exciting, then darkened. "The feds again? Ones who got Nigel?"

"Nope." I began pacing. "Feds don't stare through your bedroom window at night. I mean, they do, but by then you know what they're up to. This is different."

"Why would your—stalker, I guess—why would he follow any of us?" Chase scrubbed his short blond hair, his tell for confusion. He did that a lot.

"I don't know," I confessed. "But if you start thinking that way, you'll begin to notice details you might normally miss."

Delia couldn't hold it. "That has to be the—"

"If," I interrupted, "and this is one of the worst-case scenarios, because there are many, but if—"

"Enough!" Delia took my arm and started pulling at me, headed into the back.

"I was just about to—"

"Chase, get the boys some coffee!" Then she lowered her voice. "You were just about to make everyone quit? Is that what you were about to do? You idiot."

I stopped talking and let her pull me into the employee lounge. It too had changed, from a rest stop with Salvation Army couches and a battered desk I called my office into the best IKEA had in upscale whorehouse. She closed the door behind us and pointed at one of the plush imitation suede sofas. I sat. She stood in front of me, arms folded, tiny booted feet planted wide, and while her fury mounted I mutely looked at the walls. I'd gone with an off white, which contrasted nicely with the collection of horror B movie posters Delia snuck in. It was like we were in a museum, maybe in Barstow or Bakersfield, someplace too crappy to afford a real one, but ashamed enough to spring for fresh paint and matching picture frames.

"Darby," she said softly, the gentleness of it startling me, "what the hell, man?"

I rubbed my face. "This last month . . ." I trailed off.

"Has been a bummer. I know. You've gone from fearless leader to absentee owner. Your spark is gone." She sat down next to me and patted my knee. "Hard thing, knowing you're a sack of shit. Being called out on it. How you feel now?"

"Delia. If you could just close your mouth. Your breath smells like kale—"

"Don't you tell me what to do," she hissed. Delia quit drinking when she announced her new career plans, no doubt to help her more serious drinker of a fiancé, and now she went to yoga and drank blueberry smoothies. Sharper than ever and way, way meaner. I held up one hand in surrender and closed my eyes. She took an even breath.

"I believe you," she said calmly. "I believe everything you said. Of course I do. But listen to me, sweetheart. A year ago . . ." She stopped and I opened my eyes and looked at her. She was staring at the ceiling.

"A year ago, I was doing the daily grind," I finished for her. "Tattooing five or six days a week, fuckin' with the radiator or fixing the toilet the rest of the time. Dialed in. Battened down. Sewed up."

"Right." She leaned in close to me, a prelude to saying the really bad stuff. "And then your world changed and you changed with it. A crazy Korean gangster tried to kill you." Her voice grew quiet. "You came out of that sadder. With money, too." She reached out and curled her hand over mine. I realized how dirty I was. "Then the fucking developer blew up the shop and our lives with it. You, ah—" She still had trouble saying it out loud. "You became a l-landlord. You own half the street. You own your own bistro, for chrissake." She was whispering now. "So tell me why this is freaking you out so bad. You're the king of landing standing." She put her head on my shoulder. "It's like with nothing gnarly to do, you've turned into a pussy."

I patted the side of her head and got up and went to the

14

new file cabinet, opened the bottom drawer and got out the emergency whiskey. It was expensive enough to merit a cork, which I pulled out with my teeth. Delia frowned while I looked around for a coffee cup. In the end I took a swig straight from the bottle.

"True." I wiped my mouth. "I've even taken to the cooking shows. In the afternoon."

"Those dudes out there don't need to know anything," she said, folding her arms again. "They don't need to know that your success in life disgusts you because of how it happened. They don't need to know about your professor-bimbo-sports-bra issue, I mean girl trouble. They don't need to know about Emeril, either." She leaned back. "Body count is super high, dude. We're lucky to have anyone here at all. Mikey jumps to become a school janitor with dental and a 401(k)? Nige in the pokey? I'm sure they think my leaving isn't so much a career change as the latest rat to jump ship. We've had so many new guys I can't even remember their names anymore."

"You had a better memory when you weren't so—like you are now."

"Maybe so."

"But I am being followed." I took another sip. "Spied on. Fucked with. It isn't my imagination."

"So you're not crazy yet. Good for you." She sat up. "Think it's one of the strippers?"

Part of getting rid of the Russian real estate developer and stealing his main henchman entailed making a deal with the Armenian. He owned a business triplex that had been critically mismanaged, and that became a joint problem as part of our deal, then quickly just my problem. Now it had a laundromat with a Vegas theme, a strip club, and a convenience store. The strip club was partly mine and was run by my business manager, Santiago. Even he didn't like it. I shook my head.

"If it was a stripper she had a size 12 men's boot and a couple hundred pounds on top of it. How likely is that?"

Delia thought. I lit a cigarette. Finally, she frowned. "That isn't much. You say you've been feeling eyes on you for about a month?"

"Round about, yeah." I watched the smoke rise. "I guess I was bummed about Suzanne leaving and—I dunno. Once she was gone, I spent more and more time wandering around. Stupid, I guess, but it seems like maybe I kept seeing the same face in a crowd without really nailing anyone, just—more like a feeling. I dunno. It was after she left and I started to ramble that I began to feel like I was being watched. Like maybe I'd drawn someone out into the open when I changed my routine." I reached up and rubbed the scar on my face. "So it might have been longer. Someone could have been looking through my bedroom window at night for months."

"Jesus. How fucked up." She made a pained face. "What made you think of the mud trick?"

"Probably goes back to something I read in a comic book, but the idea came to me when I was looking at the junk in my neighbor's backyard." I sat down next to her again. "Now my brain is on auto replay. Did I smell men's cologne drifting around on the porch the other night? Has someone actually been in my house, while I was out wandering around? How many times? Did they look at my sketchbooks? The sentimental junk I keep around?"

"You feel violated."

We thought. Or at least Delia did. She no doubt considered several things all at once, then stacked variables and cross-indexed them in complex architectures I could only dream of. I thought she smelled like Play-Doh and yogurt, and contented myself with that.

"What now?" she asked eventually.

"Pancakes," I replied. "You hungry?"

"Nah. Guts are bubbly. Kombucha."

Then we watched each other, a little too much like two old gunfighters for my taste.

"I'll still call you every day," she said finally. "They have cell phone reception in Austin."

"I'll still answer every fuckin' time, too. Not like recently." I put my smoke out and rose. "Even if you turn into an arrogant little art snob, which is incidentally happening right before my eyes. Art is just like syphilis, I guess, in that in the final stage, when it consumes the mind above the rod or the beave, or"—I wiggled my fingers at her—"clam in this case, and results in a wicked crazy Republican."

Delia kissed the tip of her middle finger and blew it at me. "Leave by the back door. I'll put the word out to the remaining street life and tell Flaco. Darby Holland has a new ghost."

An hour later I was on one of Portland's cute new trolley cars, rolling over the Broadway Bridge for a second time. As we passed Union Station, I wondered in a flash what would happen if I went down there and hopped a train. Just walked into the switch yards and scrambled into a vacant boxcar headed wherever it was headed. My boots were in good shape. My bomber jacket had a big hole in one pocket, but it would keep me warm enough if I stayed out of the wind. My ATM card linked to a bank account with an unknown amount of money in it. It seemed to fluctuate—Santiago's doing—and even he had to check his computer to find out the running total. The number was stupid big. Greedy wrong. I could get off in the first city and throw my wallet away. Throw my phone away. Change my name to Dan Smathers and push a mop, get a little single-wide out in the sticks. Raise chickens and dream. Watch TV. Celebrate Christmas once a year. Find a bland woman and knock her up. Lie about my scar and say I got all the tattoos from my neighbor when I was a dishwasher in San Diego. I'd be free of all this shit, and my sketchy little empire could careen along on autopilot until the next big fire, and I wouldn't give half a shit, because I'd just be a guy with no plan at all except tomorrow. Because the cosmos has so much in common with the hammer part of a piano, that's right when my girlfriend Suzanne called.

"Suze."

"Tried to call you last night." She sounded distracted. Multitasking again. I could hear the chatter of fast fingers on a keyboard.

"Eh, well."

"Where are you?" *Clack.* The send button.

"On a mostly empty streetcar. You?"

"The office." Suzanne worked for *Outdoors Up*, a pretentious hiker/climber magazine headquartered three and a half hours north. They ran articles on the delights of Victorian campaign kits and NASA Gore-Tex gloves, bullshit about Yosemite and whatnot across from L.L.Bean ads. Every issue had at least one full page glossy of prosperous beardo hipster dipshits and their tit-job fake nature gals laughing and drinking champagne in a steaming wooden hot tub in Murkwood.

"The office," I echoed.

Ten heartbeats of silence.

"Where's this trolley headed?" Not very curious. Waiting to spring on my answer.

"I've been going in circles, actually. Got a little drunk at 'the office' this morning and I can't make up my mind. Thought I'd get off in the Pearl and bum around."

"Goddamn it." I heard something thump in her background. "What the hell are going to do in the Pearl? Get arrested for, for . . ."

"That's actually part of my plan, yes."

She hung up.

19

Suzanne was a tall, tall woman and she'd had a lonely life because of it. We'd hit it off in a special way in the beginning, in spite of all the problems I was having at the time, or maybe because of them, but as the newness faded and we began to see clearly into the strange landscape of each other's personalities, it took a downward turn. Suzanne was extremely career oriented, with ambitious but attainable goals. I'd been that way myself at one point, but the similarity in drive was all we had in common in that respect. My "career," as it were, had carried me down a dark road and I'd survived the journey long enough to reach a very curious low point, which was where I presently was.

Suzanne believed that articles and pictures and stories about people finding a new path in life was important work. Maybe it was. Sadly, even tragically, I was the closest thing to being one of those people that she actually knew. I took a different path every day, though, and that couldn't be looked on with approval from any angle. Today, for instance, I was about to pick a fight with my two least favorite feds so they'd start following me around the clock again. So they could trip up the phantom looking through my bedroom window.

This was not the bicycling-with-helmet, microbrew, artisan bacon, deep-understanding-of-foreign-movies path Suzanne had in mind for me. For us. For her, mostly.

I stared out the window, cell phone still in hand. Lovejoy Boulevard. The transformation there was complete. Once the Pearl was warehouses, big brick ones left over from a time when people put currency into the construction of things like warehouses. They grew old, and like people, they grew in character. In my first years in Portland there'd been a giant all-ages nightclub in there somewhere. Fun place. I left an ancient, smoking 400-dollar Cadillac somewhere on the street to my right years ago when it got a flat tire. People used to live all over in the area, the people who worked at grocery stores and Jiffy Lubes. Young working people. They drank at the bars that catered to their breed, and somehow, it seemed like there had been more flowers in those days. Now it was bistros, expensive cafés, boutiques, and software outfits. Upper-middle-crust San Francisco had roosted here and replicated their environs perfectly. They didn't even have to venture out into the rest of the city.

The only café in the Pearl that served bad coffee was naturally where you could find the feds and PPD detectives, sniffing their fingers and picking at themselves. It had taken me two loops on the trolley to devise a properly savage motivator for agents Pressman and Dessel, and the conversation with Suzanne had given me the kind of confusing, unfocused anger I needed to pull it off.

I got out on 10th, ducked under the first awning, and lit a smoke. Pressman and Dessel's trashed Prius was right down the street, so the first part of my plan was working. They were in there, looking at their laptops, getting foamed up right on schedule. Their odd branch of fed-state hybrid was headquartered in the Federal Building, but several months ago some political turmoil there had compelled them to spend all their time roaming the city, moving from café to donut shop to bust in a routine I'd already mapped out. I took off in the direction of the café and stubbed my cigarette out on the wet hood of their car as I passed. Time to spice up their routine.

Twenty-plus heads with matching frowns pointed my way when I walked through the door. Dessel stood out, beaming fluorescently, his curiously pubescent face lit up like a kid who'd found a unicorn at an Easter egg hunt. His partner Pressman glanced from me to him and rolled his eyes.

"Dipshits," I said by way of greeting, pulling up a free chair.

"Darby," Dessel gushed. We were on a first name basis. "Just looking at you makes my day. My week!" He dusted imaginary crumbs off his crappy suit. "Don't tell me. You were drinking under the bridge and you thought you'd pop in and dazzle us with an update on your love life. Suzanne is in Seattle, we assume to consort with men who graduated from junior high school, but we still don't know what happened." Dessel narrowed his eyes and the smile dropped.

"I'm guessing herpes," Pressman said proudly.

"Bob here started a pool," Dessel explained. "Herpes is up to, what, fifteen bucks? Right next to—"

I silenced him by reaching out and sticking my index finger in his coffee. They watched, puzzled, as I stirred, momentarily mesmerized by the swirling motion.

"Long time ago," I began, still stirring, watching the cup, "there was this pond. Thick, still water. Reeds. Old shopping cart sticking up through the algae. Mosquitoes." I let that hang.

"Your hometown grocery store," Dessel said breathlessly. "Please, go on."

"There were catfish in there," I continued. "Carp. Huge warts on 'em, looked like they had cancer. Big-mouth bass. Summertime there'd be snapping turtles. Eating the frogs, mostly. Fast for turtles, like nothing you ever seen." I clacked my teeth together.

"Slaughter." Dessel patted his chest like a scandalized courtesan.

"No shit, slaughter. But way back in the beginning, when some retired old burnout finished digging the bed for that pond and it started filling with rain, he put in this one kind of bottom feeder. To hoover up all the shit at the bottom so the other fish could breathe."

Pressman and Dessel looked at each other, quiet now.

"It was tiny when the guy dropped it in," I continued. I held up my free hand, showing them tiny. "But over the years, the decades, it grew into a kind of blind albino monster."

Pressman's monobrow pretzeled in the center. Dessel's face was blank, his eyes wide.

"One day, I see this old man out there." I lowered my voice. They both leaned in a little. "Kind of like a tree stump in dirty denim. Glassy eyes, oily whiskers. But he was focused, like how really slow people focus on TV. He had a trash bag in one hand and a beat-up plastic Big Gulp cup in the other. And then . . ." I leaned in myself. "Then, he uses the cup to scoop dry generic dog food out of the trash bag, and he slings it out over the water. The surface exploded. The catfish, you see. Size of children after all those years."

I stopped stirring and stared at my wet finger.

"The old man fed that pond, he told me, in his dead papery voice, to keep the monster at the bottom alive. He had a plan, see." I flicked. "He was gonna catch that thing someday. I asked him how and he just looked at me. It was a story with a secret at the end. The best kind."

"So-so-so . . ." Dessel studied my face, trying to read my mind. "You're feeding us dog food." He said the last like the kid in *The Sixth Sense*.

"No."

"Ahh." Dessel slumped back, suddenly drained from his efforts at telepathy.

Law enforcement in tow, I headed home. It was hard to say what Pressman and Dessel thought had just happened. The trick had been to use what I had. Red eyes. Dirty and wet. Half drunk before noon. Way morose. Toss out a story with a giant bottom feeder and dog food and I had a good hook in them. Brightened by the whole thing, I ducked into a Pearl deli and bought a chunk of artisan Tasso pork, then hailed the first cab I saw and gave him directions, sat back, and looked out at the rain.

"Got any Doobie Brothers?"

"iPod has no limits, my brother," the driver reported. A moment later "Listen to the Music" hit the speakers and I closed my eyes.

"The first live recording of—"

"No music trivia," I said, cutting him off.

Three songs later we pulled up at my place. It didn't look haunted anymore. It looked monitored instead, and I'd weathered that before. I paid and went up the stairs, then paused and looked over the street. Somewhere within visual distance was a two-man team of incredibly pissed-off feds who had repeatedly mistaken me for a criminal genius, even though Lucky was the first word in my business, and a peeping tom with size-twelve boots was about to learn that the meanest, brightest, most relentless fed in creation looked like he moonlighted in a Christian boy band. Agent Dessel might let my stalker go if he had no warrants, to see if he led back to that prize bottom feeder I'd gone on about, but he'd be sure to rub my face in it and drop a detail or two when he did, just to fuck with me. I was thinking about what to call the entire maneuver when my phone rang. Delia.

"You'll never guess what I just did," I began. With my free hand I unlocked the door and went inside. The cats looked at me once, went back to sleep.

"Don't tell me. You found Dessel and Pressman and fucked with them. Fed them some borderline crazy shit to recklessly reinstate your round-the-clock surveillance."

"Whaa?" I was hurt that she guessed so easily.

"The patrol circuit just changed outside the shop. Slow roll-bys, ten-minute intervals, same as last time. And the time before that."

"I was thinking of a clever name for this play," I said. I

continued into the kitchen and took a can of green chilies out of the cabinet. The cats would come to life when I opened it, so I took down a can of their food, too.

"Maybe something with Judo in the title," she suggested. "Or an old Kung Fu movie, straight up rip off one of the good ones, like the flick with the lady who shot snakes out of her robe."

"Flying, ah, shit. Total blank."

"Whatever you do, don't tell Suzanne you invited your friends back around." Any chance to get in a jab. Suzanne thought Delia was cute. Delia knew Suzanne's coffin size and had a burial site in a swamp all picked out.

"Right." I chinned the phone and popped the top on the cat food, dumped it on a plate, set it down. They were getting a little leisurely about eating and took their time, yawning and stretching as they made their way to the kitchen. "I guess maybe don't tell Hank your almost former boss just put us all under the microscope. Panic does weird shit to his acne."

"Hmm. I guess fuck you." Her heart wasn't in it.

"You didn't call to tell me about the new police problem because you already knew I did it. What's up?" I got to work opening the green chilies.

"Oh! Right!" Too, too bright. "Our charming neighbor Gomez just popped in."

"Shit. The back sink?" Gomez owned the bar next to the Lucky, so naturally he and Delia were close. Gomez kept to the time-honored code of fix it yourself for the most part, but for me, because we were old pals and occasional co-conspirators, and because I had become his landlord

26

when I bought the entire block, he made an exception when it came to his back sink.

"No, not the sink, sweetheart. He didn't say what he wanted. But I do know they have a giant dead dog in their freezer."

A big pot. Heat it up and toss in a pat of butter, then some diced pork. Day-old roast is fine, but Tasso is best, that spicy stuff you get at the same overpriced deli where you find exotic pears and house-made duck confit. Paprika, pepper, cumin, salt, green chilies, diced onion. Sear the fuck out of it, then splash in a shot of whiskey and stand back. A satisfying bloom of hell consumes the pot. Smile, then, as the red and gold fills your eyes. In the fire, lit with sparks and curls of aromatic smoke. you can briefly see your troubles, even project them into it, be it phantoms or frozen dogs. Add two cups of water and a bouillon cube. Last, take a bag of tortilla chips, not the fucked-up disgusting kind with nacho toxins, but the real deal. Stab a hole in it and bash the unholy shit out of it. Beat the bag savagely, like you feel the weight of the world on your back. Dump the perfectly mortised contents into the pot, lower the heat, cover.

Green chili stew on the way. And an open bottle of booze to keep you company while you wait. Serve hot, with tortillas and dreams of a better life.

Six a.m. is early for the tattoo universe, but I snapped out of a dead sleep feeling better than I had in weeks. I'd made it all the way to the bed for one thing, for the first time since Suzanne left, and even though I'd slept in my clothes I considered it a cautious victory.

Once the coffee was going, I stripped off my dirty T-shirt and did push-ups. Not many people understood why I did this morning routine, but they invariably came up with their own theories. Delia hypothesized that it had something to do with hangovers, though anymore her conjectures involved penis chakras and self-esteem, and would no doubt include my unwillingness to buy new clothes should my waistline change. I powered through the first ten at speed, but it had been a month and I could feel it.

Suzanne thought my morning ritual was a sign of paranoia. She was nine inches taller than me at a towering six feet six, and she had a swimmer's body because she swam every day. She was also passionate about rock climbing, which I secretly thought was dangerous and possibly stupid because of it, and while we had similar physiques, she steadfastly maintained that my body mass index was a product of violence and a continuous proximity to poison.

As I passed through seventy reps something popped in my elbow, so I stopped and stood. Brief vertigo. Hot now, I rolled my head around and twisted my back from side to side. More loud pops, some grinding sounds. Suzanne thought the sound of my waking skeleton was disgusting, and I enjoyed that she did. It was small of me.

I thought about the frozen dog carcass while I took a shower. The damnedest things can brighten a day. For a year, I'd been delegating things like this. Santiago, Delia, Chase, whoever. Even shoving things off on Gomez and Flaco. Having a responsible, respectable, professional woman in my life had me impersonating someone else around the clock. And I'd gotten good at it.

Jeans, boots, T-shirt. Chops and Buttons watched politely as I got their breakfast ready. While they ate I drank coffee and watched.

"I got business with a frozen dog today," I told them.

At seven a.m., the surveillance outside would change shifts. Sometimes they left the car in place and switched teams and rides if they had a good spot, and sometimes they left a tad early for a high-speed donut and coffee run. They had bottles of pee to empty by then, and a toilet to visit for a big number two, I imagined. I was watching the street through the edge of my blinds when my phone rang. Suzanne.

"Hey baby," I answered, hitting her with cheer.

"You're awake." Pause as she consulted her dive watch. "Seven a.m. Did you sleep, or did you . . ."

"Yeah, I ah . . ." I couldn't tell her any of it. Ritualistic skeleton yoga, Mexicans with frozen dog cadavers, the feds dealing with my ghost, nothing. "I made coffee. Fed the cats. They miss you."

"I miss them too," she said warmly. "No rain for us today"—sound of fingers on keyboard—"or you. Sunny in the entire Northwest. Then we both have rain tonight. Got plans?"

"I was gonna think about your legs later, but it sounds depressing now that I say it out loud." I lit my first cigarette of the day. "Delia mentioned that she wanted me to take Hank to the tuxedo place at some point, sort of manage the crisis as it evolved. Might be a good day for it."

Suzanne laughed but said nothing. I love that sound.

"I super don't want to, as you might imagine, but she'll want me to do it sooner rather than never, so I'm putting it in the maybe category."

"Be of good cheer, fierce little man. Hank weighs ninety pounds. If push comes to shove you can always out-drink him." Let the fishing trip begin.

"I'm on an upward spiral, baby," I said, maybe a tiny bit too fast. She also didn't care for being called "baby." "Not drinking anyone under the table today. Not on the menu. Nope."

"Well." She let it sink in. Is it a good thing when the guy you left for your career reaches the end of his separation bender, or does it mean he's getting over you too fast? What could it mean when even *he* doesn't know? I heard all of that in her pause.

"Confusing," I said, just to make the confusion stick.

"So, ah, when's the wedding again? Still Halloween?"

"They haven't moved it since the last time they moved it," I reported, drifting with the awkward segue. "Hank's mom is still in jail, or so he claims. The real holdouts are on Delia's side. They won't budge."

"Still?"

"Still. She's pretty tight-lipped about it, but it sounds like she's related to a pack of assholes and bitches, so I don't know why she even cares."

Orphan talk, I heard her thinking. The poor man has no idea what he's talking about. The importance of family is above his head.

"Well, if you can't be understanding, nurturing will have to do."

"Right." I dumped the remains of my coffee in the sink. Long pause.

"I miss you, Darby."

"Miss you too, Suze. As much as I can, anyway. You know, if you squeezed my entire emotional spectrum dry it would fill a Dixie cup. But your pancakes, that's a different story. And that place where your ass meets your legs is—"

"Darby."

"I can hear you blushing. Don't tell me it isn't possible."

"Yes, well. Hm."

"The guy at the desk next to yours? Clive? Calvin?"

"Todd."

"That's the fuckin' guy. You tell him I said—"

"Darby."

I heard her smiling. I listened to the background sound of her office environment. She listened to my empty house.

"Two weeks," she said finally.

31

"It's a date."

"Bye." She made a kissing sound.

I let the cats out since the sun was shining and hit the street with them, jacket over my shoulder. Suzanne's weather forecast was accurate. A few high clouds drifted through the clean blue, and the air was crisp with a bit of cool that marked it as one of the last nice days before the real rain, which would last for months. There was no sign of my new escort, but I'd learned the hard way that it only meant they'd gotten clever. Still, seven a.m. was the best time to confuse them if I was going to try. The only safe way out of my house now was over the fences and through several backyards to the café strip, and I suspected that would only work a few more times. Plus, it was painful.

My car started, which always surprised me. Parking around the Lucky was bad and getting worse as assholes like me upgraded the neighborhood. I actually *owned* a pay parking lot next to the shop, but Santiago frowned on me using it, especially since I'd given Delia my space and was taking a pay slot for free. I only drove when I had to, which was almost never. But there was a dog on this fine day, a frozen one, and cabs frown on shit like that.

Inner robot online, I drove without thinking about the sunny day and thought about Dessel instead, about the long night he had beside Agent Pressman, sitting in their Prius and watching my house. I was sure they had personally sat on my place. They didn't seem to sleep, but they also had trouble reaching out to their department for backup. They could call in the cavalry for a massive bust, including SWAT and helicopters, as they had on the night they busted Nigel and his two idiot biker connections, but for grunt work they were pretty much on their own much of the time. The two of them authentically hated me, and in the bright light of day it occurred to me for the first time that busting my stalker after I was successfully murdered might work well for them. A sobering thought.

There was one free spot about a half a block down from the tattoo shop, almost right across from my parking lot. Delia was in way early, very likely because she didn't want to miss any of the dog situation. I could just picture her, lurking inside the dark shop, rubbing her hands together, watching for me to approach. It made me feel much better about everything. I had no plan to speak of and Delia most certainly did.

Gomez's bar, the Rooster Rocket, had changed as much as the rest of Old Town in the last year, but in a surprising and novel way in this singular instance: It had gotten scuzzier. The entrepreneurial Gomez had set out to corner the entire local market on "dive," and the place had taken on a spastic glitter as a result. The bands were louder and worse. He'd put in strings of Christmas lights, which came off as lurid rather than festive. There were no artisan beers on tap. It was straight-up old man beer water from Milwaukee. Local businesspeople did their day drinking in the Rocket's dark, high-backed booths, exchanged furtive moisture with their coworkers in the grubby bathroom stalls and under the sticky tables, and conspired with their fellow cubicle inmates. By night, the twenty-one-plus crowd malfunctioned in the Rocket with great abandon. All this was good for the Lucky, of course, and Gomez was making money hand over fist.

We locked eyes the instant the dim interior swallowed me and I could intuit in a heartbeat much of the situation. It was three hours before they opened, but it smelled like pine scented mop water. Gomez had pulled an all-nighter. The door had been unlocked, so Delia had told him about my early arrival. Gomez himself was powerfully irritated, the narrowing of his bloodshot eyes said. He took a breath, but then sighed with it, as if he expected nothing more than random bad news from my direction. Resigned then that I might be of no help after all, that his situation was beyond my ability to fix and that he'd just realized it, he shook his head and produced two shot glasses. Grimly, he poured two short vodkas, the miniatures we had come to call Christian thimbles. Glasses in hand, he flicked his eyes at the nearest booth, indicating that I should join him.

We settled across from each other and drank in silence. Finally, he leaned halfway across the table and beckoned me to do the same. He had a secret to share, and even though we were alone in the bar, he wanted to whisper it. Not good.

"My nephew Santos," Gomez rumbled. "His dog has died."

"Bummer," I whispered back.

"Yes." It came out as a boozy hiss. This was not his first thimble of the morning. He glanced both ways, just with his eyes. "He is a troubled boy. Got out of juvie maybe nine months ago and we got him a dog. Bella." He grunted.

"She died and Flaco and I froze her. Mi familia, we have a few acres outside of Woodburn. For picnics, weddings, that kind of thing. It's also where we bury the cats and dogs."

"Ah." I began to see.

"No biggie, right?" It came out a little bitter and sarcastic. "Except now, we have police watching the street. Thanks to you, Darby." Gomez leveled the full force of prosperous Mexican gangster-turned-bar-owner at me. "You. Delia says you have a stalker, so you activated your federal monitors. That's your problem. Now my problem is your problem because of it. So now you have two problems. See?"

"Shit." I looked away. "How the fuck was I supposed to know you had a frozen dog in here? Delia says it's big, too. What the hell kind of nine-month-old dog is big?"

"Bella is the size of a pony, Darby. Rottweiler-mastiff mix. Wrapped in an army blanket, she looks like a fat man with his legs cut off."

"Shit," I said again.

"Yes. But I have a plan."

I sat back. Gomez sat back, too. Then he grinned.

"You're not working tomorrow, are you." It didn't come out as a question. "You never work anymore."

"Out with it." In spite of myself, an unfocused thrill was building.

"Have you ever heard of the Big Brother program?"

"Assume I haven't."

"Mm. Bueno." Gomez smiled. "Take a boy who has no father. No brothers. This boy, maybe he acts out. Why?

Because he needs a role model. Someone to look up to. Teach him the ways of a man."

I almost laughed, but his face hardened in anticipation of my reaction. He leaned in again, but this time he wasn't whispering.

"I have twenty-seven nieces and nephews, Darby, but two of them?" He ground his teeth. "Two of them. Those two little—" He stopped and calmed himself. "Santos and his brother Miguel, they did not have good lives. When they were young, their stepfather, he was not a good man. Violent. Drunk. The speed and the cocaine. Santos and Miguel spent too much time outside because of it, and the wildness grew in them. I moved them here from LA when I found out what was happening, and at first, at first it was okay. Then it went bad. They robbed a gas station and Miguel died by the gun. Santos spent three years in juvie." Gomez looked into his empty glass. "Now the boy is wrong in many ways. He does not fit in with anything. Which brings me back to the Big Brother program." He fixed me with his stare again.

"Darby. You are a massive fuck-up. You know it's true. I know it's true. We all know." Gomez considered me. "But you always land on your feet. And you have your murky principles. I know you to be a certain kind of man, and I am in no way flattering you, so wipe that fool look off your face. Now, I ask for one day. One. It is your fault I have a dog in my freezer. It would be gone by now if you had not made it difficult. Every second we sit here I risk everything. Do you know what a health inspector would say if they found even a small dog in my freezer? Flaco would be deported to Guantanamo. I would be driven from the Republic wearing tar and feathers. This is the wrong political climate for a Mexican establishment that serves food to be caught with such a thing. So one day. One. Out of your miserable life, this one day is nothing. It will be good for you. If you and Santos hit it off and become friends, then good. Very good. Maybe he will see a path with some kind of honor. The misfit's way, we will call it. If he sees in you what he might become and changes his ways to avoid becoming like you, then also good. Also very good. But I do not want Santos to become institutionalized. He must learn that there is always a different way, and no matter how you two interact, I have every certainty he will learn this from you. There is a way to misbehave and stay out of the system. Young Santos is in danger of becoming a permanent member of the prison life. A number instead of a name. A slave. He needs to meet men like you. He needs to see the joy in life, and that joy is free."

"Unbelievable."

"Santos needs an example of a fuck-up who beat the odds, and you are all I have at the moment."

"Fine." It wasn't like I had a choice. "How do we get the dog out?"

"Ah yes. My plan is a masterful one." Gomez rose to get us refills. "My plan is for Delia to figure it out."

"Mine too!" I smiled, and then I remembered for the first time that day that she was leaving.

Delia had a way of laughing that reminded me of cartoons.

Too big for her tiny frame, too loud, overfull by every measure. Maybe it was that her mouth seemed to open unnaturally wide.

"Enough," I said finally. We were in the office lounge at the Lucky. Chase and one of the new guys were cleaning out front. "The dog. Focus, Delia. I know my recap of this thing was terribly funny, I do. I laughed too. But the dog. Think about the dog."

"Right. The pony dog. This Santos kid won't be available until tomorrow?"

"Correct. He's a janitor at Saint John's Hospital. So we have twenty-four hours to figure this shit out."

"Easy enough. As in I already did. We can't move that big-ass dog tonight. Too many people around, and when they all go home it'll be all the more obvious. Plus it would thaw out and start leaking. Did you see how big?"

"Not yet, but think massive. Rottweiler-mastiff mix. We're talkin' monster here. Gomez has it wrapped in an army blanket, says it looks like a fat man with his legs chopped off."

"Vivid and disturbing. These are the salient factors," she said. "We have police roll-bys every fifteen minutes. Your car is marked. But thankfully Gomez has a car collection."

"I like it so far. The cars, I mean. As in not my car."

"First, our colleague Chase Manhattan. This will be his formal initiation into our inner circle. About time anyway. We're gonna have to see if he lives up to his rep."

"Go on." It appeared she had developed an idea with multiple applications. I knew Chase from the old days, and it would be nice to know if he'd gone soft. But it was more than that. We routinely came across complex situations, and it was more than just an evaluation of his mettle she was after. If he blew it and one of us got busted with a dead dog in someone else's car, it was not the end of the world. Just disappointing. But if Chase went James Bond on the situation, that would be disappointing too, because we'd have to fire him. Players play, after all, and that eventually comes full circle. He'd be a threat then, scheming to rule it all. Chase was going to have to hit the middling ground.

"You leave your car in your parking lot tonight. Santiago will just have to deal with it. Then you go out and make a scene. Get drunk and raise hell. Make it clear that you're way too blasted to drive home, which is why you took a cab. With me so far?"

"I like your plans, Delia. They're always so convincing that I fall for them myself, even when I'm the key player."

"Of course you do. Now, in the morning I want you to wear a very specific outfit."

"Ah ha!" I leveled a finger at her. "You're scheming to pick out my clothes. You love doing that."

"Like putting a sweater on a cat. It's hysterical. So. Jeans, white tee, bomber jacket, your Dead Moon baseball cap. Then you ramble around looking cool and come in at 9:30."

"All doable. Believable."

"Chase gets here at nine. Red pants, red shirt. He has them, I've seen it."

"Christ."

"No shit. Now." She got up and began pacing. "Here's the tricky part. Gomez and Flaco will have moved the frozen dog into position by the back door of the Rocket. You and Chase switch clothes and Chase blazes out in your ride like he's running from the devil. As the tires are screeching, you hump that frozen dog into the back of one of the lowriders of Senor Gomez and blow out in the other direction."

"I'm not wearing Chase's clothes. And why aren't the cops going to wonder why Gomez has a car parked in the alley?"

"You don't have to wear the red pants, idiot. Bring your own in a bag. Gomez and Flaco buy a ton of shit at Costco every week. Tomorrow morning they will be loading in bag after bag of it."

"So they finish unloading and take up their stations, I toss the dog in and blow, go pick up the kid."

"Then give him spiritual advice while you help him bury his dog, yes."

"Excellent." I considered. "What the hell am I going to tell him?"

"That's the hard part." Delia sat down next to me again. "What do you want to tell him?

"Are you crazy?" I stared at her. "I don't want to tell him anything! What if I fuck him up somehow? It sounds like he already has problems."

"Let me rephrase that. What would you tell your young self?"

"Don't get caught." I shrugged helplessly. "Maybe wear a rubber. Check out the Doobie Brothers. Shit." I thought about it. "I guess I should tell him to try to beat the odds on a minute-by-minute basis. That kind of thing." I looked at her. "Doesn't everyone know that already?"

"No." It was her turn to think. "What's the most important thing you've learned since you were a teenager, Darby? That would help a kid like this, I mean."

"I have no idea," I admitted.

Delia smiled. "Then this will be good for both of you."

She left me sitting there thinking about this. While she mopped in front and listened to Bathory at D for Deaf sonogram level, I ruminated on the next best step. Santiago was probably down at the restaurant already, combing over receipts and scrutinizing incoming fish orders and drinking espresso with his pinkie up. He'd be good to bounce this Santos bummer off of. Plus, I had to visit Nigel and tell him what was going down. For a guy who never worked anymore, I had a ton of stuff to do. I decided to start with Flaco and a second opinion. He'd give me one whether I wanted it or not, but it was worth the two bucks it would take to hear it. No education is wasted.

Flaco's squalid little hole in the wall had just opened. The smell of white onions and cologne wafted out, nauseating at the best of times, and the old man beamed at me and chortled in delight, knowing exactly what my morning had been like. Flaco's Tacos had withstood the beautifying tides of Disneyfication with the same implacable gusto as the Rooster Rocket, but with different results. The signs, painted on old plywood, had somehow failed to take on a magical "antique" or "authentic" aura and instead remained boldly crappy. The white and yellow base was peeling around the edges where the wood was warping, and the scrawled, semiliterate descriptions of the food, all in Spanish, had been rain-blasted away in places and redone with Sharpie, also fading. The tiny stainless steel counter was bent and dented from a service life it had endured years before it was installed. Its time at Flaco's had added an additional patina of scratches and dings and even a hole or two. The sticky bottles of hot sauce looked straight-up evil. To top it all off, Flaco had taken to leaning out the window as he was now. Perhaps as a sorcerous talisman to ward off errant health inspectors because of the frozen dog situation, he'd added a hairnet to his ensemble.

"Two juniors," I said gruffly, cutting short his morning bullshit. "Hold the dog hair."

"Culo!" he spat, the huge grin instantly replaced with fury. He glanced both ways. "Keep it down! This is all your fault anyway." He yanked himself back in and glared at me.

"Two juniors," I repeated.

Flaco made a hissing sound and whacked a giant metal spoonful of congealed red meat product down next to the tortillas on the griddle. My stomach made a *sproinging* noise at the sharp sizzle.

"I'm responsible, how? And I should keep it down, why?" I leaned casually on the counter. It had a sign on it saying not to.

"This would not be an issue," Flaco said quietly, "if you had not put the Lucky back on the radar. You have surveillance, then so do we."

"Whatever." I took two dollar bills out of my wallet and tucked them under the edge of the window.

"Delia says you have a stalker." He spread the meat out, avoiding my eyes.

"She talks."

"It's a woman, Darby." He sighed dramatically. "One of your many curses. Your Amazon moves north and like magic the next one appears, as troubling as the last. I know this curse well, my ignorant friend."

"Flaco, dude, just because you read the story section in your porno magazine does not—"

"You should listen to someone, someday," he continued.

"See a therapist under an assumed name. Maybe a priest in your case. Wear a fake beard into the confessional." He looked at me suddenly and the grin was back. "I know! An Indian shaman who is also a lawyer! But soft, with a grandmother's belly. She can help you."

We both laughed. A car sloshed past and I glanced at it, then up and down the street. No sign of my federal tail, but that didn't mean anything. I turned back in time to see Flaco sniff the onion tub and scowl.

"Tell me about the kid," I prompted.

"No, no," he said slyly. "Gomez already did. I have nothing to add."

"Huh. That actually tells me a great deal, Flaco. Thanks."

He stopped working and squinted at me.

"Gomez knew I was going to pump you so he told you to keep your mouth shut. Means the situation is worse than he let on, right?"

"I said nothing." He tried to cover his alarm by sniffing the onions again.

"Yes you did. Loud and clear. And your face, Flaco. Jesus, man, you're an open book."

"Madre de—" His mutter went too low to make out. Angry again, he pulled down two sheets of wax paper and laid them out, slapped the tortillas in place, two thick, and used an iron spatula to scrape up the meat and dump a load on each. Then he sprinkled them with the questionable onion and thrust them through the window.

"So this kid, Santos, right?" I shot a blistering line of squeeze-bottle hot sauce on the first junior. "Piece of shit? The black sheep. Batshit lunatic vato outcast with—"

"Santos is a good boy!" Flaco said with suppressed fury. I ate casually while he continued. "The men of the Familia, especially the young ones, there is always trouble there. Like a shadow, it follows us. It is in our minds, you see, and a man must learn to trick his way past it or he goes away. If a young man cannot learn, it is because he has the wrong teacher. Simple. Santos is not bad." Flaco gave me a shrewd look. "We have just not found his guide."

"I'll be damned." I picked up taco number two and gestured at him with it. "You part Hindu? Cause that sounded downright Bhagwan, dude."

"Hmm." Flaco flashed me his grin again, but with less energy this time. "So playful. Such . . ." He looked for the right words. "So much dick in you, Darby. So much asshole." He shook his head and turned back to the flat top. "Gomez is wise."

I didn't have a snappy comeback for that, so I left. The street at eleven a.m. was so different than it had been five years ago. I owned part of the block and almost every yuppie I passed averted their eyes. Some of the brave ones scowled. I scowled back every time, but it was tedious. At the end of the block, the restaurant that had replaced "mitri's izza," my old landlord's failed pizza joint, was already alive with lunchtime traffic. I went in and the atmosphere washed over me in a startling way, just as it did every time.

Alcott Frond was tasteful where other bistros were uniform in their adherence to the stony code of New Portland chic. The reclaimed barn wood and art-meets-steel, exposed brick and visible but possibly fake ductwork, was not Santiago's vision. Instead, Frond reminded me of a '70s French movie, with Alain Delon, transvestites, and something else, something I could never quite put my finger on. But it had clean lines, tablecloths that didn't drape, none of the waiters had beards, and there was no chalkboard special menu. It was unique, in a city that had largely sold that quality. There was a single open seat at the long bar and with a nod to the hostess I took it.

"Soda water, little bit of lemon," I said to the bartender. His name was Rob or Bob. We knew each other enough to chat every once in a while.

"You got it."

I felt the heat in the air against my back before he spoke. Santiago is that big.

"You on the wagon, little man?"

I turned and looked up into his wide face. "Who you callin' little, you fruity midget?"

"C'mon then." Santiago tossed his head in the direction of his office. "I got maybe three minutes. And some measuring tape."

With a nod to the bartender, I took my pink glass with fruit and followed my giant business manager through the polite diners to his office, which was far nicer than mine. He closed the door behind us after a quick word with the hostess and we both sat down, Santiago at his cluttered presidential desk and me in the plush chair opposite it. He steepled his fingers.

"Delia tells me you have a stalker," he began evenly.

"Shit." I didn't have it in me to try to be pissed. "I do indeed have a stalker." I shook my head. "Went and shot my mouth off to Dessel and Pressman so they'd follow me again."

"Good. Those two motherfuckers will find out who's messin' with you. Might be a little bit of a challenge when they do, but good. You better go see Nigel, though. He needs to know if the feds are back in the mix. They might try to crack him again, squeeze a little more dirt out of his head."

"Yeah."

"Do it today. I'll call and book you for a visit."

There was a knock at the door and one of the waitresses entered with a shot of espresso. Santiago thanked her warmly as he took it and I watched, smiling at his perfect elegance. When I first met him, he was working as the enforcer for a Russian criminal, and even then he'd had an air of grace. As soon as she left I went on.

"So, Oleg. Your old boss. You think any of his people may be out to even the score?"

"I would have heard about it," Santiago said. He had big eyes that went a little smaller when he talked about his former boss. "When Delia called me, she asked the same thing. Oleg's network is dead. The Russians seem to want to forget all about him, which means they also want to forget about you. And me. If the feds hadn't seized all his money we'd both be in trash bags by now, but they did. There's no angle there. What, ah—" He sat forward a little. "What about this guy you were having trouble with before I came along? Dong Ju, the Korean from San Francisco?"

"No angle there, either," I said. "He's in Argentina,

maybe. Somewhere the feds can't get to him." He was in the river, dead, but Santiago didn't need to know that. It wasn't that I didn't trust him. I did. But it's bad manners to turn someone into an accomplice to a crime they had no hand in.

"Delia asked about our strippers." He said it flatly, like he didn't really want to talk about it.

"*Your* strippers, dude. I never go to the club, never will."

"Prude." He shook his head. "We make a ton of money off that place, Darby. Least you could do is stop in once in a while."

"And do what?"

"Act like a nice guy, you arrogant little dipshit. Jesus."

"I don't think so." I waved dismissively. "But you did rule that out, right?"

"As much as I could." He shook his head again, like it was naïve to even ask. "What about your shady tattoo pals? Any weirdos there? Old customer with some kind of crazy busting out? Old employee with a grudge?"

"Always possible," I admitted, "but unlikely. This feels like something else."

"I'm here for you. I don't want to put anyone in the trunk, but if push comes to shove." He let that sink in.

"I have to help this kid bury his dog tomorrow," I said, changing the subject. "Gomez's nephew. Supposed to give him some kind of good advice, too. He's maybe a year out of juvie, they don't want him getting used to it."

"Hm." Santiago sipped from the little cup and considered. He'd done time before he worked for the Russian. "That is a real danger. They like to turn the kids early. Get 'em used to the system, think of it as a way of life. Free labor. It's a modern slave racket."

"Gomez said the same thing. Fuck that."

"What do you plan on telling him?"

"I was hoping you might have some ideas, actually."

"What, because I've done time? Or because I'm out now and I have a good life?" Santiago tilted his head. "Not gonna be that easy, Darby. Gomez wants you to do this because he thinks you have something in your head the kid might be able to use. He didn't ask me, homie. So don't go looking around in my head for your answer. You ask Delia? You did. Of course you did."

"Yeah. No dice."

"Huh. You hungry?"

"Nope. Just ate. I guess now I have to go see Nige and then I'm supposed to go carry on and make a scene for the tail I have."

"Why is that, exactly? Not that they won't enjoy it."

"The dog in question is frozen. Gomez has it in his freezer and I have to smuggle it out tomorrow morning. My getting too loaded to drive home tonight is all part of Delia's master plan."

"Then it's good that you're going to see Nigel after this," he said distastefully. "Put anyone in a drinking mood. But when you get back, don't park in the lot. We're booked solid tonight and I need every space for—"

"Take it up with Delia," I interrupted.

"I will." He finished his espresso and rose. "Speaking of Delia, how're we doing on the wedding? She get her famous chicken yet?"

I froze. "What the hell are you talking about, Santiago?"

He laughed and shook his head one last time. "Ask her yourself. But I expect to see you for dinner at nine, before you get too loaded to drive home. Agreed?"

"Jesus man." I got up, too. "You're like the mother I never had."

"You've lost weight since Suzanne left," he said firmly, eyeing me. "When does she visit again?"

"Couple weeks."

"Right then. Let's get you back into fighting trim, shall we?" Santiago worked out two hours a day, six days a week, from five to seven a.m. "In anticipation of all the fighting you'll be doing."

I handed him my empty glass.

Traffic had gotten worse as the city swelled, but it still wasn't nearly as bad as LA. I got on I-5, the freeway that seemed to go both everywhere worth going and everyplace to avoid, and headed south. As I drove, I thought about the way things were shaking out.

It was possible that massive boredom had made me into a different animal. I could be in the eye of the perfect storm, on a level I was just too dim to recognize. But that didn't make any sense, not really. Santiago would have called me on it. Delia, of course, would have beaten me with such a thing. And Suzanne. Suzanne would have maybe noticed if I'd slipped into some kind of one-way funk that had more than her as an ingredient, but I had to be honest with myself about how dishonest I was with her.

I lit a cigarette and checked the rearview. No sign of my tail, but I knew they were back there. Santiago would have called ahead, so my appointment with Nigel would be on the books. I smiled grimly at the thought of it. I'd be going to the one place my tail wanted me to go, but way ahead of schedule. When I took the exit for the Oregon State Prison, I was the only car to turn off.

I guess my tail just kept on going.

It was hard to say what Nigel hated the most about prison. The food, the drug prices, the toilet paper, or the round-the-clock affirmation that he'd been bested by the boy wonder Agent Dessel. As long as I'd known Nigel he'd been of a questionable disposition, and our friendship had been one based on mutual goals and common enemies. Those goals were no more, and those enemies had consumed him alive. As the metal door opened and a skinhead in wrist and ankle shackles hop-walked to the scarred table where I sat waiting, I again realized that distance. Nigel sat and stared at me without speaking. I stared back. One of his eyes was swollen shut, and had been for long enough for the skin around it to go from black to purple and yellow, and there was a fresh-looking swastika on his neck. He smiled without humor. Missing a front tooth.

"'Sup," he said finally.

"Dude." I hated visiting anyone in prison. Visiting Nigel was somehow worse. "I, ah . . . I put some dough in your account."

"Pretzels." Nigel picked at a scab on his knuckle, still watching my eyes. "Maybe I'll get crackers."

"Yeah." I touched my neck where his new tattoo was. "Makin' friends?"

He tapped the table. It was wired.

"Shop is doing good," I went on. "Wedding date is Halloween, firm. Taking Hank to get fitted for a tux next week."

"You should kill that guy."

I laughed it off, playing it like a joke, but I flared my eyes at him. "He's okay. Kid's got no future in music, but who does. Jiffy Lube is always looking for the Hanks of—"

"I'm serious, man." Nigel glanced up at the camera behind me. "Take that kid to the Greyhound station and buy him a one-way ticket to wherever the fuck he won't come back from. You're rich. Set him up. Pay him off to take a ride."

"Why the sudden change of—I thought you kinda just—Hank's a harmless idiot, man. Right?"

"This whole fuckin' thing surprises me, dude." He looked down at his hands. "Delia." He snorted. "Your little fuckin' Delia. And you're gonna let her get married to that little junkie skag? Exactly how fucked up are you?"

We were quiet for a minute. Prison smells like public school hallways, bad mop water, and sweat. Iodine. Wet iron. Fear. I listened to the distant clanging of hollow metal on harder metal. Somewhere, a man screamed in rage. Nigel looked back up at me and waited. When I didn't say anything, he went on in a slow, low growl.

"You got blinders on, dude, and she does too. Hank's a piece of shit. He cheats on her for one thing, has the whole time. So it's more than just the drugs. But that fuckin' guy will bring her down hard, Darby, all the way down to where she can't get back into the light. Delia goes down, then so do you."

"Ah." I gave him a tight smile. "You're worried about your commissary money. The dough I send your lawyer. You're not worried about Delia. You're not even worried about me. You're worried about my money."

"Dude, you don't owe me for this shit." Nigel raised his hands and rattled the chains. "Not really. I know it. You know it. And who the fuck cares anyway. It was only a matter of time before I got busted for something. I hated you in the beginning, though." He shifted, trying to get comfortable. "When that mad fucker Dessel came after me, I thought it was because of you, because that guy fuckin' hates you so bad. But it wasn't. Pressman told me months ago. I was just another case they were working the whole time, so it might have been the other way around. They maybe first came across your name as a possible accomplice of mine." He leaned back. So did I.

"Fuck," I said finally.

"Yeah. You didn't know that, but you keep in mind who told you. Me and you, we were solid for a long time, Darby. S'why I'm telling you about Hank. In the interest of keeping the goodwill flowing."

"Huh." I considered. "So Hank's a junkie? You know this?"

"Straight up. Mexican tar. Smokes it."

"And the cheating thing?"

Nigel laughed bitterly. "Skank named Becky, looks kinda like Delia but she has big tits. Hank's one true love. Works at Sho's Diner. The night shift."

I must have looked confused. A wicked smile spread over Nigel's face.

"Delia, she's the smart one. You're cunning, Darby. Like an animal. But the junkie mind is a sneaky kind of brilliant, baby, borders on witchcraft. Delia has money. Hank has a habit. You think he could ever get real with a woman he's turned into something like food? No, dog. No respect there. No love, deep down where it counts. She's his sugar momma, and when he gets access to the sugar bag with no one watching . . ." Nigel made a *poof* sound and gestured "gone" with his hands.

"Nigel." I licked my lips. "You picked a dangerous time to tell me this."

"When was a good time?" he hissed wrathfully. "When I suspected all this shit? You would have thought I was full of shit, that it was just more Creepy Nigel, shooting his mouth off to stir the pot. Or should I have ratted him out when I was sure, when I saw Delia give him money and I bumped into him at that stripper palace on Lombard making a score twenty minutes later? Then it was too late, because when the smoke cleared it would leave me in the shade just the same."

Nigel had never been the kind of guy who believed people could change for the better, even when he was free, roaming the streets with a pocket full of cash and a woman on either arm. He was more of the mind that people became harder versions of what they always were to begin with, but not in a clean way, like an emerald emerging from a bigger wad of shit-colored rock, or a Darwinian weeding of a garden, where all the flowers and fountains were destroyed, leaving only a single tree with a utilitarian function. His new view of humanity was lower, I could tell. It was that the hard person in all of us just became more obvious.

"Time's up," I whispered. We watched each other.

"Thanks for the peanuts."

I let my mind wander on the drive back and listened to it ramble through unrelated small rages, rumors I should have paid attention to and couldn't remember clearly, suspicions I'd had but dismissed as random paranoia or flagrant assholery. On 205 North, I took the airport exit without thinking, distracted as I was, and drove on autopilot to the cell phone waiting area at the 82nd Street exit.

I pulled into a spot, and after I checked out the other cars, I angled the rearview to keep an eye on the entrance. Then I lit a smoke. The view before me was a panoramic sweep of grassy field with low white buildings with blue doors off in the distance. To my right, in the direction of the terminals, a few planes and a handful of square little airport vehicles sat idle. The sunny day, as Suzanne had predicted, was ending, and the clouds moving in were fast and gray and low. The first scattering of drops were large and far apart. I didn't leave the engine on for the heat. I didn't turn on the radio, either.

I thought about Hank.

Nigel had admitted he was the kind of man to drive a wedge between people if there was even one small percentage point in it for him. That's what all the mincing around had been about. But so was the between-the-lines admission that there was no angle in it for him, that he needed to point the light at this because it could disrupt his money flow if the wheels came off. I turned it this way and that. Happiness, when it came to other people, had always annoyed Nigel in a cynical way, but not to the point of going to the dark side like this. Prison couldn't have driven him that crazy, either.

No, Nigel liked Delia. Not in a romantic way, though. Nigel was the kind of method mover who shied away from smart women in general. In fact, he was probably scared of Delia. He'd told me so more than once, but I'd always thought he was joking until now. The patter of the rain on the roof was loud. The tall grass in the field swayed and rippled in an unseen wind.

With our long alliance dragged from shaky ground to quicksand, Nigel would lie to me just as often as he lied to everyone else, but no matter how I turned it, I had a bad feeling he'd been telling me the truth. Nigel was definitely scared of me, too, and even in prison he wasn't safe if I was pissed enough, and he knew it. So, Hank.

A Miata pulled in. Older woman, too heavy to be a fed. The cell phone waiting area had been designed for guys and gals with my lifestyle. Good view, one way in, no helicopters, close to the freeway. I'd fallen into the habit of sitting around there doing nothing almost a year ago, just to piss off Pressman and Dessel, and later to eat lunch because it was peaceful. That led me to the last part of my speculation.

Hank was probably exactly as guilty as Nigel claimed, and Delia had no idea. She would have told me. No, she was in love, the worst kind of love, crazy and deep and tragic, and that kind of love would make anyone blind. And I'd failed her, for all kinds of reasons, and I was failing her right then, at that exact moment. I'd been too wrapped up in my own shit to notice what was going on in her life and I still was. And I was going to continue failing her unless I did some highly inventive shit in the immediate future. Without the benefit of her insights and feedback—behind her back, even—and all while I was under surveillance and being followed by some shithead at the same time.

This was why people invented booze. I was supposed to go drop off my car and get drunk in Old Town, make a scene, leave my car. It was like the cosmos was smiling on me in a sad way.

A night on the town, when you're supposed to seem like you're spending the night on the town, partying with great abandon and being exactly like the worst possible you, does not start easily. Especially when you're being followed by any number of people, all of them also possibly following each other as well.

I drove into Old Town and looked for a parking spot for a while, distracted and cursing, until I remember that I was supposed to park in *my* parking lot. More cursing. The lot was always full, so I bought an all-day ticket from the little robot kiosk, paid myself with my debit card, and idled while I dialed Delia and waited for her to pick up. It rang five times and went to voicemail three times in a row before she finally picked up.

"Working, dude," she snapped. "Don't tell me this is your one call from the pokey, 'cause if it fuckin' is—"

"Move your car," I snapped back. "Jesus. I'm in position for phase one of whatever we're calling this, Operation Frozen Dog, or the Troubled Vato Conspiracy, or—"

She hung up.

A moment later, she bounded out of the shop, waved and blew a kiss at the ever watchful Flaco, who caught it and pressed it to his heart, then bounced my way. As she did her face hardened. When she stopped and rapped sharply on my window, I was almost afraid to roll it down. I was more afraid not to, so I did.

"Santiago told me that he accidentally ratted me out," she said, in a flat way, like she was spoiling for a fight about it. "I don't want to hear one damn thing about the chicken, Darby. Your borderline fucking with my wedding is pissing me off, so just shut your fuckin' mouth."

I stared.

"You're talking with your face, dude," she said coldly.

"Ah, man." I rubbed my scalp. "You, ah, you got plans tonight? We can get loaded like the old days, play pool. Hit the dives that haven't been closed down."

"You'll have to call one of your other friends, dear."

"Ouch." Then I remembered her annual health food kick. "Wait. You can watch me get loaded and make fun of me. We can hit a wheatgrass enema place and, ah, fuck it. Move your fuckin' car."

She did. I pulled into the vacant spot and got out, then stood there for a moment, thinking. I was being watched, I was sure, so I tried to decide what I would normally do. I'd just visited someone in prison. Most people would get hammered after that. But where? And with whom? Without Delia, I was coming up short on drinking partners. Chase was out. Santiago was working. Getting blasted with the Armenian was never a good idea. Suzanne was gone. Getting hammered in the Rocket seemed depressing. One by one, I ticked my options off the list. The light rain that had been falling on and off for the last half hour turned back on and made my mind up for me.

With grim resolve, I started walking toward Burnside. When I got there, I crossed and drifted into downtown proper, traveling under the awnings to stay relatively dry, and as I did my mood lifted and I started to get into the spirit of things. There were a few dark, smelly bars left between Second and Fifth, the kinds of places with old man drinkers, women with big hair, that kind of thing. The Olympian was one such establishment. I ducked in without a backward glance. Night was just coming around as I did.

The inside was suitably grim. It smelled like old beer, BO, and burnt plastic. I took a seat at the bar and motioned at the bartender. Some kind of rubber band around my heart popped loose at the sight of her. She was old school, a punk gal with bleached hair and a sore on her lip, hard and lean in the way long years make a body, the way yuppies go to the gym to achieve. The New Portland bartenders, who all looked like executives at Urban Outfitters or accountants at REI, made me irritable and cheap.

"ID?" she asked. She shrugged and pointed up at the camera at the end of the bottles.

"Last time I was here you guys were camera-free." I dug out my wallet and passed her my license.

"Boss is afraid we're stealing olives. Mostly 'cause we are." She passed it back. "What'll it be?"

"Dunno." I surveyed the rows and rows of options. "I have to get half wasted tonight. But I'm gonna sort of sneak up on it."

"A long slow burn," she said, nodding.

"Yeah. I also have to stay halfway sane through the whole process. So, hmm."

She turned and looked at the bottles, too. "I'd say either go top shelf or all the way down to the well. Nothing in between."

"Yeah?"

"Sure. Top shelf, you run out of money before you puke. All the way down at the bottom the shit's so bad you don't even want to drink it, so same difference."

"Christ. One more philosophy that would backfire on me in a wicked way. But I see what you're saying."

"You celebrating anything? Good or bad? I mean, what's your deal?" She turned back, more bored than interested.

"I'm . . . fuck. I guess I'm . . ." I trailed off. She nodded and turned back to the bar, took down the Jim Beam, poured a shot, and set it in front of me. Then she poured a beer back of something watery from the tap.

"Beam. The exact middle of nowhere whiskey. They should advertise a weedy highway median in their *Rolling Stone* ads, but no one ever does the kind of shit that makes sense anymore." She pointed at the beer. "Crap."

"Let the games begin." I picked up the shot glass and drained it, slid it back and gestured for another. While she poured, I took my phone out and looked at it.

The tattoo industry standard was the iPhone. It took great pictures, you could check your email, social media, do Google image searches, everything. I had no email, social media was a bad idea on many levels, and using Google images was too close to cheating for me. My phone was the kind that Cricket gave out for free. It had many interesting features, too. Flashlight, for instance. It took pictures, too, and I even knew how to do it. I hit the little camera button and then hit the little reverse button at the top of the screen, then set it down on the bar and dug a twenty out of my wallet, put it down next to the new shot.

"These cameras," I said. "Guy can't count drinks with pour spouts? You got 'em on every bottle."

"You'd be surprised how a bartender can run a burn on a place," she said. "Water the bottles, swap contents. We had a guy a little while back who would put his own bottles into the rotation, skim the money out of the till as it went in. No way to bust that move without a camera."

"No shit. Nothing is sacred."

"Way shit. You get ten of your own bottles in rotation, easy couple grand a month."

I looked at my glass. Then I looked at the camera. I drank and flipped the camera off. The bartender snorted.

"I guess one more of these little beers," I said. I drained the one I had and then leaned into the bar, picked up my phone. Without moving much, I took five pictures of the room behind me. I'd been turned away from the door for long enough for all kinds of people to file in and take a seat. While I'd been chatting up the bartender, the lone waitress had been busy.

Dessel was at a table on the far wall behind me, drinking coffee and half hiding behind a *Portland Mercury*, our snarky hipster rag. Suitable torture. There was no sign of Pressman, so he was stuck in the Prius or sitting on a toilet somewhere—he had a history of bowel trouble. The other drinkers were innocuous enough. Two construction workers, tired and muddy but happy enough. A chunky boozer lady staring at a phone. Old guy with thinning hair, nursing a coffee and picking at what looked like French fries.

There was a time when I would have known at least one person in a bar like that one. I never did anymore. One of the biggest changes in the city was all around me. I'd become more anonymous than ever. People were so poor these days, too. The old guard, the heads and bodies that once filled places with cheap booze, now drank at home to save a few bucks. Or they'd moved. If you listened closely, you could always hear elements of the master evacuation plan. Rainy Portland, that had once drawn artists and musicians and misfits because of the cheap houses and the shitty weather no one else could stand, had been replaced in the swirling undercurrent of street gossip. No one came here to start a band anymore. People came to cash in on the last of the boom in the real estate market. And the dive bars had cameras. The bartender drifted back over and raised an eyebrow at my empty. I shook my head.

"I know you from somewhere," she said, giving me the eye. "You used to work for UPS or something?"

"Nah."

"You were on *Portlandia*." She said it like I had something to do with the sore on her lip. I saluted her with the last of my beer.

"Something better. The news."

"All the news is fake unless it's harpooning the fake president. Which franchise?"

I motioned for her to lean in. She did.

"You see that guy behind me? Drinking coffee? Looks

sort of like he lives in his mom's basement, maybe has a weird fear of ants?"

She expertly flicked her eyes over my shoulder, then back to me. Miniscule nod.

"Fed. He's a dick, but right now he works for me. That little piece of shit is responsible for the popularity of my face, though. I made a few changes since his promo campaign." I touched the scar on my cheek.

"You're the tattoo guy who went on a murder spree," she breathed, enchanted. "You charge by the hour or the piece?"

"Depends. Whatcha lookin' for?" I cradled my chin, casually swirled my beer.

"Something difficult," she confessed. "Messy. Tedious. Time consuming. Trashy, but in a classic way, so blurry too."

"Say it ain't so."

She laughed without much wind in it. "What the hell are you doing in my bar?"

"Getting drunk. The fed boy is following me to see if he can pick up the trail of some shithead. Long story."

She batted her eyelashes. "I picked a bad day to have my lip act out."

"Your hair looks nice," I replied. "I have a girlfriend anyway. At least I do for the moment."

"Figures. So your fed guy over there, it be better if we made him uncomfortable?"

"No." I set my beer aside and picked up my phone. "But there is one thing you can do for me. I'm not entirely convinced he's all that good at his job. I mean, the kid is smart as a fucker, but I've given him the slip one too many times. When I leave, he'll split a minute later. You wanna do me a favor, snap a picture of whoever follows him out of here and send it to me."

"And for this I get?"

"Extra twenty bucks." I gave her my ready leer. "And the rest of the story."

"Gimme your number."

I left an hour of solitary drinking later, half wasted and just in time to hit the liquor store four blocks over before it closed. Life in the bar had picked up, mostly slumming college kids from PSU and the downtown office crowd. From the liquor store, I walked up to the Park Blocks and strolled, head down against the rain, which had turned into the light, constant drizzle Portland was famous for.

The Park Blocks had once been a hotbed of speed dealers with mullets, and that had given way to a decade of trashy punk kids, my decade, and then it had dried out and become real estate. The streetlights were gold and the trees were old and big, and I had to admit it was pretty. I stopped in front of a *Mercury* dispenser and took one out, then wandered over to a park bench and used it as a seat pad to keep my ass dry.

People drifted past and I watched them come and go, sipping the Beam I'd been developing an appreciation for. The overhanging trees soaked up enough of the rain to let me hang out for a little while without getting soaked, and my bomber jacket was waterproof. Eventually I set the bottle down and lit a cigarette, blowing smoke into the wet night.

Dessel was out there somewhere, watching me drink illegally in a park. Someone might or might not be watching him watching me. But I kept thinking about Hank. Hank Dildo. Hank from Empire of Shit. Delia's fiancé.

Hank unfortunately had very dark dirt on me. About a year ago, I'd hired his entire stupid band to help me out with a shitty situation. I was desperate, and at the time I hadn't thought Hank or any of the Empire kids were players of any kind. They'd posed as waiters while I rufied the shit out of a rich Russian man and Santiago, then the rich man's bodyguard, and afterward they'd helped me transport them to a run-down motel on 82nd. They had no idea what happened after that, but it would be bad if they ratted on me. I'd airmailed the rich man (in a transmission box) back to Russia, where he had warrants. After I beat the shit out of him in an unfair fight, Santiago and I had made a lasting peace that had turned into a real friendship, and it could go conceivably bad for him if it came out that he had been involved with the Russian real estate developer's untimely return home. Though he was not directly connected with the disappearance of Oleg Turganov, having the case reopened would not bode well for him. He was on probation and he was doing well with it. It was not hard to imagine an enterprising guy like Agent Dessel bending the facts and making something stick to Santiago, if only to get to me.

So beating the truth out of Hank regarding his mistress

was out. Kicking his ass for fucking around was out. Essentially, it would be hard to act on Nigel's claims without proof, and even if I got it, it would still be hard. But nothing was impossible. I put it together in different ways, turning it this way and that. It boiled down to the same thing, over and over again.

I didn't want Delia to marry the guy.

I didn't really care if Hank was a junkie. I didn't give half a shit if he was in love with another woman. The kid was an idiot if he thought he could rip Delia off and get away with it, so even that didn't especially bother me. What bothered me was that I knew, I *knew*, that Delia would stick with the piece of shit once she took that vow. She would, no matter what it took, stay true to her guns. She'd blame herself. She'd believe, deep down, that his running away had something to do with her, that he'd seen something in her, that in some way she'd come up short. That she just had to try harder, or differently. And that meant she would have a sad life.

Delia was a lot like me in that way. It was how I felt about Suzanne.

I got up and walked. The opera was a block down, and well-dressed people were going in. I headed up and a little north, to the nearest row of food carts. Most of them were closed for the night, but the taco wagons always held on till the bitter end. There was no line when I stepped under the awning of one of my favorites.

"Gimme, ah, five *pastor*," I said. The squat Mestizo woman didn't even nod, just got to work. While she did, I checked my phone. No new messages, no missed calls.

Nothing. I thought about that as I looked out at the rain. Fake party night had a bitter, lonesome quality to it that I hadn't anticipated.

"Seven fifty."

I turned around and paid, then unwrapped one and ate it while she watched me with flat eyes. It was bad form to stand there, but no one was waiting. She had the heat on and the temperature had been dropping while I thought about Hank, and the spicy warmth felt good on my face. I wolfed down one more before her gaze got to me, then headed out into the rain with a white bag of tacos and a brown bag with a bottle.

Ten minutes later I was in the alcove in front of Ming's Boot and Shoe Repair. I tossed down my new *Mercury* and sat on it, fished a taco out of the bag, and ate slowly, watching the cars pass. It was a little after ten by then and it had been a long day. I was tired, but restless. After taco number four, I set the bag aside and opened the Beam, lit a cigarette. While I drank, I took my phone out again and looked through the photos I'd taken in the bar one more time.

Other than Dessel, none of them looked familiar. I used the browser button Delia had shown me and spent a few minutes typing in "Stolen Car" by Bruce Springsteen. The Patty Griffin version came up, but I was too drunk to fight with my phone all of the sudden, and I liked her version anyway. I listened and watched the rain and smoked.

A particularly scrofulous bum wandered past and stopped by the TriMet trashcan in front of me. I watched as he rooted around in it for a minute, finally coming up with a beer bottle. He peered at it, holding it closer and closer to his eyes, trying to make out the redemption value, and there was something poetic enough in it that I called out to him.

"Fancy restaurant up on Sixth, you go by around one and they set out leftovers."

The bum looked around for the source of the voice, eventually found me with his eyes. I raised the bottle and saluted him. He ambled my way.

"You say what now?" He was painfully thin, and he'd lost his dentures too, so that he was all Adam's apple and bulging eyes. Reflexively, I glanced at his shoes. Big, but they were filthy basketball sneakers with no laces.

"Alcott Frond," I said. "They have specials and what-not. End of the night they put out what's left. Free for the taking."

He nodded and looked out at the night. The guy was drunk as I was. I raised the bottle.

"Care for a taste?"

He squinted at me. "What is it? Beer tears me up anymore."

"Beam."

He took the bagged bottle in one dirty hand and raised it to his lips, took a healthy mouthful, swished it around and swallowed, repeated, then handed it back.

"Ain't drank no Beam in goddamned years," he said. He shook then, and I thought he might throw up, but he didn't. A tremor passed through him and he wiped his lips with the back of his hand. "Oklahoma."

"You mean that's where you last drank Beam, or that's your name?"

He stared at me, confused.

"Oklahoma," I said. He nodded.

"That's right. Rodeo maybe. Back when I was workin' in fencing. Cattle wire. All that's done now."

He got lost inside himself again. I drank and waited for him to say something or move on. When he didn't, I remembered the last taco.

"You hungry, man? I got a taco here."

He looked back at me, then nodded and stepped into the alcove. I passed the bag up to him and he took the last taco out and ate, gumming it as best he could. Judging from the little grunts he made, he liked *pastor* as much as I did.

"Tacos drop in quality the further you get from I-5," I observed. "You got maybe all the way to the ocean on the one side, but going inland? I say maybe fifty miles. A hundred maybe if you get into farming country. Beyond that, you pretty much got shit."

He nodded.

"Course, that's about where steak country starts. You into food?"

He finished the taco and nodded. "Fairies in this shithole town, swear I ain't never touching kale with my mouth again. I'll pick it, but I won't even wipe my ass with it, much less my tongue."

"Right on."

I took a cigarette out and lit it, and before I could offer

him one he wandered off, headed for Burnside and the last homeless shelter. I watched him go. Once, not long ago, the typical homeless guy had been just like that. Drunk, from the south, with no idea how they got so far from home, but with no real desire to go back. But the demographic had swelled to include the working poor. There was no place to rent that a bottom-rung worker in retail or the service industry could afford anymore. For a few years, it had been feasible for them to pile into apartments two to a room, but as the class of landlord changed, so did the rules. If those rules changed and you didn't have the money to split town, then the eviction notice was a one-way ticket to the streets. The shelters were overflowing as a result, and many of the old men and women who had relied on them most weren't able to reliably make it in. They'd die by the dozens once winter settled in, but the news would turn them into a number, or at worst an irate whine in a gossip rag like the one I was sitting on.

The Beam had delivered me to nowhere, just as promised. I got unsteadily to my feet and stepped out of the alcove, then remembered my paper seat. I scooped it up and went to the trashcan and stuffed it through the hole, then drank the last of the booze and dropped the empty in after it. Then I turned and walked in the opposite direction the Oklahoma bum had taken, headed deeper into Old Town.

Walking drunk in the rain at night with no destination in mind is a semi-psychic maneuver, often revealing your deepest wishes or your darkest secrets, sometimes both. As the train station came into view, I realized in a lucid flash my exact place in the universe. I was a single drop of rain, falling through the darkness, ready to splatter, and at the same time I was a heavy thing in unlikely motion, like the water drawn up into the sky only to fall again. Like the rain in the clouds, I wanted down. I wanted down and out.

"How fuckin' dumb," I muttered to myself. I wiped water from my face and kept going.

The switchyards were past the station, but you could see them clearly from under the last awning. I stopped there and sat down on a bench, wiped my hands on my shirt under my coat until they were dry enough to light a smoke, and then I considered the dark lines of steel, all of them bound for somewhere else. I was thinking about that when Agent Dessel sat down next to me. I glanced at him and then looked back at the trains.

"I bet you just ran out of cigarettes," I said finally. Dessel laughed bitterly.

"Even drunk as shit you . . ." He trailed off. I took my pack out and shook one loose. Dessel took it and a match flared.

"Where's Pressman? He want one too?" I didn't bother to look at him. He smoked for a minute before answering.

"Bob has the night off. Just me."

"That why you just blew your cover?"

"Why are you looking at those trains, Darby? Sitting here drunk, you look like some dummy on prom night, watching his best girl bob for apples in another guy's Camaro."

Then I did turn and look at him. Dessel was tired. I could see it in the skin around his eyes. The handful of whiskers he'd collected in this life were three days long. He took a deep drag and I noticed his fingernails. Yellow.

"You look like shit, Dessel. I mean, worse than your usual bad."

He shrugged and looked out at the switchyard, maybe hoping to glean some insight into what I was doing.

"What the fuck could you possibly care what I'm doing, man?" I turned on the bench to face him better. "You're supposed to be my shadow, hunting the stalker and all that. He sees you sitting here, well." I laughed bitterly. "My whole plan goes to hell."

"Trains." Dessel gestured with his cigarette. "I bet I know why you're here. Looking at the slow ride to anywhere." He looked almost sad. "It's 'cause I finally beat you, Darby. You're worn out, aren't you? Took long enough."

I didn't have anything to say to that.

"Toast," he continued. "Couple years of being on the radar is all the time scumbags like you have in 'em. Then they, well, they get drunk and stare at something like trains. Sometimes TV. Dreaming of a way out of all the shit, the crazy bad life they built up. The lies and the violence and the sleepless nights. They just want it over with." Dessel took a deep breath. "The big burnout. End of the line."

We smoked in silence, both of us thinking.

"Delia's getting married," I said finally.

"Who cares."

I sighed. "I do. You, ah, you got a girlfriend? Boyfriend, whatever? Significant other?"

He took another deep breath through his nose, let it out. "No."

"Why? Actually, don't tell me. I really would have sleepless nights."

"I did have a woman I was close to." It took him a little while to keep going. "It didn't work out. Law enforcement is hard on relationships."

My laugh sounded evil because it was. "Goody."

Dessel laughed, too. "It is good! Weeds out the bad ones. Last thing I want is to have to come home and lie about what I did all day. That's for guys like you. Not me. The details of this life, well. You know. Your story is one of them." He laughed again, quieter this time. "The Comings and Goings of Darby Holland. It's a colorful life. Leads to problems for me."

"Jesus." I gave him an appraising look. "Either you're totally fuckin' with me or we actually have something in common."

It was his turn to chuckle in a bad way. "I don't think so. Unless . . ." He squinted at me. "Suzanne."

"Fuckin' A right, dude."

"Figures. She was too good for you." He shrugged. "Loretta was too good for me. Wouldn't it be weird if we were both total wads? I mean, I don't like you. You break the law. You're smug about it. Thus, a piece of shit. But you feel the same way about me. I know you do because you remind me of your profound feelings now and then. But what if they're both right? The women in our lives, I mean."

"Might have a point." I thought about it. "This Loretta of yours turns eighteen, maybe her mom will let you have another run at her."

Dessel sighed. "Smoke for the road?"

I gave him three and he stood.

"'Night, Holland. Don't stay out too late."

"'Night, Dessel. Hope Bob feels better."

That got me a sharp look, and then he was gone.

I looked back out at the dark trains. I was tired. Tired and wet and cold. Something about the conversation with Dessel had hit me in a strange way, and I'd already been in a strange mood. It was his eyes. The way he said the name "Loretta," maybe. I didn't think Dessel was a piece of shit. It was more complicated than that, and also a great deal worse.

Men like him, even boy men, seemed evil to me in a special way. The death of the City of Roses was a prime example of that evil. The tide of blandness. The encroaching quality of white bread with no crust. Pill sleep, with no dreams, for one and all. It was hard to make art in the world anymore, to exist on the fringes of the machinery of convention, to be the lone singer in an endless, faceless chorus of voices making the telephone busy signal sound. Many people think that dreams come out of nothing, that they're born from the vacuum inside empty heads, but that isn't true. And bold dreams come out of people brave enough to think differently, people like Delia, even Chase, even Hank fuckin' Dildo. It took more than guts to light fireworks in the mundane shopping mall the world had been transforming into. The developers like Oleg Turganov, the rich thieves like Dong Ju, they were money men, bad to the bone, but real menace came in the form of misguided do-gooders like Dessel. He wanted the world to be without color. His job was to press down the bumps in the carpet, to smooth out the unsightly wrinkles in the fabric of society. Guys like that, in the metaphorical sense of the word, didn't have souls. And most importantly, they didn't want you to have one either. Deep in his heart, where shit was hard to change, Dessel believed it was his calling to enforce *normal*.

And that was what really bothered me. If a clear blue zero like Dessel blew it with a woman named Loretta on the grounds of passion for anything at all, then the rest of us, with clouds in our skies and the occasional rain, with thunder and lightning and tornadoes and meteorites, we had no chance at all.

I don't remember how I got home.

I woke up to the sound of my phone ringing. It was on my chest, and that couldn't be good.

"Wha? Oh god."

"You did it!" Delia squealed. "I can hear it in your voice! I bet you don't even know how you got home."

"Shit. I think I got so wasted I called Suzanne."

"Ha ha. Cue sad clown song. Rise and shine, dumbass. It's seven a.m. and you have a fun day of all kinds of fun shit to do. I just called Chase and woke him up too. Dudeboy's all psyched to wear his red pants, the nimrod."

"Oh god," I repeated. I sat up. I'd made it to the bed again, and I'd even taken off one boot. The cats were staring at me, unsympathetic. I looked around for evidence of night chaos. Keys, wallet, change, all on the nightstand. No strange murals on the walls, so that was good. No foreign panties, either. Double damn good.

"You want me to come over? Hank is still asleep, the poor baby. Band practice ran late last night."

"Nah. I gotta get my shit together." I took a deep breath and let it out. "My hangover is bad, but not snake-bite-to-the-melon bad."

"Okey dokey. Remember your outfit. I packed you and your new little brother a lunch. And I want you to take one of the vitamins I left in the fridge. Don't try to chew it or you'll barf, just—" I hung up.

I stripped, fed the cats, got the coffee started, and while it was brewing I put a cup of cornmeal and water on low heat and took a shower. Santos. A massive frozen dog. Evading feds in a sinister lowrider. Misadventure. Mayhem. Therapy of some kind, true. I couldn't help it, but the feeling that I was doing something with the potential for fun in it again made me feel better. I dismissed all thoughts of Suzanne for the moment. I hadn't checked the call log, but if I'd drunk dialed her at two a.m. she was sure to have made a list of some kind, charting and ranking my violations, then cross-indexing them with the latest studies in *Emotional Scientist Magazine*, and I'd get the results both barrels. The text message button had a miniature six above it, so her first essays were already in. They could wait.

So could my morning workout. I'd be humping around a hundred pounds plus of frozen meat under crisis conditions soon enough, and then I'd be digging a big muddy hole in the ground. I dressed as Delia instructed, which I felt sure she had included in the plan just because, and then I made the kind of breakfast I needed to fortify me through the experience.

The cornmeal was polenta by then. I fired up the cast iron skillet and dropped in some bacon fat, and while it went from translucent to runny I stirred some milk and olive oil into the cornmeal and added half a can of green chilies, making a thin batter. The cats watched me do this, bored, waiting to go outside. Then I poured a big burp of it into the pan and watched it sizzle. When the first pan-cake was done I put it on a plate and doused it with hot sauce, eating it while the next one cooked.

"No going outside today, dudes," I announced. "Nothing personal. Some lunatic is out there and I don't want you to fuck him up before I do."

Chops lay down right in the middle of the floor in pro-test. Buttons sniffed my boot and then stared up at me with wide, imploring eyes. I tore off a crunchy piece of green chili pancake and offered it to him. He sneezed on it dramatically and lay down, too.

"I'm going to bury a dog today," I reminded them.

When I was done, I washed the dishes and packed my change of clothes in a backpack, then thought for a moment. What might I need on a day like this? I used to carry big ball bearings on questionable outings, but I'd stopped doing it some time ago. A knife seemed excessive. I didn't own a gun. A sword? No. I had one under the bed, but it would send the wrong kind of signal to the kid. In the end, even though I knew it was a mistake, I decided to bring no weapons at all. We'd have shovels, ostensibly, and that would have to be enough.

This is the kind of logic that creates my most lasting problems.

The cab ride to the Lucky was uneventful. The Prius was in the rain behind me somewhere, but I didn't bother look-ing for it. Dessel's late-night appearance left me assured of their participation. The driver dropped me off in front, and Delia opened the door before I could unlock it. She looked me up and down and nodded her approval.

"Nothing gone wrong yet?" I went inside and she locked the door behind me. The shop was dark except for the spill from the neon. I could see the glowing outline of the door to the employee lounge, so the party was back there. It smelled like Delia had just mopped, and of course it smelled like Delia. Birthday cake frosting and margarita mix.

"Not quite yet," she said, "but you have to be patient."

We headed for the back room, quiet for some reason. Chase looked up from the comic book he was reading when we entered, smiling, not a care in the world. He was wearing red pants, red wingtips, and a bright red shirt with a big collar, which he instantly fingered.

"Hey boss. You sure you don't want to trade jammies straight up? The red don't get you laid, you've gone extinct."

"Please," Delia said.

"Jammies?" I rolled my eyes and Chase laughed.

"Okay, boys," Delia said, dropping into her lecture mode, "here's the drill. Gomez and Flaco are about a half hour out, maybe less. They pull up to the back door and start loading in crap from WinCo. Bag after bag of it. About halfway through, Gomez hangs back long enough to drag the dog out of the freezer and position it by the back door, then he starts helping Flaco again. With me so far?"

I nodded. Chase shrugged and glanced at the comic book. Delia picked it up and put it behind her back.

"Right. As soon as they're finished, Gomez calls my number. Their ride is idling, doors open, trunk up like they're still unloading. We get the call and our team goes. The shop lights fire up. I go out and start yelling on my phone, totally made up, and that will draw attention to the front. Thirty seconds later Chase, wearing Darby's fetching ensemble, blows out at Olympic speed and sprints to the parking lot, gets in Darby's car and tears out, straight to Burnside and then to I-5, head down. I'm out front watching because I was already out there having my phone conversation. The instant I see Chase exit the parking lot I call you, Darby. You get that fuckin' dog into the waiting ride and casually drive away, go pick up that kid and do your thing. Questions?"

Chase politely raised his hand.

"Chase Manhattan," Delia said formally. "The floor is yours."

"Where am I going again?"

"North or south," Delia replied. He nodded and held his hand out for the comic. Delia shook her head. "Get changed. The clock is ticking."

Chase and I began stripping. He had a huge owl tattooed on his stomach that I'd never seen before. I handed him my shirt and he put it on without sniffing the armpits, which was unexpectedly courteous, and as he was about to take his red pants off he glanced at Delia, who was watching us, arms folded.

"You, ah . . ." He trailed off.

"Delia." I tossed my thumb at the door.

"I'm about to get married, you assholes. Like I care what

you two look like naked. Plus, this might be my last chance to see a man other than Hank without his clothes on."

"Beat it," I said. She stormed out and slammed the door. Chase winced but said nothing as I handed him my pants.

"Your car have any problems?" he asked casually.

"Nah. I'd head south if I was you. Traffic eases up sooner. CDs in the glove box. Doobie Brothers, Ramones. Some Creedence."

He made a face. "So, ah, where you takin' this dog? So we don't head in the same direction."

"Maybe don't ask too many questions in these situations, homie."

"Unasked." But he said it with a smile. Pants on, he held his arms wide. "I look like you or what?"

"Kinda." I started lacing my spare boots on. "Pull the hat lower. Don't let Delia whip out her makeup kit. She'll do it just to fuck with us."

As if on cue there was a knock on the door.

"Time to do your faces," Delia called.

"No," Chase and I called back together.

Silence. Then, "T minus five minutes. Anybody has to pee, do it now."

We looked at each other. Chase shrugged. I did, too. We lit cigarettes instead. I sat down. He sat down, too. My phone rang and startled us both. I took it out and looked at it, put it back in pocket.

"Suzanne," I told him. He nodded.

"Ah."

"Pretty sure I called her last night after I'd been drinking."

"It happens."

"Yeah."

"Shit already tense?"

"Totally."

"Huh."

We smoked. And then suddenly it was on.

"We are go, people!" Delia screamed. "Darby! Back door position! Chase! Prepare for evacuation!"

"Luck, dude." Chase rose and straightened my pants.

"Back at ya."

He went out and I went through the side door down to the bathroom and our back door. I could hear an engine idling, then Flaco cursing. A moment later he was joined by a cursing Gomez. Then it was just the engine. The shop lights went on and I heard the front door open and close. Thirty seconds later it opened and closed again as Chase barreled out. Ten seconds after that my phone rang.

"You know what you're gonna say to the kid?" Delia asked quietly.

"Do you? Do I go now?"

"Soon as you tell me, I give you the thumbs up or down."

"Stay true." It just came out of me.

"Go." She whispered it.

I opened the back door and peeked out. A white minivan was squatting by the back door of the Rooster Rocket. Gomez had selected the worst ride in his entire car collection, the supremely pitiful 2001 Chrysler Town & Country EX his seventeen-year-old niece had rejected as offensive. The doors were open and waiting. Flaco's head appeared. He looked both ways and gestured for me to hurry.

I scrambled to their back door and then took a step back toward the van, appalled. The dog was huge, as described, but the army blanket had slipped off its head. The frozen tongue was projecting out at a right angle, almost straight up and dark purple, and the eyes were open in a lazy, sleepy way, glazed with freezer rime. Flaco elbowed me.

"Move it, culo!" He retreated back into the bar as fast as he could.

Cursing, I grabbed the cold front legs and leaned back, dragging the carcass over the trim. The blanket tore free as the body hit the alley surface and the friction increased. I clambered into the van and in one huge heave I pulled the body up inside and on top of me. Flaco reappeared and threw the blanket over us in a flash and slammed the bar door.

Cursing, I crawled out from under the dog and pulled the sliding door closed, then clambered into the front seat. There was a straw cowboy hat on the passenger seat no one had told me about, but I put it on, slouched low, and put the van in reverse. Just then, my phone rang again. I stopped and dug it out. Suzanne again. I tossed it on the passenger seat and let it ring as I backed out of the alley. Without a glance in either direction, I put it in drive and headed for the Broadway Bridge and the freeway that would take me to the owner of the frozen dog behind me.

Suzanne called twice more as I drove. I didn't answer. Once I was safely out of Old Town I called Delia instead.

"They followed Chase," she reported. "Flaco says you got the dog in the van? They gave you a fuckin' van?"

"Sure as fuck did. The little white one nobody wanted."

She laughed. "Please take a selfie. I know you don't do that kind of thing, but if you could do it just this once. For my scrapbook."

I had to smile. "This dog? It's even bigger than I thought. Also, no shovels. And I'm wearing a cowboy hat."

"They forgot the shovels." Delia made a *tsk* sound. "I told Flaco to put the lunch I made for you and your psycho-in-training in the glove box and he swore up and down he did. But then he forgets the shovels. Right here is where everything starts to go to shit. You have a plan?"

"Not yet. Suzanne called, like, three times."

Delia laughed again, but ominously said nothing.

"Alright," I growled, cutting her off. "Call me if anything develops."

"You too. As far as shovels go, maybe—"

I hung up and drove. It was overcast and drizzling, but the uniform gray sky was the kind that didn't have real rain in it. It wasn't cold, so at least we wouldn't be freezing while we dug. I lit a cigarette and considered the kid, but the closer I got to the hospital the less I had in the way of camp counselor material. I'd managed to convince myself that half of the rules I lived by were dangerous bullshit by the time I turned into the parking lot. My heart sank instantly.

Santos stood out in every way, a shining, glossy beacon of East LA gangster apparel, his slender, dapper frame radiating casual violence, intelligent reproach, and too much dick for his own good. He was beautiful, but in a terrifying, demented, Catholic way. He'd left the protective overhead of the Emergency entrance so he could smoke. There were signs everywhere indicating there was no smoking at all, anywhere, including one right behind him, but his demeanor made clear that he considered the warnings to be for other people or merely polite suggestions. White button-up shirt, all the way to the throat, black slacks, patent leather shoes, no jacket. He looked like he was on his way to a fashion show or a bank robbery, but not a hole digging. Santos must have weighed in at an even one hundred pounds, but every teaspoon of it was prizefighter. I pulled up and zipped down the passenger window. He swayed back to peer in.

"I help you, white boy?" Quiet, like he expected me to read his lips.

"Santos?"

In answer, he flicked his smoke in the general direction of the NO SMOKING sign and got in. Then he stared straight forward. He smelled like aftershave and hair tonic.

"I guess you don't have a shovel either," I continued. He turned and looked back at the lump of dog under the army blanket, then back. He made a wan flick of his hand in the general direction of forward.

"I-5 South."

I smiled. We were already bonding.

"Santos," I began as we headed out of the parking lot, "your uncle tells me you did some time in juvie awhile back."

Nothing.

"You, ah—" I searched for the right words. "Fuckin' raw news, little dude. Teen years, you think about pussy more than you'll think about anything else for the whole rest of your life. Not that you don't keep thinking about it, but not like that. You crazy? I mean, that shit drive you nuts? I'm just trying to get a handle on how fucked in the head you are."

That got his attention. He swiveled his head and stared at me, his face carefully blank. He said nothing.

"I'm a fuck-up, too," I continued. "But I never got caught. Different time. Different town." We came to a stoplight and I took out my cigarettes, shook one loose and lit it. "No bragging, not exactly. But that's, ah, you know, some information. To get us started."

"White boy," he began, "my uncle—"

"Don't call me white boy," I interrupted. "Name is Darby."

"Darby," he repeated. "My uncle says that some of the shit that comes out of your head sometimes makes sense. Now, this dog back here?"

"Jesus!" I said. My phone was ringing. I dug it out and tossed it to him.

"You want me to answer this?"

"Fuck no. See who it is."

He looked. "Suzanne."

"Well. That's another problem. But let's start at the beginning. Shovels."

"What about 'em?" He sat my phone in a cup holder in the divider, took out his cigarettes.

"Where are they?"

"Dunno." Santos fired up. "Store, I guess."

"Lemme guess, you're broke."

"As a joke. Fuckin' janitor at a hospital, yo."

I drove. He had a point. We needed supplies anyway. The kid smoked in silence, not exactly brooding, and it occurred to me for the first time that he might still be upset about his dog.

"Sorry about your dog," I volunteered.

Nothing.

"What, ah, what was his name?"

"She." He took a drag, blew it out. "Bella."

"Bella," I repeated.

"Who's Suzanne? Your old lady?" He glanced over at me with the same blank expression. The convict dead eyes. He had them already.

"You have any idea how much shit I went through to be in this fuckin' van right now?" I asked. The glaze in his eyes wavered. "I'm under federal surveillance right now, homie. Had to do all kinds of shit to give them the slip and they're gonna be pissed tomorrow if they find out. Then, then!" I stopped. He angled a little bit in my direction and I realized he wasn't wearing his seat belt. It shocked me that I'd noticed. I wasn't wearing mine, either.

"Then?" A hint of a smile, and not an arrogant one, either. Young Santos appeared to enjoy a good yarn with fuckery involved.

"Then we have a plan to smuggle Bella out of your uncle's bar that involves, I shit you not, a dude in bright red pants. In a mad convolution of reason, this same guy hotrods the fuck out of the scene wearing *my* pants! That's a side story we can get to later. But boom, we pull it off, and—"

"There!" he said, pointing. "The big Fred Meyer's! For a shovel, *ese*." He looked at me and winked. "And some cerveza."

I took the exit. As I did my phone started ringing again. Santos picked it up and read aloud.

"Dirt Mouth." Delia.

"Answer and tell her I'll call her back."

Santos nodded.

"Hello, this is the phone for Darby, the furious white man." Santos paused and listened. "No, Mrs. Dirt Mouth, we are currently free on our own recognizance." Another pause, this one longer. He looked at me. "Yes, he still wears the cowboy hat." Pause. He turned the phone away and before I could grab it he snapped a picture and hit send, all with the unnatural karate speed kids have with phones.

"Dick," I snapped.

Santos listened more. "Yes, Madam. I will do my best." He hung up and put the phone back in the cup holder. "I'm to keep us out of jail today. Evidently you have to help that foul-tempered woman go chicken shopping tomorrow."

I pulled into a parking space and cut the engine, turned to him.

"Guard Bella. You a Mexican that actually drinks Mexican beer?"

"Not even," Santos replied scornfully. "Think twelve-pack, maybe Stella, like a Euro lager."

"Figures. You gonna lose your shit and steal this van, anything dumb like that?" I gave him a pained expression. "I mean, you cracked in the head? Fragile and whatnot? I just don't know what I'm dealing with here, like I said."

"Dude." Santos blew out a breath. "Listen. I just talked to someone on *your fucking phone* that makes me think I should be asking you the same questions. So shovel, beer, don't fuck up in there." He squirmed uneasily. "Jesus, you want me to go in there with you, fuckin' babysit? I'm nineteen, dog. I go, we don't get the beer. No beer is no *bueno*. So chop-chop." He clapped his hands together and turned forward, went still.

I picked up my phone and calmly got out. If he stole the van and went broken arrow on the operation, I'd be able to call a cab. Plus, he struck me as the kind of kid who would look at all my messages.

Fred Meyer's was the Oregon response to Walmart, a giant place that specialized in nothing in particular. I had a bad history with them, too, going way back. My first violation on their turf had come right after I moved to Portland. I was the mop guy at the Lucky in those days, no older than Santos, and with a few bucks in my pocket I'd gone to see the Butthole Surfers and Smegma. Afterward on the way home I'd cut through the local Fred Meyer's parking lot, where I got jumped by two drunk guys, right in the middle of the empty lot. The comical conflict ratcheted up a notch when the night security guard showed up to see what the hell was going on. The situation warped and we all three decided to fight the guard instead of each other. In later years, I'd been banned from two more Fred Meyer's for various incidents. But not this one.

Not yet.

I'd parked by the home improvement entrance. There was no greeter, but I got an informal nod and a second glance from the first clerk I passed. Unfortunately for all, it was the upper-middle-class franchise abutting the Raleigh Hills, and they didn't see much in the way of middle aged punks with impressive facial scars. I saw rakes pointing out of the top of a distant aisle and headed that way.

Right on the money, and five different kinds of shovels to choose from, too. I could never really understand why there were so many. Obviously, I didn't need a snow shovel. The shovel with the broad, flat head looked like it was more for scooping, so I immediately moved past it as well. The remaining three had spade-shaped heads, with what looked like varying weight and minor differences in size. I selected the one that would make the best weapon and took it out of the rack.

The heft was good. I visualized a foe in front of me and made a few practice stabs and a lunge or two. Not too heavy, but just heavy enough. Then I whirled it and whipped it around, tossed it up and caught it in a spear throwing position. That was when the first security guard appeared at the end of the aisle.

Satisfied, I put the shovel over my shoulder and headed in his direction. He glowered at me as I approached, so I stopped in front of him to say hi.

"Gotta go bury a dog," I explained. "But it's a crazy fuckin' world man. Crazy. A mofo needs a shovel to double as an edged weapon."

I headed for the beer. Behind me, the security guard kept a discreet distance as he called in reinforcements. It had been some time since I'd been inside one of the really big stores. There were more advertisements than ever, packing every available surface, and many of them were electronic. There were also many more cameras, and not just the black half globes on the ceiling. The electronic ads surely had cameras in them, if my tech customers were to be believed, but I'd read in one too many places that there was also a camera or two wherever there was a cash register, and the damn things had multiplied.

I paused in the first food aisle. Chips and more chips. Santos might enjoy suckdog fare, but he had good skin so he likely wasn't a junk food kind of guy. I strolled past without entering it and had made it past cookies and then lukewarm jumbo plastic multicolored sodas without incident. The security complement had grown to three, and when my phone rang we all paused together so I could answer it. Delia.

"Fred Meyer security," I answered, leering back at them. "Is this the jackwad's lawyer? Cause this motherfucker is—"

"Don't tell me you're in a Fred Meyer's," Delia snapped. "Where's the fuckin' kid?"

"He's safe." I turned around and headed straight for the three security guards then. They were big, but in the way their mothers might have described as husky. Overweight, mostly around the middle, and too young to have ever been real cops. "I didn't want him to have to deal with these"—I was right on top of them, so I fake lunged at them—"spastic rookies!" All three of them jumped and I laughed.

"Sir," one of them began. I kept going. I'd finally seen the beer.

"Did you just do that right in front of them?"

"Yeah."

"Darby." She took a deep breath.

"What the hell is this shit about a chicken? Because if that was the first sign of dementia in young Santos, it's not too late to turn around."

"Did Suzanne call today?" she asked, neatly changing the subject.

"Three or four times. She sent a bunch of messages, too. She sends these really, really, really long ones." I hit the beer aisle and turned into it. "Suzanne knows I don't have email, but she's somehow figured out how to send massive letters that can only be considered letters, or emails as it were, to my message thingy."

"Everyone can do that, dude. We will get you to join this century. I'm working on it. Consider it my going away present. The gift of technology."

"The chicken," I repeated. I stopped in front of the Stella Artois and I'll be damned if they didn't have it in twelve-packs. I lowered the shovel and managed to grab it with the same hand. Then I turned and headed back toward the security guards.

"The chicken," Delia began, "is a small piece of a larger—" She kept going, but at that moment I was close enough to the guards for them to hear the phone. I held it away from my ear and mouthed in a hoarse whisper, "My boss talks and talks. WHICH WAY ARE THE DONUTS?"

They scowled and I blew past, headed for a line of registers at speed.

". . . the sanctity of the ceremony." Delia ended on a firm note, as though she had said something reasonable.

"Gotta pay for this shit," I said. "Call you later. Any word from Chase?"

"He's somewhere near Salem. I told him to head back in about an hour. My car is in the parking space right now. When he gets close, we'll swap and he can run right back inside. If they bust him it won't matter at that point, but I figured it'd be good to at least try."

"Right on. Okay then. Shovel, beer, smokes, we're set."

"Jesus."

We hung up on each other simultaneously. I put the phone away. The line at the register I picked went fast. I paid without saying another word, and all three of the guards followed me to the exit. There were two more waiting outside. I stopped.

"You guys gonna follow me to my car?" I asked. "I didn't steal anything. Paid in cash, right in front of you."

None of them replied. By then I had the shovel in one hand and the beer in the other. I raised the shovel.

"Anyone follows me to my ride gets a spankin.'"

One of the new guards stepped forward and took a picture of me with his cell phone, then stepped back.

"Don't return," he said. "We reserve the right to refuse service to anyone. It is the policy of Fred Meyer's to ensure the safety and security of—"

I started walking. It was raining a little harder, but the temperature had gone up a notch. When I got in the van, I handed Santos the beer and gently put the shovel next to the dog. As I started the engine, he tore open the top of the case and took a beer out, cracked it and passed it to me, then opened one for himself. He gestured at the cluster of security guards by the exit, who were still watching.

"'Sup with those guys?"

"Bored," I replied. He shrugged.

"You call your woman back?"

I pulled out and headed for the freeway, thinking. He had a point. The longer I put Suzanne off, the worse it was going to be. But calling her from the road seemed like the wrong thing to do. If she asked what I was doing, I'd have to lie about it and I didn't want to. I didn't want to tell her that I was driving around with a young criminal, drinking beer and chatting about the high burnout rate in crime, the merits of calculation, the philosophy of true freedom, the ethos of a life unchained by "responsible" behavior, or how to deal with the weight of individuality. I was making all of it up as I went, and talking to her of all people mid-ramble would derail me. That was telling, in a bad way, in a way Delia would point to as proof that she was right about my relationship with Suzanne. But if I called her tonight and she asked what I'd been doing all day that was so much more important than her, I could truthfully tell her that I'd been helping some kid bury his dog and leave it at that.

"No," I said finally.

Santos drank and said nothing.

"You got a gal?"

"Sometimes," he replied. "Big family picnic last month. You know a waitress named Cherry? White girl? Big butt? Works at the Rocket every once in a while?"

I knew her. Cherry was a sweetheart. She liked dogs too, I recalled. At least she talked about them sometimes. Blond hair, blue eyes, maybe ten years older than Santos. She'd been a regular waitress at the Rooster Rocket before the explosion that changed all of our lives. I was glad she and Gomez were close enough that she still went to his family BBQs.

"Sure. I know her."

"She gives good head."

"I hope she says the same of you, young Santos." I glanced at him. "Does she? Cause if not, you should shut up about her cock-smoking chops."

"I bet she does," he said lightly. "I hope so, anyway. But that is as close as I can get. The flirting, then the dancing, then the small love."

"Probably a bad thing, dude. You gotta be ready to have your guts ripped out. That kind of prophylactic thinking is a sign of the times. People confuse sad with depressed, think it's unnatural. It isn't."

"You're happy?" He was actually curious. "I mean, really?"

"Nah. But I'm full. S'okay for now, and who knows. It might lead to this 'happy' we all dream about. I'm trying."

"And you believe this is wise."

"I didn't say that." I glanced over at him. "But it's smarter than swapping head in a parking lot. You gotta think to the future, kid." I put my eyes back on the road and considered. "Here's one thing. Little bit of insight. Lemme ask you a question. You think being in juvie gave you the right view of women? Take Cherry. She's sweet.

Little too old for you, but who cares, really. A woman like that could be a good thing. Talk. Tell me why not."

"You first."

"What?"

Santos finished his first beer at the same time I finished mine. While he got us another round I lit a cigarette. Once we were both drinking and smoking, he continued.

"You have more to say than I do on the topic of women. First, you have one you say is the one you are with. She calls, you don't answer. And you've been doing it all morning, evidently. Then you have another, Mrs. Dirtclod or whatever, who calls and you answer immediately. She also speaks as though she's your wife. So what is it, white boy? Tell me something about women I should know. I'm listening."

"Jesus."

City was gradually giving way to countryside. I relaxed into my second beer and tried to enjoy myself. The road was clear of traffic for the most part. It was a weekday. So what if the kid was a smartass? I was too, and it never faded. I thought about what he'd said. Women, well. They weren't a topic, like rocks or trees or rain or wind, as near as I could figure. They were more like something I could only approach with a telescope and never understand in a real, concrete, tangible way. But that didn't make any sense, because I touched them all the time. Or at least I wanted to. Had. Intended to in the future. It was all very confusing.

"It's all very confusing," I said at last. "Here's how it

shakes out. Suzanne, that's the woman I'm with. In the same way you were with Cherry, but in a bolder, more consistent way. We can't keep our clothes on for too long in each other's company. I love her, but in this one way. And that way? That is a strange way. Unique." I paused, considering what I was saying.

"Go on," Santos prompted.

"Maybe it isn't unique. Maybe it's the same shit all over again, or worse, maybe it's what I expected. But either she's too good for me or she isn't, ah—we can't get on the same page in the deep down way. She either wants me to be something I'm not or believes I'm something I'll never be."

"I see." He finished his second beer but refrained from a third and smoked instead. Eventually—"And the other one? The rude one?"

"Delia. She's my friend. She's getting married to some sack of shit I should probably have brought with us to bury, but she's—she is one of a kind. A total fuck-up on the surface, but so not once you get to know her."

"Ahh," he said knowingly.

"Don't 'ahh' me, dumbass. I have women problems. Real ones. External ones, like on the outside. Yours are in your head, little dude."

"Hm. And I should *export* these problems, you say. Share them with the world and make them real, as you've done."

I glared at him. "What are you, some kind of idiot? Of course you should. Haven't you been listening?"

Santos laughed, and eventually I did too.

"I thought you were going to be a hard-ass," he said after a minute. "My Uncle Gomez, he speaks of you like people speak of him."

"And how do your people speak of my friend Gomez?" I couldn't help it, I was curious.

"My uncle is a hero to many people. Here and in Los Angeles."

"He is?"

Santos looked at me. "You didn't know?"

"Well, I ah, you see—"

"This is part of my problem with the family. So many heroes. So many legends. My brother Miguel and me? Fuck, *ese*. No way we could live up to any of that shit."

"Huh. That why you guys robbed a, what was it? A gas station?"

"A gas station. A gas station." Santos said it bitterly. "Miguel, he was three years older than me. We had this little apartment, me an' him. The bedroom was his. We had this old couch we found an' that was mine."

"I lived like that when I was your age. Sucks."

"Yeah. We could have called Flaco and bitched. Uncle Gomez would have come and brought us up here, to the rain and all the church on Sunday, do this, do that, go to school, blah blah, you know? But fuck that. It was too late. Hard to convince people that you aren't a man but you aren't a boy either. And people talk to you a certain way after they know you were hungry. So fuck that."

Unfortunately, I knew exactly what he was talking about. He could tell, too.

"Yeah, dog. You know. I can smell it on you. So Miguel, he gets this idea one day when he finds a gun." Santos laughed. "Right there! In front of this little store! Just fuckin' laying there, like it fell out of a bag and someone just kept on walkin', man. He picks it up, walks right the fuck into that little store and it's like shopping! Three bills, just like that!"

I didn't say anything. When I glanced over, Santos had his eyes closed.

"We ate chicken that night. A whole chicken, man. And we had beer, too." It came out quieter, and I could tell that he had savored that memory many times. "A few days later, maybe a week, we used the last twenty to buy another gun. So now we had two guns."

"Two guns," I repeated.

"Two guns are better than one."

"And then you robbed the gas station."

"Then we robbed many gas stations, man. We robbed all kinds of things."

Neither of us said anything for a while. I wondered if Gomez or Flaco knew this, and I somehow suspected they didn't.

"But then something went wrong," I said. "You got popped."

"Something went wrong all right. Miguel and I, we came to Portland for a wedding. It was right out here, where we're going to bury sweet Bella. We had to come. If we didn't, my uncle would have known we had left my piece of shit junkie mother and her husband. He would have been so angry with all of us. After that, we went back and forth. We had a car by then. Miguel had this woman. It started to get expensive, man, and so it became, er, risky."

I didn't say anything.

"I was into the coke. This one whole weekend, I don't remember shit. One day it's Thursday and I score big. Then it's red lights and blue lights and music and, ah man, I don't even know. And then someone is shaking me awake, screaming. Consuela, Miguel's chica, and she's screaming that Miguel has been shot. He tried to rob a gas station without me." He stopped.

"Fuck, dude."

"Yeah. The bitch took off. I did the last of the coke and I got my gun. I was gonna go and shoot the fuck out of everyone at that gas station, kill every one of them, but the cops got to me first. They came to the apartment. And there I was. Fifteen years old, high as a motherfucker, gun in my hand."

"So, so they didn't get you for robbery? I mean, you weren't even there."

"Nah, dog, I wasn't." Santos gave me a watery stare. "But they could smell it on me, see?"

"Shit."

"Yeah. I dunno. I was in maybe a month, broke this rapey guy's arm and I got an extra year pinned on. Fucked up again, took me all the way to my eighteenth birthday."

"That's fucked up," I said finally. "Gomez, Flaco, they don't know about this?"

"Sure they do. Now, anyway. Both of them, once upon a time, a long, long time ago, they did crime. Especially

Uncle Gomez. But a man has to forgive himself, they say, before he can change his ways. So they wait. And watch." He sighed. "And watch."

"Family, man." I shook my head. "You know how lucky you are? Those people care about you, dude."

He frowned and said nothing.

"I don't have any kind of family. That kind of life, you got no safety net. Break a leg, you die. Get too sick, you die. So a part of you gets tired way before it should and it just keeps wearing down, year after year, until there's nothing left of that part of yourself but dust and echoes. Then you carry that empty around until the end."

Santos looked at me, but his story was over for the moment.

"I think I understand why Gomez wanted me to talk to you," I continued. "Maybe a little. It might be that you've confused the system for your family. They fed you and put a roof over your head. You're a smart kid, Santos. I can tell. So think this through. You don't think that in some way you've been tricked? You go back in as an adult, you know how much money they'll make on you? All the years of your life, working for free? Juvie manufactures slaves, dummy. The system is *for profit*. What part of that don't you understand?"

"You're just like they are," he said, disgusted.

"No, dude." I laughed then. "I'm not. That's my problem with Suzanne. The conversation has come full circle." I whacked him on the arm. "See, there is no reason in the end to obey every fuckin' goddamned thing. You live by a code is what you do. Look around with free eyes, little man. We live in a country where rich people eat the poor, where kids like you are set up to fail so some wad in a suit can live in a bigger house. 'Business as usual' is a disgusting proposition for me too. It's so fucked up I don't think I ever even considered it."

That got him. He was paying attention now.

"But I do have rules," I continued. "I break them from time to time, and when I do I feel bad. But one of those rules is to stay free. Don't get caught. Someone wants to trade you on the New York Stock Exchange, little homie. Your response should be twofold. One, to say fuck that. Two, to spend your life robbing those fuckers for even trying that shit in the first place. You're pissed off at what's happened to you, but you aren't pissed off at the right people."

Santos snorted.

"I had all night and all morning to think up wise and wholesome shit to dump into your empty head," I confessed, "but I came up empty, too. I guess all I have to say is this. Half of what is labeled 'crime' is something else. You be your own judge. Your own boss. The world is broken and you won't fix it by obeying the broken rules. But two guns are better than one? Robbing gas stations? That's criminally stupid."

"We're getting close," Santos said. "Five more miles or so, we take a right. Dirt road, maybe a quarter mile in to the big clearing."

"Time for one more road beer."

The turnoff to the Gomez family wedding festival and animal cemetery was unmarked.

I took the narrow one-lane entrance and hit the mud and gravel road slowly. It was lined with tall trees, second growth that was at least twenty years old, and the forest floor still had the mossy stumps and fallen logs left behind from the last clear-cut. The canopy let through enough light for ferns to grow, and everything was covered in an emerald moss. Driving that slowly through it, I felt transported as I always did when I got out into the woods, and I wondered again why I didn't leave the city more often. Suzanne always wanted me to, and maybe that had something to do with it. My face started to relax. Beside me, Santos stared out the window, lost in his memories. I cracked the window and the air was green smelling and fresh. The clearing came up two bends and five minutes in and I stopped. Tall grass, a little more than knee high, swayed gently, deep green, tipped with gold. Peaceful. We sat there appreciating it for a moment before Santos spoke. He pointed off to the right.

"There's a big tree over there, one of the old ones they missed when they cut everything down the first time. My uncle bought this right after he first moved up here. It was all stumps then except one or two trees the hippies had driven nails into."

"That where we should dig?"

"Yeah." He opened his door. "Maybe I'll go look first. Take a second to just, I dunno."

"Sure. I'll get Bella out of the back. No rush."

Santos got out and slowly walked away, deep in thought. I watched him go and wondered what he was thinking. Probably about the last time he was here. Dancing with Cherry, music on the boom box, grill fired up, maybe strings of lights. The smells of sizzling meat and posole and fried bread. Laughter. I'd been to the parties his family threw, none of them out here, but they were good ones in a special way. He might have been daydreaming about fooling around with Cherry in the back seat of her car and wondering if I was full of shit. But he was probably remembering eating and drinking and feeling like an out-sider, like he'd been tainted in some way he was having trouble washing off. I got out and walked around to the side of the van and opened the door. Reluctantly, I pulled the army blanket away. Bella had thawed enough for her eyes to go wide. Her purple tongue was no longer stiff, but had become sticky instead and was glued to the side of her face.

I put the blanket down and yanked the dog out onto it, folded the blanket over the top. We could drag her over the wet grass, I reasoned, and save the sweating for the actual dig. I lit up a cigarette and looked around, leaned up against the van. On the far side of the clearing, there were three picnic tables visible, old wooden ones that had turned ash gray with exposure. It was wide enough for more than a hundred revelers to comfortably do their thing. I wondered why Gomez had let the forest come back rather than plant grapes. The answer was probably the stumps, which were too huge to remove. Clearing the land after a clear-cut would have been too much work.

Santos appeared a moment later and made his way to the van. He was still lost in reflection when he looked at Bella.

"You didn't tell me what happened to her," I said. He looked up.

"Cancer. Bella had it in her stomach. The vet told me she had a year, but she was in pain." He looked down at the covered body and shrugged.

"You take the shovel," I suggested. "I can pull her along the grass. Sound okay?"

Santos reached into the van and took the shovel out, slowly started walking back the way he came. I leaned in and put my cigarette out in the ashtray, then grabbed the edge of the blanket and followed. Dragging the big dog was far easier than carrying it, but even so I took my time, leaving him to his thoughts. Santos got to the edge of the trees before me and vanished into the woods. I stopped at the edge when I got there and peered in. He was twenty paces away and digging fast under a massive old Douglas fir. I walked in to take a turn, and as I did I understood why he was working so fast.

"Hornets!" I shouted. Right as I heard the buzzing sound the first of them flew up my shirt and stung me on the chest. Santos looked up, frantic, and I was amazed.

One of his eyes was already close to swollen shut. "Santos, get out of there!"

"It must be here!" Santos screamed back. "Here! Here!" Then he was digging again, hacking at the soil with all his might.

I lurched back as another hornet hit me right in the chin. Then I was running, tearing my jacket off and using it as a giant fly swatter. I sprinted into the middle of the clearing, flailing the air around me, then stopped and looked back to shout again. Another hornet flew up the back of my shirt and I tore it off and threw it, then rolled in the grass. The hornets had found me, though, and nothing was going to stop them. Cursing, I scrambled to my feet again and ran toward the picnic tables, then shook out my bomber jacket and put it back on, zipped it all the way up.

"Santos!" I yelled. "Santos!" It echoed into the distance.

Nothing. I cocked my head and listened. He was still digging frantically. A patrol hornet zipped past, and before it could circle back and send out the alarm I jogged back to the van.

When I got there, I opened the door and took out two beers, cracked one and drained it and put the cold glass against my chest, held the unopened one on my chin. My cell phone started ringing and I was glad it hadn't broken in all the rolling around, but not glad enough to take it out of my pocket and answer it. A lone hornet zipped past and I remained still until it was gone.

I was going to have to recommend therapy. I couldn't believe it. The kid was fucked in the head in a way nobody even suspected. I'd never even heard of something like this. I held my breath for a second and listened, and abruptly the digging stopped. Santos screamed and I dropped the unopened beer.

"Kid! I'm by the van!" I wasn't up to dragging him out while he was still capable of yelling. "Run for it, man! Run!"

Santos sprinted out of the woods at top speed. He was carrying a muddy metal box, clutched to his chest, and even at a distance I could see the angry halo around him.

"What the—"

"Start the engine!" Santos shrieked. "Hurry! Ahhhh!"

He was coming and there was no stopping him. I slammed the side door and ran around to the driver's side, jumped in, and started the engine. Then I reached over and locked his door as he skidded to a halt. His eyes widened as he realized I wasn't letting him in. I put the van in reverse.

"What the fuck, man!"

"Fuck you!" I yelled back. "Get those bees off of you!" I floored it and tore backward as fast as the van would go. Santos bolted off into the woods again and I watched him go. It became clear that he meant to lose as many hornets as he could in the trees, so I backed down the road another twenty feet and waited for him to circle in. As he did, running a little slower now that he was alone, I leaned out and unlocked his door. He jumped in and slammed it, then glared at me, panting. I glared back.

"You crazy dumbass," I said.

He'd been stung several times on the face and hands.

Shaking, he put the muddy box flat on his lap and fished out a beer, cracked it, and gulped down half before he came up for air.

"We made it, *ese*." Santos let out a strange, broken giggle.

"Santos, you insane little fucker, if you dug up someone else's dead pet I swear to god I'm leaving you here."

He laughed and finished the beer, dropped the empty on the floor and took out another one, handed it to me. Then he patted the top of the box. It was a little bigger than a standard briefcase, off beige, and it looked like it had been in the ground for a while.

"Debbie," he said finally. "Debbie!"

I looked at the box again. My skin crawled. Santos turned his wild eyes on me.

"My brother Miguel's last words. 'Tell Santos the money is with Debbie!'"

"What? Who the fuck is Debbie?"

"Three years in juvie I wondered who Debbie was! We don't know a single Debbie, not one. So who is this mystery woman? Who is this fucking woman with all of our money? All of the money from the robberies Miguel had been saving so we could have a new life. The bitch had stolen it all. You see?"

"No." But all of the sudden I did. My mouth went dry.

"He said *the bees*! The money is with *the bees*! He buried it here where no one would ever look!"

My first punch was a right cross to his jaw. It bounced his head off the door and dazed him, so I reached across and opened his door, then leaned back and awkwardly kicked him out of the van. Santos lay there unmoving, his eyes wide and unfocused and pointed at the sky. I climbed out and stared down at him.

"What did you do to that poor fuckin' dog, you piece of shit!" Then I kicked him in the side.

Santos was just as tough as I feared he might be. He rolled with the kick and then he was on his feet, lightning fast. The metal box bounced off my shoulder and as it did he came at me swinging, poised like a street fighter, his body tight. I barely ducked out of his first punch and whipped in and chopped him once, hard in the stomach, then kneed him in the forehead before he could straighten out of the curl. He went down again.

I kept my distance, but he didn't move. He was breathing but he was out cold, so I walked slowly back to the idling van and got in. The day hadn't worked out well at all, I thought. I had no idea what I was going to tell Gomez. His nephew was a rotten scumbag to the core. He'd killed his dog to get a ride out to the family plot so he could dig up his dead brother's loot. His loot, buried out there with the dead animals under a hornet's nest. I wanted to get back out and hit him a few more times, but I didn't. Instead, I made a laborious three-point turn and started back up the muddy gravel road to the highway. Santos could find his own way back, and if he returned to Portland, he could face the music of a different symphony. I was out. I had no idea what would happen to him next, but it wouldn't involve me. There was not one damn thing I could do to fix a kid like that.

I lit a cigarette and blew out the smoke, coughed a little.

My hands were shaking, and I felt sad and nauseated and dazed. The hornet sting on my chin hurt, but the one on my chest burned like fire. The first bend in the road was fifty yards up and as I rounded it I slowed, then stopped and stared. There was a gray Lexus blocking my path, parked sideways across the road. A tall, extremely thin, dapper man in a suit the same color as the car was standing ten feet in front of it holding a gun, pointed down but clearly visible. He smiled at me, and we were close enough for me to notice his dentures, which were perfect.

It was the bum from the last night, the one I had given some of my nowhere whiskey to and then listened to him jabber about kale and Oklahoma. He pointed the gun at me and gestured with it, making a winding motion, smiling his artificially perfect smile the entire time.

"Out of the car, Holland," he called. His voice was high and loud and clear. "Come over here with your arms above your head. You do anything else and you die a little harder and a little sooner than planned."

I got out and slowly raised my hands. He kept smiling.

"You the guy who's been staking me?" I asked. "Looking through my window? You fooled me with your whole 'bum' thing. Like it came natural to you, digging around in the trash. Nice choppers, FYI. White. Like, seriously."

"Darby Holland." He lowered the gun a little. "Of all the names you could have picked, you pick that one? It means something, right? Something to do with a band, or one of the little books you love so much? I have to know. I won't tell anyone."

"What the hell happened to your original teeth?" I stayed right where I was.

He shook his head. "I was told you'd try to bait me into a fight. You can keep trying if you like. Later on when I'm torturing you I'll remember it. Come! I want you to see something in the trunk here."

"Fuck no."

He pointed the gun at my feet. "Right foot or left. God gave you two, so pick the one you like the least. Thirty-eight hollow point, so everything from the ankle down will be gone forever." He cocked the trigger.

I started forward, as slow as I thought I could get away with, looking for any kind of play that would give me the upper hand. There wasn't one. He backed away as I approached, staying too far away to rush him. He didn't need to unlock the trunk because it was already ajar.

"You turned out to be a remarkable guy," he continued. "You slip your federal monitors long enough to what? Come out here to the woods with a shovel and a young gangster? And now you're returning alone?" He laughed. "Slick. I'd offer you a job under different circumstances."

"How long have you been following me?"

"I wonder what your nine-foot-tall girlfriend would make of this behavior of yours. Drinking and driving, and at this hour. Burying boys in the forest." He made a *tsk*ing sound. "Maybe I'll tell her. Just so I can see the look in her eyes."

I was between him and the clearing by then, which was good. Behind him, fifty yards back, a bloody-faced Santos staggered into view. He had the shovel in his hands.

"I disappear and Suzanne will have federal on her forever." I paused to give Santos time. "I bet she could kick your ass anyway."

"Open the trunk," he ordered. "Then you hop in. We're going for a drive. Someone very important wants to say hello to you. Hello and so much more."

"I knew it," I said scornfully. "You're a butler of some kind."

He laughed. It was a dark, wrong sound. "I am indeed. A butler! I like that. It has a nice ring to it."

I stopped next to the Lexus and lowered my hands a little. He raised the gun and pointed it at my chest.

"Easy now. I want you to strip because I have no idea

what kinds of weapons are in your clothes. You do it nice, like you don't want to scare me. Then climb in and slam the lid, hard. I want to hear it latch. And after that you be real, real quiet, understand? That lid closes, not one peep until it opens again. If we stop and you start yelling, believe me when I tell you that you will find Jesus long before your last breath. Got it?"

"You, you want me to take my clothes off?" I made a disgusted face. "Christ. What if I leave my underwear on? What kind of knife or gun am I going to have in my underwear, man?"

"I start counting, I won't stop. It will just be so you know when to take a breath to scream."

Santos was halfway there and moving quietly. I pointed down at my feet.

"Boots," I explained. "I have to unlace them, but don't fuckin' shoot me while I do."

"No sudden moves," he cautioned.

I knelt and slowly rolled up one pant leg, then untied the top of my boot and struggled with it, taking my time. When I finally got it off he made the winding motion with the gun again.

"C'mon, Holland. Get a move on."

I moved a little faster with boot number two. When I was done, I rose barefoot and glared at him. Santos was maybe twenty feet behind him. He still looked dazed, and I had an awful flash that the poor crazy kid didn't know where he was after the blow to the head and he was bringing us the shovel because he thought it was ours.

"What do I call you?" I asked.

"Me?" This surprised him, or at least he made it seem that way. "Oleander. That's the only question I'm going to answer, too. Now, jacket next, then pants and socks *and* your underwear. Hurry the fuck up. You aren't naked and in that trunk in one minute, I shoot off a chunk of meat."

I nodded and began stripping fast. Santos heard that last part and it galvanized him. He couldn't sneak along any faster, but he had some kind of idea what was going down. I was being abducted, and that meant riding around naked in the trunk of a new Lexus. The kid didn't have any reason to like me after getting his ass kicked, but he clearly didn't care for kidnapping, either.

"Okay, Oleander," I said when I was naked. I lifted the lid of the trunk and looked in. Empty. "Try not to hit every pothole between here and hell, okay? Can I pee real fast first?"

"Get in." No more smiling.

I raised my hand and flipped him off. His eyes flared and he snarled and pointed the gun at my stomach just as Santos swung the shovel with all his might and delivered a hard blow to the side of Oleander's head. Time slowed as Oleander fell, shooting as he went down. The bullets went wide, three of them, and Santos raised the shovel high in both hands like a spear, the head pointed down. Oleander twisted and landed on his back, tried in vain to bring his gun to bear on Santos, who stood snarling above him, poised to strike again.

"No!" I yelled.

Santos brought the shovel down into Oleander's neck as hard as he could. I was frozen then, stunned, and so was

Santos. Oleander's gun went off and the bullet ripped past Santos. Oleander made a gurgling sound and tried to raise his free hand to his throat while he jerked the gun around. Santos brought the shovel down again one more time, right into the neck again. The gun dropped and Santos stepped back, panting.

The man who called himself Oleander was dead, his eyes wide in disbelief. His final breath came in the form of bubbles through his gory neck, and then he was still.

"I needed that fucker alive!" I yelled into Santos's face. My voice was loud and cracked in the post-gunfire silence. I yanked the shovel away from him and we both stared back down at the body.

"Too late now," Santos replied. He looked at me. "Clothes, homie. You should get your clothes on. This would be a lot less fuckin' strange if you were wearing clothes. I mean, *Madre de Dios*. I feel like I should make the sign of the cross but I have blood on my hands. I . . ." He trailed off.

"I, ah, shit." I looked at him. "You in shock, dude? I just beat the shit out of you and you killed a guy. With a shovel. I might be in shock too. So I'm just asking."

"I don't feel good," Santos confessed.

"Beer in the van."

I dropped the shovel next to Oleander's body and walked back to the Lexus, where my clothes lay in a pile. While I put them on I watched Santos get a beer out of the van and try to open it. His hands were shaking badly. Mine were only a little more steady. When I was dressed, I walked over and stood next to him. Neither of us said anything while I fished a beer out and wrenched the cap off. We drank and listened to the wind, high up in the trees.

"I did kill Bella," he said eventually, long minutes later. We were both looking at the sky. "Heroin. She went out on a cloud, *ese*. But it isn't what you think."

I waited.

"I never even wanted a dog," Santos continued. "I enjoy the company of cats. But dogs, I think they smell. Uncle Rodrigo thought it would ground me, whatever that means. But I loved that stupid dog after five minutes. One morning I was taking her for a walk, she ate a used condom." He glanced at me. "How the fuck you supposed to love a thing does shit like that? But I did. Bella was a good dog. She had a soul. A big one."

"And you killed her."

"Hardest fuckin' thing, too. It started out small, her sickness. She couldn't keep her food down at first. I thought maybe she ate a spider, or a condom like that one time, maybe it got stuck in her somewhere. I wasn't lying about the cancer. We got her drugs from the vet, but it was only a matter of time. She slept right next to my bed, and right there at the end I would wake up and she'd be staring at me, wondering what the fuck happened to her. I could see it in her face. I couldn't stand it anymore. Neither could she. That fucking dog wanted out, dude. You don't believe me, we can fight again. You got in a sucker punch the first time. Won't be so lucky again."

"And this shit with the bees? That box?"

"I wanted to bury her out here. She liked this place. Couple weeks ago, when I was out here for the party?

Cherry an' all that? I thought back an' I remembered when me an' Miguel discovered those fucking bees. We snuck away to do some blow an' he got stung right on the ass. But then, couple nights ago, it fuckin' hit me, just like that. The money was under that fuckin' hornet nest, 'cause nobody was gonna fuck around under that thing. Nobody but me and my brother. Bella's time came and here we are."

"Huh." I looked at my beer. "Well. Sorry, I guess. For jumping to conclusions an' all that."

"It happens, man. And I am so fucking sick of that happening, too." A deep, real anger crept into his voice. "Always, always, this judgment shit. I was a starving fucking kid. I did bad shit to stay alive. Maybe I lost my way, but I'm not gonna find my way back if every motherfucker keeps pushing me into the dark at every fuckin' turn." He threw his beer down and glared at me. "I don't accept your half-assed apology, piece of shit white boy."

Santos walked over to his box of money and picked it up, then walked over to Oleander's body. I watched as he fished the keys out and put them in his pocket. When he took the wallet out of Oleander's pocket, I walked over and joined him.

"You want any of this shit?" he asked. "The money and the credit cards are mine. So's the Rolex."

"Keep it." I looked over his shoulder. "What are the names on the cards?"

"Chester G. Goodwin, Robert Gold." He kept them and handed me the wallet. "Fake."

He pocketed the bills, a few hundred, and the cards.

The driver's license was out of New Jersey. Robert Gold again. AAA card. No slips of paper with phone numbers, no hotel cards, nothing. The wallet felt new, too. I saved it. All of it was about to come in handy.

"Cell," Santos said, holding it up. "You want it? They can track these things."

I took it. An iPhone, locked. I put it in my pocket, too. Santos rose.

"Let's check out my new ride," he suggested. We walked over to the Lexus, leaving the body for the moment. He noticed my apprehension and gave me a tight, bloody smile. "Nobody comes out this way except on party days."

"Still. Dead body in the road."

There was a briefcase in the back seat of the Lexus. Santos used a key on the key ring to unlock it and we both stepped back. Inside was an even five grand, neatly bundled, and a stack of photographs. Santos took them out and looked through them, glancing my way now and then as he handed them over. The photographs were all of me. Drinking in the alcove in front of Ming's. Hanging out at the Lucky. Drinking at the Rooster Rocket. Walking with Suzanne, holding hands. Drinking with Delia. I looked at the last photograph for a long time.

We were in a bar on Stark, the Twilight, eating their onion ring bacon cheeseburgers and drinking bourbon. That night had been almost two months ago, right before she stopped drinking, the night she announced her move to Austin. The night she told me she was engaged to Hank.

"Shit," I said. Santos glanced back at the body.

"Creepy, man. Dude has been, like, stalking you."

"Yep." I tossed the picture back in the briefcase. "And he worked for someone. Someone within driving distance, too. Someone who had something important to tell me before they killed me."

"You got more than woman problems, man."

"Sure do. So." I looked back at Oleander. "I guess I gotta bury that dude. Wanna help?"

"I still have to bury Bella. We can help each other."

An hour and a half later, Santos and I stood by the Lexus and the van. We'd buried Bella far out in the woods, Oleander in a thicket in the opposite direction. I'd taken the photos out of the briefcase and stashed them in the van, and Santos had buried the briefcase, too. We drank beer and ate the lunch Delia had packed us, pastrami on rye, spicy pickles, and potato salad. Santos had washed his face in a tiny stream, and even though his white shirt was utterly destroyed, he looked much better as he consulted Oleander's Rolex, now on his wrist.

"Dude. It's two in the afternoon. Fuckin' A we get shit done, no?"

I clinked beers with him, then tossed my head at the Lexus.

"Where you headed?"

He shrugged. "I got money, wheels. Maybe Idaho. Sell weed, that kind of shit."

"I been to Idaho. Nice. Boise. Twin Falls."

"Many Mexicans in Twin Falls," Santos said thought-fully. He popped the last of his pickle in his mouth. "Maybe

I find the right place, fit in. Work in a restaurant so I can meet people."

"What should I tell your uncle?"

"I been thinking about that." He looked down. "I feel bad, man. He tried. They all did. But it wasn't enough. It was no one's fault though, you know?" He looked over at me. "How the fuck are they supposed to know all the shit that goes on in my head? But you're right about not getting caught, Darby." He looked out at the trees. "The world is too beautiful to give up on. I only just got started."

I looked out at the same trees. "Stay true, dude."

"You too, man."

At the end of the road I paused. Santos took a right in front of me and he was gone. I was turning left. The highway was quiet, so I lit another cigarette and took out my phone to face the music.

Seven missed calls from Suzanne and two from Delia. I checked my text messages. There were nine in all. The first two were from Suzanne, and I immediately confirmed that I had indeed called her last night. First she was concerned but amused. Then she was irritated. The third text was from Delia, reminding me to bring the clothes I was wearing.

The fourth was from an unknown number. I opened it. The bartender had taken a picture of the first person to leave after Dessel. It was Oleander, the dead man buried at the edge of the clearing behind me. The rest were from my irate girlfriend. I didn't read them, and instead stared at the picture of Oleander. He'd been wearing a different suit, darker, older, with no tie. There hadn't been any clothing in the Lexus. So he had a hotel room somewhere in town. I was still staring at the picture when my phone rang, almost giving me a heart attack. Delia.

"You okay? How's the kid?" Before I could say a single word, she continued. "My mother called this morning. She and my father are going to be on vacation for the last two weeks of October and try as they might, they can't change their plans. But they did offer to send me a ticket if I want to go with them. One. Ticket."

"Fuck those people," I said. "So, the day took an interesting turn."

"Easy for you to say," she went on. "Hank. God, Darby. His family is so fucked. And now this. It's like our wedding is cursed. Is it? I mean cursed? Is that even possible?"

"I don't know."

"You're done? When are you getting back?"

"Ah, hard to say." I looked out at the empty highway. "Tonight."

"Good. I have a special treat for us tomorrow. Something I need your help with. Fair trade since I rescued you with all my clever planning, right?"

"This treat has something to do with chickens, doesn't it?"

"Please, Darby," she whined. "I've been good. Really, really good. I even picked out your clothes this morning. And I packed you lunch. Was it good?"

"It was good."

"Then it's a date!" Delia hung up before I could protest.

The intermittent drizzle had given way to an overall gray downpour, and abruptly I wished that I could spend the rest of the day anywhere else than Portland. I didn't want to turn around and spend the afternoon at the Gomez family party graveyard. I didn't want to hunt for the dead man's hotel, which might lead me to his boss. I vaguely wanted to go bitch out Dessel for being so crappy at his job, but not enough to actually go do it. I headed for I-5 and figured I'd make up my mind when I got there.

As I drove, I realized it was the same impulse I'd been having for months. I wanted to be free again. It was hard to say when and where I lost the sense of freedom, but there was no denying it was gone. If I was to be honest with myself, some of my problem with Delia leaving had a little to do with envy. To move, go to a new place, do something different. My life had grown chains.

A half hour later I hit I-5 and headed north. I did it without thinking. The clock on the dash read 3:39. I could make it to Seattle by the time Suzanne left work. She left at the same time every night, and if I drove fast and straight through, I could be waiting outside her office when she walked out the door. Maybe I could stop one time, really fast, and buy flowers.

I'd made it almost forty minutes into the drive before Oleander's phone rang. The ringtone made me panic and I felt a flash of insanity, a terrible certainty that I'd lost my shit. The iPhone's ringtone was the bleating of goats.

"Mother fucker," I answered.

"Darby?" The voice was digitally altered, but even so it sounded sarcastic. "Darby Holland?"

"That's right." It came out low.

"So good to talk to you again. So good. You still don't know who I am, do you?"

"I know all kinds of shit about you, dumbass." I paused and listened.

"There is only one reason we are talking, Darby. I love the way the game is shaping up."

"This is a game?" Behind the scramble of the voice I could hear what sounded like traffic. A car horn. My heart skipped a beat as I realized what was happening.

"My move."

I hit the turn signal and skidded to a halt on the right shoulder. A semi blew past, howling, and the van sucked back and forth on its shocks. I dropped the iPhone and took out mine, frantically scrolled through it to Chase's number. He answered on the first ring.

"Boss!" He sounded like he'd been laughing. "I fuckin' lost your feds, man! Straight-up *Dukes of Hazzard*, dude! Walmart parking lot just now and I—"

"Chase!" I yelled. "Someone else is right behind you! *Someone was following the feds!* Ditch the car and run like the fucking—"

The line went dead.

I took the first exit and came to a stop in a gas station parking lot. Chase didn't pick up. I tried again. Same result. I got out, holding the phone. The forest had given way to agriculture, and I could see for miles in both directions. The gas station was at the peak of a low, gradual hill. The cold wind cut through my jacket and made my eyes water. After a minute my phone rang. Chase.

"Dude! Your car! Sorry, man—"

"What happened?"

"You were yelling!" Chase was out of breath. "All I heard was get out and run, so I did! I did, man, and your car blew the fuck up, dude! I can see it right now! It's like, like, like—"

"Chase! Are there any police?"

"Cops just pulled in, one car. If I run I can—"

"Go and stand next to the cops. Now."

"*What?*"

"Chase. I'm not asking you to get arrested. Go and stand as close to them as you can get. Listen to me, man, someone is watching you right now. You leave the scene and you are dead, dead, dead. Got it?"

"What a fuckin' bummer." It came out breathless.

"I know, homie. Car on fire, the fire trucks, ambulance, all that shit will be everywhere. Exactly where are you?"

"I was circling back, man. Off of 82nd. Three blocks from the Walmart."

"Stay there. I'm coming to get you."

Quiet. "Okay." He took a deep breath. "I heard you were rollin' hard these days, man. But this is blown-up car territory."

"Sorry, dude." I took a deep breath too.

"Not ready to turn pussy just yet. I'm ah, I'm gonna go chill with the police."

"You're wearing the right clothes."

I picked up Chase almost an hour later. By then my car had been reduced to a blackened skeleton. Most of the emergency services vehicles were gone, and a lone fire marshal wagon and a single cop car remained. Chase didn't say anything when I pulled up, just squinted through the windshield to see who was driving the van, then came around and got in. I pulled out and we headed toward Burnside. Eventually, he spoke.

"If this was a real job, I'd ask for a raise about now."

"Real?" I kept my eyes on the road.

"Real world. You know what I mean."

"Yeah. And?"

"I guess I want a raise anyway."

"I can see that." I was relieved. People had quit for far less, and quit as in they went far away and changed their phone numbers.

"Let's get some coffee at a drive-through," he suggested. "Then we chat. Okay to smoke in here?"

"I didn't ask," I replied, wondering for the first time. "But it's too late now."

We both lit up. I hit a Starbucks drive-through and we both got double espressos. There was a police car in the small parking lot, the cop behind the wheel taking a break. I pulled up next to him and turned to Chase.

"Let's have it."

"I want in."

I raised an eyebrow. Chase smiled.

"There's some next-level shit going on at the Lucky, man. You went from small time to rich in the last year or two. Now, don't say anything. This is what I know. Nigel is out. Doing time because he slipped mid-crime. Big Mike works at a car parts place or some shit. Delia, and dude, here I gotta say I love that gal, but Delia is leaving. You need me, man."

"I always liked you, Chase. Delia likes you. I remember how nice you were to Obi when he first started out."

"Your old apprentice Obi." Chase laughed. "Love that guy too. Got him that job in Monterey. Those six months we worked together were smooth and cool, dude. But you see my point."

I glanced over at the cop. He was five feet away, sipping coffee and looking at his phone. Then I looked back at Chase. "Exactly where do you see yourself in the shady side of my operation?"

"In the shade." His smile widened into a grin and he cocked his head.

"Here's the deal, man. It's not like I run a criminal empire on the side. But Old Town—fuck, man, this whole city—as money pours in, a tide of shit moves with it. And every time some kind of burning scam rips across my part of that desperate place, I take a piece out of the fucker who lit the fire. So in the strangest possible way, the Lucky is Old Town's immune system."

"Rad." He liked that. I could tell. I smiled back at him.

"You really actually want a piece of that action? Look at my face, man. Sometimes you pay a high price."

"Sign me up, my brother." He didn't even need to think about it.

I stuck out my hand and we shook.

"Right on, Chase Manhattan. Welcome to the party."

Whatever kind of tail Chase had been leading around had moved on when my car was vulcanized and they realized he wasn't me. Either that or they were using drones. I saw no sign of them, but after I dropped Chase off at a MAX stop with instructions to go home and change, I ditched the van in a parking garage and headed out on foot. I didn't want to face Gomez or Flaco yet. I was going to be hard, telling them how bad I'd screwed up with the entire Santos deal. What was I going to tell them? *He's fine. He has money and a car and he had a good lunch before he set off to become a weed dealer in Idaho. Don't worry. Oh, and he killed and buried a guy.* It was too painful to even think about.

I still didn't have a shirt, having left the last one out in the field with the goddamned hornets, and Chase had been unwilling to give me mine back, so my first stop was clear. I took a cab from the parking garage to the Ross Dress for Less below Pioneer Square. It was going to be a complex start to a complex operation.

The register lady gave me the same look the cab driver had flashed in the rearview. Mild shock, then business as usual. The bee sting on my chin wasn't as bad as it could have been, but it wasn't good either. Plus, I was muddy. Under the glaring lights, I walked to the men's section with my head down, pretending to look at something on my phone. The security guard stationed at the door followed me, but for once I didn't feel like making an issue out of it. I picked out some twenty-dollar fake leather shoes, bargain black waiter slacks, a white dress shirt, and a made-in-China dinner jacket with irregular sleeves and paid in cash, then went straight to the nearest Starbucks.

It was just getting dark by the time I made it into the restroom with a double espresso. I changed quickly. The filthy jeans and the boots filled up the trashcan. I put my muddy jacket in the Ross bag and then studied myself in the mirror. Not bad. Not great, but not terrible. I washed my face and hands and then rubbed some soap into my hair to simulate gel, knowing from experience that Starbucks bathroom soap is the next best thing, and from there I went to the Mallory for a chat with Jane Shannon, the bartender.

The bar was what I thought of a bar standard when I ducked in—not too dark to make out all the faces, but not bright enough to see the bags under anyone's eyes. The Mallory was high end, rivaled by maybe fifteen other hotel bars in Portland when it came to the glamour of the drunks. Jane was tending bar with one other jockey, smoothly working the upper-crust winos with practiced charm. Her eyes flashed my way as I came in, then moved on. I took a solitary stool at her end of the bar, as far away from everyone else as I could get. A few minutes later, she headed my way with a glass of scotch and a smile. Jane made good money off of me, especially when I messed up.

"Fighting with bees, Darby?" She beamed and set my

drink down, leaned out to pat my hand. "Or was it a spider?"

"Hornets." I tasted the scotch. "Wanna make some money?"

"I'm here, aren't I?" She gestured at the bar. "Top of the world and all that. You don't need stitches again, do you?"

A year ago I'd been left for dead in a dumpster and she'd nursed me back to a semblance of health. I shook my head.

"Fuckin' no way, psycho. Your stitching is crazy bad." But I smiled when I said it.

"So's my ketchup and bagel pizza roll. But you eat anything, don't you, my wittle snookums." She tried to pinch my cheek and I pulled my head away.

"So, ah, I need you to check this guy out. Scumbag, but my instincts tell me this is high-end scumbaggery." I took out Oleander's wallet and passed her the driver's license. She looked at it, shrugged.

"Can't say I recognize him."

"You and the concierge still pals?"

"Barry? Sure." Her eyes lit up. "You want me to see what the concierge network reveals? Good idea, but expensive."

In the two weeks I'd been holed up at Jane's we'd played endless card games and watched countless old movies. I'd listened to many of her stories, too. She'd been constipated with them, it turned out. A life of listening with no one to listen back had come out of her on those long winter nights. One of them was a funny story about the concierge network. The high-end hotels were in communication, after a fashion, to keep track of guests who tipped big, guests who were dangerous, and where to get opera tickets.

"How much?"

"I don't know." She frowned. "I don't even know if Barry will do it."

"What if you feed Barry a line. Tell him something like—"

"Darby, don't ask me to lie to a friend of mine."

"—like your friend Darby, owner of the Lucky Supreme Tattoo Parlor in Old Town, co-owner of Racy, and big investor in Alcott Frond, is being stalked by the guy in this photo. Even hundred for you for asking. Even hundred for him for asking his pals. Even five for whoever gets me a room number in the next hour, plus free dinner at Alcott for you, Barry, and the lucky concierge."

"Barry likes blow." Jane wiggled her eyebrows.

"And a gram of blow for Barry. I can have some delivered in the next ten minutes by bike messenger."

"I bet he goes for it, except the driver's license photo. That's a weensy bit too sketchy."

I took my phone out. "Texting you a picture now. Taken by another bartender, actually." I found the photo and sent it to Jane.

"Be right back."

She took her apron off and had a quick word with the other bartender, who glanced my way and smiled. I drank and tried to unwind. I'd always liked the Mallory. The first time I'd ever gotten shitfaced in the place was more than ten years ago, on one of those nights where the rain had turned to ice. I was with a guitar player in a heavy metal band, a poor choice for both of us, and the only reason Jane had served us was because the bar was totally empty.

After the guitar woman got a call from her real boyfriend and split, I'd told my miserable story to Jane, who laughed and laughed, and by last call we'd not only bonded but I'd managed to acquaint myself with one of the clerks from the hotel, Brenda. My smile faded when I thought about her. Thinking about her made me think about Suzanne.

It would have been great to see her. Way better than hunting through expensive bars all night in a crappy disguise. Cheaper, too. Probably less dangerous. I stared across the bar at the mirrored backsplash. The gold light and the glitter of the bottles didn't hide the expression on the face that was pointed back at me. I missed that woman. I missed my old life, too. I missed the boots I'd just thrown away in a Starbucks bathroom. I thought about that, and gradually circled back to the train station. That dumbass Dessel bumming cigarettes off of me. He was going to be as pissed as Gomez.

I signaled the lone bartender for another round of whatever it was I was drinking and finished what remained in the glass in one smooth move. She nodded and was pouring when my phone rang. I looked down at it. It came up as "private" so I answered on the evasive.

"This is Dan."

"Holland, you dumbass," Dessel spat. "Where the hell are you? I need you to come downtown right the fuck now."

"I don't have time to join a lineup," I replied. "Ask someone else. I didn't do it no matter what it was, and even if I did, recall your record when to comes to—"

"Holland." Dessel's tone went icy cold. "Listen to me.

For once, listen to me. Your little stunt today, burning your car with that buddy of yours in it? That was cute. But it shook something loose. I need you to look at something and I need it to happen right now."

"Oh, so now you believe me." The bartender set my drink down and I winked at her. "Dessel, I can't tell you how impressed I am. But I'm busy."

"Where are you?" He paused and said something muffled to someone else. "I can come to you."

"I'm doing the kind of shit you wouldn't approve of," I said honestly. "You have your lead and I have mine. Be a big boy and do what I'm doing. Run it down like they do on TV." I hung up.

The phone rang three more times before I turned it off. I was just about to flag the bartender down again when Jane returned, a smile on her face. She swept back behind the bar and put her apron back on, then drifted in my direction like we were spies.

"You got yourself a deal, mister," she whispered. "But that coke? You better get it fast."

"How fast?" I asked, taking my phone back out.

"Soon as you want that room number," she replied. "Barry already came through."

I dialed Paco. He picked up on the first ring. Ten words later he was his way to the Mallory at top speed. Jane watched me operate out of the corner of her eye. When I hung up and gave her the thumbs up, she nodded.

I'd met Paco five or six years ago. Most ranking tattoo artists knew a Paco, or knew how to get one, but my particular Paco was something else. He was a bike messenger for one thing. He was also one of the more successful drug dealers I'd ever known. I'd had a hand in his rise to power in a way, and he felt as though he was in my debt, which was convenient from time to time, as it was now.

Paco moved from San Francisco to Portland to pursue a career in weed smoking, banjo, food cart tourism, and hairy women, in that order. He was a bike messenger by trade and by necessity he kept that job. In the first year of plying the rainy streets he delivered something to the Lucky, I forget what, but he liked the place well enough to get a tattoo a few weeks later. It was shortly after that that his life changed in many ways. I happened to be along for part of the ride purely by accident.

Paco discovered that one of the other bike messengers had established a drug delivery system for the downtown executive class. The other messenger approached Paco, as a cool guy and potential dealer/helper, and they struck a deal. Messenger one picked up the money, messenger two dropped off the goods ten minutes behind him.

Paco was into fitness and so was the other dude, so there was no danger of them getting sucked up in their own product, at least in the beginning. The spiral down began when they increased their product line. In addition to weed and coke, two standard, easy-to-sell staples, they added pills. Shortly thereafter, things got complicated. Paco's partner got popped, but got off with three months in county. They had money by then, enough to get a pretty good lawyer, and it paid off.

I entered the scene when I ran into Paco outside of the Radio Shack on Fifth Street. I was buying a new soldering iron, he was going in to buy a new burner phone. We chatted and he told me about his wheeling and dealing over a couple beers at a bar down the street. He knew I wasn't a druggie, but reasoned that I might know people who were. A few days later I ran into him again, just as he was about to sell to a cop I'd tattooed a year or so before. I warned him off, and it turned out it was the very cop who had busted his partner. Small world.

So Paco owed me, which is why he showed up so fast. Plus, a guy like Paco needed guys like me as much as I need guys like him. I never knew when it was going to come in handy that he owed me. He didn't know when it would be good news for me to feel the same way about him.

Eleven minutes after I called him, Paco came through the bar door, dressed for the Mallory in a way I wasn't. He was wearing a suit, tailored by the look of it, and he had a stunning blonde on his arm. She peeled off to the bartender at the end and Paco runway-strutted up to the stool next to me and took a seat. He flashed Jane two fingers and pointed at my scotch, almost blinded her with his smile, and then turned to me.

"My brother." His eyes narrowed when he took in the scar on my cheek, the bee sting on my chin. "What's up?"

"Same old," I replied. Jane set our drinks down and drifted out of earshot. Paco and I toasted each other. I leaned in a little closer to him. "Gotta bribe this dude. Your blow any good?"

Paco smiled. "You know it." He passed me a bundle

under the lip of the bar. I took it and dropped it into my jacket pocket. "Gram sets you back forty, but get me and my chick over there a comparable bottle of bubbly and we'll call it even."

"Deal. What's up with the suit?"

"I wear 'em all the time now," he replied. "I still sling hard, but I have a couple side operations. Crime has a high burnout rate."

"Hear, hear." We drank to that.

"Biz is what it is." Paco shrugged. "What about you? I heard you got hurt last year, saw some shit in the news. What the hell happened?"

"All kinds of crazy," I replied. "But today I got stung by a fuckin' bee. Can you believe that?"

"Might be the last day of the year that can happen, too," Paco observed. "Cold out there now. Me and Tabby there are headed to dinner." He glanced over to where she had just taken a seat and blew her a kiss. She blew one back.

"You've upgraded all around," I said. He turned back to me and smiled.

"I did. We good?"

"Your bottle is on the way."

"Keep in touch," he replied. He finished his drink and went back to Tabby. I watched them, smiling, until Jane came back over.

"Janie, send a bottle of sparkling wine to my pal and his gal there," I said. I slipped her the bundle. "I'll pony up, too. Got people to fuck with."

A minute later she came back with my check. I tipped

big and added two hundred. While I was counting she delivered the bottle to Paco, who saluted me one final time.

"Always so good to see you, honey." Jane tucked the money away. "Stop by for movie night sometime. You still haven't seen my new carpet."

"I will."

She lowered her voice. "I'll give this to Barry in a sec. He'll meet you in the upstairs lounge in front of the elevators. Five minutes."

"Tell him quicker the better. Trail goes dead fast."

Five minutes later, a dapper man with a runny nose gave me a complimentary magazine containing *Portlandia* trivia and restaurant reviews. He left without a word, so I opened it. The ad on the first page was for the Heathman. It was circled in red and "ROGER" was written across it in red. The Heathman was close, a five-minute walk. I buttoned up my new coat and made it out just in time for full dark and the rain.

Fall was definitely in the air again, and for the hundredth time I cursed the luck that had brought me into contact with hornets, a crazy Mexican kid, and a dead dog. The rest of the people on the sidewalk were hurrying in one direction or another. I took my time, checking reflections as I went, but if my car bomber was with me I couldn't make him. Oleander's wallet and his phone felt warm in my pocket.

The hotel was dazzling. I walked across the marble floor, past the check-in desk, and found the concierge office. The door was open and a well-dressed man in his late thirties was sitting at the desk talking on the phone. I stood in the doorway until he saw me and when he did he motioned for me to enter, then covered the phone when I did.

"Get that door?" Then he was back to his conversation, wrapping up what sounded like tickets for two to a gallery opening. I sat and waited patiently.

"You the guy with all the, ah, you're Darby Holland?" he asked almost apologetically.

"One and the same," I replied. "You're Roger?"

"I am." He spun his monitor around. "Your guy was here this morning. Checked out around nine a.m. Trevor Connor. 7119."

"Shit. How many days was he here?"

He checked his monitor, tapped for a minute. "A long time, actually. Same room, sixty-four days in total."

"Expensive."

"We've had people stay here for more than a year, so it's not that unusual. Depends on who's paying the bill and what kind of work is involved. Government, no way, three nights tops. Corporate, the wives and whatnot. Mistresses. Foreign business, we see a percentage of that. What was your man up to?"

"Spying on me. What did he drink?"

"Looks like nothing. Not even bottled water. Twelve days ago he made his first and only minibar purchase, two shots of Glenlivet 15."

I thought back. I had no memory at all of what I had done twelve days ago, if I might have inspired some kind of celebration. I was unsure what day of the week it was, for that matter.

"Room service?"

He tapped. "Several hits, all late afternoon." He looked up like he had bad news. "Salad man. Your investigator is a vegetarian."

"Aw, man." I sat up a little.

"I printed out his signature and his credit card information." He handed me an envelope. I took it and rose.

"Deal is a deal. Is there anyone in the room right now?"

"Nope. Already cleaned, too." He sat back and looked back at me, clearly done. "New guest in less than an hour."

"Can you burn me a key so I can check it out?"

"Sure. I'll need to hold your credit card, but sure. Be quick though, okay? I have broad discretion, but that's the kind of thing I like to keep."

I gave him my debit card and the five hundred dollars while I was at it. He pocketed the cash without a word and put the card on his desk. That thinned out my wallet quite a bit, but I didn't mind. While he made the key, I took my phone out and checked the messages. One from Suzanne, one from Delia. I didn't read either one.

"Here," he said, handing me a key card. "Be quick, okay? Just bring the room card back to me and I'll give you your card back. Seventh floor, elevators are out the door to your right."

"Be right back."

I rode the elevator up alone. The Muzak was some kind of classical, muted and dull yet cloying in the way only fancy elevator music can be. My warped reflection in the polished brass door was at least comical enough to make me smile. The bee sting was just angry enough to give me Bruce Campbell's jaw.

When I got to the door I paused before I slotted the key. Sometimes in the movies detectives will do that, to listen for activity on the other side of the door, even when the room is supposed to be empty. That's not what I was doing. Instead, I was probing myself for the haunted feeling I'd had while I was being watched. I closed my eyes and willed myself to become calm, to allow paranoia and fear and darkness to wash over the buzz I had going. I searched my skin for the subtle crawling feeling, listened to the nerves in my stomach, felt for the suggestion of breath in the hair on the back of my neck.

Nothing.

I slotted the key and the little light blinked green. Oleander's old room was big, with a double bed, large windows, a flat-screen inside a towering oak cabinet, beige on blond with pastels. I stopped in front of the painting. The Oregon coast in winter, very Turneresque kind of sky. I went to the windows and pulled the heavy curtains, looked out at the rainy City of Roses.

This was what the dead man who had been watching me had also seen. The man who had been looking through my windows had also looked through this window. From where I was standing, I could see the irregular grid of the city, the slope down to the river, which itself looked slow and richly black. I wondered what he'd thought when he looked out there. Probably all kinds of things. Like me. Suzanne. The Lucky. Delia. Old Town. All of it. He'd checked out after a long stay, and that was consistent with him having completed his work here. He knew who I was, he'd verified everything; he had my life mapped out.

He'd been mapping out my life.

I was being set up for something.

I sat down on the bed. Then I lay back and stared at the ceiling. The same ceiling Oleander stared at, night after night, day after day, whenever he took a break from learning all he could about the Old Town hustler named Darby Holland.

The bleating of goats didn't even surprise me. I took the iPhone out of my pocket and answered.

"I wondered if it was possible to track these things," I said. "I mean, for realsies. S'why I brought it along. Now I know. What's up?"

"How do you enjoy the Mineral Man's room?"

"Fine." The voice modulation sounded the same. I closed my eyes to scan the background again. Faint music. Muzak.

"The clock stopped ticking. Time is up."

"That's bad news for you," I said slowly. "Your guy? The flower dude? He was sniffing around my patch long enough to learn the most important thing you need to know about me. Give you one guess."

"That you've finally turned into a killer?"

"Nah." I sat up. "It's that I always win."

I let that hang as I walked into the bathroom. It was twice the size of mine at home, but I liked my old claw-foot bathtub way more. I walked over to the toilet and unzipped, let loose a bladder full of expensive booze. All that came through from the other end was spooky breathing.

"Wasn't always that way."

I cradled the phone under my chin while I zipped up. "We

learn," I said. "We adapt. We—" I dropped the phone in the toilet and watched it sink to the bottom. "We drop dead people's phones in their toilets." The last part was just for me.

The concierge, whose name I had already forgotten, was puzzled when I told him I'd found a phone in the toilet but left it there. I got my card back before I told him, so there was nothing he could do about it. I recognized the Muzak, too. The caller was somewhere in the Heathman, in a public area where the music was playing. This time the background sound was just to toy with me, so I walked out without bothering to look around.

It was close to midnight and I was exhausted. But there was a psychopath somewhere in the rain watching me, playing some kind of game at that very instant. I turned my face up to the sky and let the drops hit my hot skin.

The clock had stopped. That meant that whatever kind of well-planned disaster had been crafted for me was complete.

Show time.

I lit a cigarette and the urban sorcery of doing so caused a cab to pull up. I bit the filter off and had one last good drag before I got in.

"I could have waited," the driver said. It was a guy in his mid-twenties with a wide-open face. I shrugged and gave him my address.

"You eat there?" he continued. "The French badass who got the stars for the place moved, but I heard it was still good."

"I was just visiting," I replied. Suddenly, I was hungry.

"Bar is awesome, I hear." He glanced in the rearview and wiggled his eyebrows. "Uptown girl, you know what I—"

"Dude," I interrupted. "That's a Billy Joel song, right?"

He looked back at the street and went quiet.

Traffic was light, so we made good time through downtown. I stared out the window at the sporadic homeless people framed against the huge display windows showcasing shit they would never in this life be able to afford, the rain swirling through the gold halos of the streetlamps, the beaded windows of the cars we passed, and then we were going over the bridge.

"Burnside used to be a mud chute they slid old-growth logs down," I said. The driver glanced back.

"That right?

"Skid row. A skid row."

"You know Hawthorne used to be called Asylum Way?"

"No." I looked out over the dark water. It was different from this angle, reflecting the lights of downtown. One of the tiny speckles was likely from the room the man Oleander had been in, lost in the trillion shimmers. "That doesn't sound good though."

"Yep. Great big insane asylum right at the end of it, around where 40th is now, I guess."

I sighed. So much for small talk.

"Yeah," he agreed. "Old Portland. More of it gone every day, but some of it probably never needed to be there."

"I feel like that all the time these days."

He glanced back and went silent a second time, and this time it lasted.

My street was quiet. The unmarked car the feds were using was visible three houses down, just sitting there. Whoever was inside was on his phone reporting that I'd arrived. I went up the stairs, more and more tired with every step, and when I finally got to the door I wasn't surprised to find a note taped to it.

HOLLAND, WE ARE ON THE EDGE OF SOMETHING YOU SHOULD KNOW ABOUT. STOP BY TOMORROW WHEN YOU'RE SOBER. —DESSEL

I wadded the note up and carried it in. The cats weren't all that happy about being trapped inside all day, but they didn't have the energy to mope, a condition unique to cats. I stripped off the top part of my disguise and left it in a pile on the couch, then went into the kitchen and opened them a can of food, poured myself a drink, and threw the note away. There were some leftovers in the fridge, two-day-old braised pork shank and shaved Brussels sprouts with hazelnuts from Alcott that I ate without tasting. When I was done, I took a shower and changed into pajama jeans, old and worn almost to nothing, and carried my final drink back out to the couch. Once I was settled and the muscles in my back had turned into something other than wads, I picked up my phone. Almost two in the morning. I dialed.

"You better not be calling to give me shit about this chicken thing," Delia said. "I don't think I could take it. I was on the phone all day trying to get black roses and I know they have the fuckin' things. I've seen them, like in real life. But nooooo. You want a few dozen of them and you might as well be shopping for a baby albino. People think it's ghoulish to the point that they, no shit, hang up on you."

"Tell me all about it," I replied. I closed my eyes and listened.

I woke up just before sunrise on the couch, exhausted, my phone on my chest. After I fed the cats and got the coffee going, I did fifty push-ups and as many pull-ups on the bar in the bathroom doorway before I was empty. After that I took a shower, slammed two beers, turned the coffee off untouched, and split as soon as I was dressed.

The car situation was a bummer. I had an old Alfa Romeo in the garage with a bunch of other crap, but it was a total piece of shit. The Armenian had tricked me into buying it as an investment for an even grand, and afterward Santiago had told me that the blue book value for it was around five hundred. It ran, but it leaked everything, including rain, and the battery never stayed charged. I opened the garage door and moved bags of packing material I'd been hoarding for unknown reasons and unplugged it from the charger it had been hooked to for the past several months. Anticipating nothing at all, I got in and turned the key. When it started, I almost laughed out loud. Almost.

I pulled out and closed the garage and it was still running, so I drove to the airport cell phone waiting area, stopping once at a Starbucks drive-through, and made it there as the horizon began to glow in earnest. Steeling myself, I called Suzanne.

"If you're calling from jail you should have called some-one else."

Ah. A sign. I sipped my coffee.

"Where exactly are you?" She was walking, fast and angry.

"Drinking coffee out by the airport. My car, ah you know how it is, so I'm driving that little red Alfa."

"Serves you right. Did you get my messages?" A door opened and closed.

"I was afraid to check them," I admitted.

"Darby." Suzanne stopped whatever she was doing and gathered herself for the summary of her text essays. "When you called me the other night you sounded different."

"I was drunk. My bad."

"It wasn't that." She was being careful now. "I could hear it in your voice. Something I've never heard before. You—how do I put this? Are you happy? Not with the way things are between us, but in general. If you had never met me and this relationship was not a factor in your sense of well-being, how, I mean, what, would you be happy?"

I thought about it for less than a second. "Nah."

"Why?"

"Suze, this is a bad time to get into my emotional land-scape. Now is just what it is. Now. Yesterday and tomor-row are—"

"It's always a bad time to ask you questions like this." Firm. She was right and she knew it.

"Then why the fuck did you ask?"

"Move here. Move to Seattle."

I froze. All the air in my lungs was gone.

"Did you hear me?" she continued softly.

"*Why?*"

It was her turn to be speechless.

"I mean, Suzanne, I don't mean that in a bad way. I mean, why would that make me different or better or somehow more worthwhile? Why would that make a difference?"

"I wish you had read my messages. This is it in a nutshell. Darby, I love you. You love me. I know you do. But this life you have, the Lucky Supreme, all the terrible shit that happens in Old Town, all of it, it's all bad for you. Don't you realize that? Is your life really so good you can't walk away from it? The other night when you were wasted you went on and on about how you wanted to go to the train station and go somewhere far, far away. Why not here? Seattle? With me?"

"Jesus." I didn't know what else to say.

"Delia is leaving. Old Town is the new San Francisco. Everything you worked for is done. You have money. You're still young enough to do something different. You've told me a million times how much of a nightmare it would be to wind up like your old boss. Think about it! A fresh start! And I would be right there with you the whole time! We don't even have to live here! We could go anywhere! As long as it was new, and your old life was just that. Your old life."

"I—I don't know what to say, Suze." I scratched my head and realized my hands felt cold and numb. "That's— that's either the nicest thing in the world or something else entirely."

"Don't say anything," she gushed, and right then I could hear how much she loved me. My face went hard and sad and my chest hurt. I wanted to smell her hair more than I'd ever wanted anything in my life.

"Suze."

"Just think about it," she whispered. "I'm coming down on Sunday, don't have to be back for three days. We can go to the coast like we used to, stay at our little place, the one with the BBQ."

"What day is it?"

"It's Wednesday, Darby. Wednesday."

"Okay."

"I have to go." She was far more upset than she was letting on, I could hear it. She didn't like talking about her feelings any more than I did. She did write and text about them, however.

"I'll call you way before then."

Sniff. "You better, mister."

I lowered the phone when she was gone and looked out at the long, swaying grass. I didn't blink until my eyes hurt.

Delia gave me the X-ray treatment as we walked through Oregon's Best Feed and Stock. I was pushing the wheelbarrow she had been loading with Halloween wedding objects: shovels, burlap, rolls of wire fencing, hand trowels, the three-pronged dirt claw things, and now we were strolling through the live chickens. Delia was in search of the rare solid black Surinam rooster. Black heart, black eyes, black liver. No doubt she intended for Flaco to make posole with stained corn out of it for some kind of hellish pre-honey-moon snack. I'd still been sitting in the cell phone waiting area when she called to make sure we were still on, and she'd been immediately suspicious when I sounded enthusiastic. She still was.

"I like this chicken," Delia said, pausing in front of a striking red and gold model. He crowed violently and gave us the evil eye.

"Seems like the right kind of bastard to me," I agreed. "Let's fuck him up."

Delia gave me a curious look, the hundredth in the last half hour, and continued with her hands clasped behind her back. She was dressed in skintight black jeans, giant red engineer boots, and a kid's King Kong T-shirt, riding high. She'd left her oversized raincoat in the car, which was maybe good because she'd spray-painted it with stenciled revolvers. The gun imagery might have made the wrong kind of impression. Her hair was scarlet and her lips and eye shadow were orange, appropriate for chicken-shopping when it came to the old guy at the register maybe, as he quickly looked away when she winked at him, but it had an alarming effect on the birds.

"You say you spent the entire morning at your airport picnic area in quiet contemplation." It wasn't a question. "I can admire that. Did you talk to Suzanne?"

"She's what I was contemplating. But she's super excited about the wedding." It was premature to tell her about the "move" or "abandon my life" discussion we'd just had. I had no plans at all to tell her about Santos or the dead man buried in the field, so I was on a roll. Delia snorted. I went on before she started talking.

"Farm slash horror theme Halloween wedding gets you style points all around, kid. You can see why Suzanne's excited." No way I was going to tell her about Nigel and his bad news until I was absolutely certain, either.

"Maybe she can write a *Portlandia*-style article about it," Delia suggested innocently. "Make some money. Then your ill-gotten gains, your reckless lifestyle, your shitty pals, all of it will feed back into her tidy American ATM machine." She gestured at a chicken. "Down payment on a Saint John's condo for her right there if we sacrifice him to Odin or—"

"When am I supposed to take Hank on this tuxedo mission?" I interrupted. Delia wheeled on me.

"So that's what this is about!" she spat, instantly furious. "You think you can get out of it if you help me shop for party supplies? You spiteful cock-smoking—"

"No, no," I interrupted again. "I just want to take him out for drinks. Before or after. It was your idea, you mean little bitch."

She moved in like she was going to punch me and I flinched and dropped the handles of the wheelbarrow. Instead, she stuck her index finger in my face. It smelled like peaches.

"If you have some kind of genius motherfucking plan," Delia whispered, "to fuck with his mind or make a 'man' out of him, I will peel your tiny dick, Darby. I will dry the skin and wipe my—"

"Delia!" I cocked my head at her, willing her to calm down with my best thoughtful expression, never very convincing. "I can't believe I'm saying this, but you need either a hug or a Valium."

She crashed into me and hugged with all her might. I patted her back and we stood like that, surrounded by chickens, who took that moment to make their presence known.

"So much could still go wrong," she said into my sternum. "Our luck does not extend to weddings."

"I know, sweetie," I said softly. "But I'm going to be on my best behavior. I mean, I'm going to do the right thing."

She pulled back a little and looked up into my eyes, frowning.

"Why do I feel like you added 'the right thing' as a modifier to your behavior vow? Darby, this is no time for any of your shit, man. Your creative interpretation of the 'right thing' has a police record."

"It's different here," I assured her. "I won't let you down, baby. Not now, not ever." Delia nodded and pressed her cheek into my chest again. I focused on the meanest rooster, a real bastard posturing right behind her. "Gonna take Hank out for drinks. The whole nine yards."

She pulled away and sniffed, gave me a smile, then began strolling again. It was a nice morning to be at a chicken and hardware store shopping for wedding supplies, I had to admit. The air was crisp and cool, and patches of blue sky were visible. The place smelled like hay and birds and roofing tar, and it all combined to create a relaxing effect.

"Your day yesterday with the kid," she continued. "You never did tell me about it."

"Kinda boring. He wants to move back to LA and give it a try with this gal, says Gomez is cock-blocking him, something like that. I wasn't listening."

"Huh. So no heart-to-heart bonding bullshit?"

"Not really. Lunch was good."

"Darby Holland." Delia made a *tsk*ing sound. "The lies you tell."

I laughed. "I don't know what you mean, Cordelia." Delia had kept her real name and her roots as an upper-crust wingnut secret and probably would have indefinitely. Dessel had filled me in on her personal history. Her parents weren't coming to her wedding because they were snobs. Her two sisters were the same.

"Go ahead, toss that out there." She shook her head. "I'm too tired to fight anymore this morning."

We walked. She stopped in front of a rack of hoes and stared at them.

"You, ah, you were fighting with other people this morning?"

She looked at me. "Hank."

"Ah."

"I don't want to talk about it. Not right now."

We kept strolling, slow, and as we went I watched her. I was tired and so was she, and my mood shifted then, from enjoying her company on one of the last nice days of the year to wanting to beat her fiancé to death. I cleared my throat and she turned back and looked at me with sadness in her big eyes.

"Let's go get lunch," I suggested. "We can hit up the Vietnamese sandwich place on Halsey and then go blow five bucks in nickels at the video game place."

"Dealio." She smiled, and I could see in a flash some of the things that were weighing her down. One of them was me. Just like I was, she wondered at that instant if it was the last time we were going to eat up an afternoon doing not one goddamned thing.

It was dark by the time we got to Delia's house. A year or two ago she'd moved from her longtime art studio with a futon and she never talked about the new place. It was odd, considering that she talked all the time. I'd never given it much thought. When we hung out outside the shop, it was always at my place so she could spoil the cats, or at a bar. Where I bought the drinks.

So I'd never been there, but as we rolled in I began to suspect that we weren't going to her place after all. It was Beaverton, for one thing, in an area of the suburb where her red vintage Falcon stood out like a boil among the family sedans and newer BMWs. When we pulled into her driveway, I looked around and was about to ask if we were stopping off to perform an impromptu robbery, but a dark look from her, particularly piercing, stopped me. Silent, I followed her in without a word. At least I was silent until we got inside.

"Question." I didn't have one. Not exactly. It was all I could think to say.

"Of course I have beer," she said, answering what would

have been my last question first. "Hank is a Blue Ribbon kind of fella." Delia hung her jacket on the coat rack by the door and left me frozen in place on the doormat. "Wipe your feet, please," she called over her shoulder. "The real estate agent is showing it again tomorrow and I don't want to mop again."

Delia's condo was entirely out of keeping with her character. It was in a good neighborhood, for one thing. White, too, with a tidy little yard. The living room before me had beige furniture, high-end hotel stuff, with matching walnut end tables shining with polish. There was a coffee table that came in the same set. Freestanding lamps with pale blue shades. Two big oil paintings, sunflowers on one side and sea grass on windswept dunes on the other. Hardwood floors. I heard a refrigerator door open and close.

"Has . . ." I stopped before I stuttered. She poked her head out of the kitchen and waited. Nothing further came to mind.

She rolled her eyes and disappeared.

I wiped my feet and walked into the kitchen doorway. Delia was staring into the sink.

She glanced over at me, back at the drain. The kitchen was spotless. New stainless steel juicer and a matching blender. A single magnetic hook on the refrigerator with a single pot holder, unadorned black. A lone miniature wooden barrel with cooking implements fanning from it in a careful bloom. And a wad of plaid that could only be Hank's briefs sitting next to a can of Pabst.

"I'm a bitch, Darby."

"No you aren't," I said instantly. We were in a show

condo, I realized. No one lived here. But then there was Hank's underwear to prove otherwise. "I give you strange, as in weirdo, but—"

"I'm not in control," Delia said flatly. Then she glared at me and passed me the beer. "Look at this place. My father bought both of my sisters houses, but I rated condo. I'm not offended, I mean who cares, right? But it was deemed the better investment short term, because art is a stupid career so I'd need to cash out first. So, a condo. This isn't a home, like your place. Total irony there, I know, so shut it." She shook her head. "I live in an investment. An investment. Me." She turned around and faced me. I didn't say anything. She wasn't done.

"So I live here. Or sleep, whatever. But I accepted it. This judgment. This daily fucking reminder. Fucking shame. And I'm beginning to realize that this piece of shit place is a symbol of some kind of awful shit that was built right into me." She gestured encompassingly and let her hands drop, shook her head. "The closer we get to the wedding the more I act like my mother. Makes me want to wash my mind off in sewer water."

"What—"

"His underwear!" Delia thundered. She balled it in her fist and shook it in front of me. "Darby, I made an appointment to get his teeth cleaned! Like he's my fucking dog!"

"Wait a—"

"Remember when I told you . . ." She tossed the underwear back on the counter and stepped in front of me, looked up, searching my face with watery eyes. Her lower lip was trembling. Heat was rising from her tiny frame like she had a fever. "Remember when you and Suzanne met and all that shit was going down? And I told you she was already trying to fix you, to paint your windows over and stop the light? Remember?"

"That was—"

"I'm doing the same thing!"

I put my hand on her shoulder. The contact seemed to shock her, and she sipped in a fast breath. She'd never told anyone what she was telling me. I could see it in her eyes. It was the first time she'd even said it out loud and put the thoughts into words, and it had stunned her.

"Delia. Listen. You and Hank, this is different than me and Suzanne and I'll tell you why. Me and Suze, I've come to realize that love is the real deal, as in huge, the biggest journey there is, but complicated people have a different time waiting at baggage claim. Suzanne is waiting for her cameras and her sports junk. I forgot what my bag looks like, but I know the cops are waiting for me to take one. Same plane, same airport, but a totally different experience. This house?" I gestured with my free hand. "This condo thing? This is your empty bag. Hank doesn't even have a bag, sweetie. You see?"

Delia sagged and I pulled her in.

"We're almost there," she whispered.

"I know," I said gently.

"Just, no band practice. No fucking impromptu parties, with spray paint and bong water explosions. This place will sell in the next few weeks in this market, and by the time we get back from our honeymoon we'll be set. Then we get the Dildo Palace." Her voice grew quiet and dreamy.

"Austin City Limits. Little adobe with a garden, and my dumbass husband can start the rudest country band of all time. But for right now . . ."

It wasn't adding up. None of it. It was simply impossible that she was marrying Hank out of some kind of teen rebellion after being "gifted" this terrible condo. It came to me then that maybe some part of Delia was tired. Tired of the constant fire she was burning. Maybe I was seeing it all through the warped lens of my own exhaustion. Maybe that's why I felt as lost as she did. It could be almost anything, this wanting to run she obviously felt as much as I did. The City of Roses was shedding its carnival side. The odd, once so cherished, so much the soul of the place, didn't feel at home here anymore. Austin was as good a place as any. Better, in fact, than my own destination of Nowhere.

"For right now," I said, staring at the clock behind her, "we hold our shit together."

I left Delia to clean up the mess from the horrifying pear and kale smoothies she'd made. She was in a better mood, laughing, and the skin around her eyes had lost its tautness. She was a secretive woman, but so much of the truth is in the burden of it, I knew from experience, and sharing it lightened it, changed its gravity. She was relieved that her bland investment life hadn't stunned me all that badly after the initial shock wore off, and what I'd said about love and Hank and empty bags had spackled a hole in her. Lying so often to the boy genius Agent Dessel and the next-level criminal scumbags who were fucking with my game in the last few years, shuffling around the facts for Suzanne, it had all culminated in a mastery of the cowardly science of deception. So I felt dead inside.

I couldn't pick out the tail behind me, but I knew they were back there. The rain had dialed down to medium thick. I drove aimlessly, waiting to feel better. Instead, I felt gradually worse.

Hank's shithole of a bum squat second home looked abandoned when I drove past it. The lights were out and the official Empire of Shit van was gone. I didn't slow, just rolled past without turning my head. A few minutes later I pulled into the parking lot of Sho's Lounge, where his secret girlfriend worked. Four cars, no van. I turned the ignition off and sat in the spill of neon from the sign, smoking and thinking.

If Hank was inside, the jig was up. Plus, I'd get arrested. My tail had pulled into the lot across the street behind me, a 2000 Generic White Nothing, and if a 911 call came in reporting a savage beating in progress, I'd get busted even if I got away and whatever was left of Hank didn't rat.

Four cars. They were beaters, too, so they probably belonged to the employees. Sho's was run down in the same way. No one there was making any money, so if Hank's one true love was working, it might be my only chance to say hello. I stabbed out my cigarette.

The inside of Sho's was dumpy casual, with red over-stuffed washable plastic booths and formica tabletops, a deluxe bar with a righteous display of middle-of-the-road booze, and low light from regularly spaced sand dollar lamps. It smelled like old beer, cheap hamburger, and mold. I scanned the place from the doorway next to the gumball machine like I was looking for someone I knew.

She was just as Nigel described her. Short, with Delia's pug nose, but a wide mouth with big red lips, long hair with loose, heavy curls, and the chest of a woman twice her size. She was chatting up the bartender in a familiar way, a towel and an empty drink tray next to her hands. Both of them glanced my way.

"Sit anywhere," she called. She had the throaty, smoky voice of a Lauren Bacall. I nodded and slid into a booth. She picked up her tray and a menu and casually sashayed in my direction.

"Drink?" She put the menu in front of me and gave me a sleepy smile.

"Old Crow, rocks."

She glanced back at the bartender and he nodded that he'd heard. When she turned back she cocked her hip.

"Cool scar," she said, meaning it. She touched the side of her face where my scar was. In spite of it all, I liked her, right then and there.

"Cool hair," I said back. She stuck a finger in a curl and twirled.

"The rain does it." She sighed and looked out the window. I squinted at her nametag.

"You from here, Becky?"

"Nah. LA. Specials tonight are the prime rib, okey dokey if you're in the mood for a hungry man platter, and the red eye chili comes with cheese and onions."

"Just the drink for now."

"You waiting on company?" She twirled her hair again, and then she smacked her gum for the first time. Becky was the laziest gum chewer I'd ever seen.

"Yeah, sorta."

She drifted back to the bar, picked up my tumbler, and brought it back, all in slow motion. I watched the whole thing blankly. Becky was undeniably beautiful, and in a tragic way, one of my favorite kinds. Bloomed, but in a dark place, and with the perfect curves and unconscious, languid grace that could never last. If Delia was being played by Hank, then the angel with my booze was a victim of a higher order. You had to love a woman like that through what was coming next for her, the hard years of decline from that accidental and magnificent high, and maybe Hank knew that, maybe he didn't. But the womanizing little scumbag was not that man.

"Who you waiting for?" she asked. She chewed again. "You look sorta sad, man."

"Barroom telepath, eh? That's a grim sorta talent." I squinted up with one eye closed and gave her questioning and innocent, as much as I can make that face. "Just makin' sure I don't owe anyone here money."

Becky snorted when she laughed. It was that real. "And? You sat down, so . . ."

I knocked back half my drink and tossed an arm along the back of the booth, slumped into a relaxed posture. "What brought you here from LA, young miss? You don't mind my asking."

"My mom. Sick. Took care of her for the last year, stuck around. Now I work here." She smiled wanly. "Sho's Diner, where good girls go to get rich."

"Get back to LA ever?" I sipped. She shook her curls.

"Nah. But me an' my dude are moving back in a few months, so full circle. Get a little apartment in Santa Monica, maybe, finally live under the same roof. He's a musician. He's gonna start a country band, maybe get a little skate shop going. I'll still be waiting tables, but I bet I'll make more money."

"Right on." I peeled a ten and a five out of the roll in my pocket and finished my drink, set the empty on the edge of the bills. "Keep it."

She stepped back as I slid out. When I stood, we smiled at each other. Her beautiful junkie glow might hold for a little longer, I reasoned, and I had a wild impulse to rescue her, to get her away from the dummy drain she was circling, to somehow shine light into her head. I could only think of one way to do that, and in that instant, looking down into those dream fog eyes, I missed the cutting mind of Delia. My way would have to do.

"See ya."

Becky went back to the bar, the bills in her apron pocket, and I knew I was already forgotten. The rain was coming down harder when I stepped outside. I ducked into the dark corner of the entryway and lit a cigarette. Sho's parking lot had been big chunk gravel at one point, but it had worn through in most places into deep, oily puddles. I watched the passing lights reflected in them, warped and choppy by the impact of big black drops, and all I could think about was Delia again, and Hank, and the surprising time bomb element of it all.

The waitress Becky had beautiful eyes, and they were full of love. Tragically, it wasn't horndog love or dick-sucking worship love, but the real kind, with breakfast involved. This rain didn't mean shit to her because she was getting out. None of it did. The eerie new bummer vibe in the city, the dead daytime skies, the shit job. She was going home, a wonder woman, in a controlled habit delusion, with a trophy guy fresh from a score, into a semi-retirement leisure fantasy of bong hits, cowgirl boots, tender garden sex, and a part-time job. She was that close.

She was that close. I could see her new place, too. Little one-bedroom with the best IKEA and garage sales had, and with a cat, too. All of it, down to the airfare, paid in full with the money Delia would get from selling her condo of shame. I didn't feel the cold wet as I walked to my car. I don't even remember unlocking the door. I got in and stared at the Sho's Diner sign, and then turned to the woman sitting in the dark in the passenger seat. It didn't even scare me.

She was in her late thirties, her black hair pulled back tight enough to make her hard face even more severe. Blue windbreaker. She held up her badge and she didn't smile.

"Lopez," she said, then pointed out at the neon sign with edge of her ID. "Did you want to show me something? I was going to jump you tonight anyway for dissing Dessel, but if you did, this is a definite 'meet cute.'"

"Jesus Christ." I gripped the wheel and looked forward. "I'm having the worst fucking luck with women today." Then I looked at her again. "You are a chick, right?"

"Pressman is retiring," Agent Lopez said. "I'm the new guy." She looked away, out the windshield. "I read your file twice, Holland. The first time because it's my job and I like horror movies in my personal life, and the second time because it's fascinating, and I need more dark Coen brothers imagery in my soporific reading. Smoke?"

"No, thanks."

"I mean gimme one."

I shook two out of my pack and we lit up. Lopez was hard to read in the bad light, but her motions and tone were calm. Calm is not good in feds.

"How are you still alive?" she asked finally. She continued before I could answer. "It's like hell rejected you. Just like the judicial system." She patted my knee and I almost jumped. "Rejected by everything but the high-speed gutter running through Old Town. And that gutter is drying up."

"Okay. I get it. You're cooler than Pressman. Let's start there."

"Fine. Let me put it all together for you, Holland. Someone is ghosting you, and whoever it is has professional skills. We know that now. However you caught wind of it in the first place, maybe through your network of escapees from the Island of Misfit Toys, was a test of some kind.

You activated your federal monitors to see what we might flush out, and here we are."

"Did you hear my fishing story?"

"Listened to the recording, read the transcript."

I sighed. "Then I might as well tell you. I caught wind of this ghost myself. Sort of felt it, I don't know how. And then I found boot prints outside my bedroom window. Someone knows my schedule. When I'm home, when I leave. How to hide around my house. And that someone knows how to remain unseen. You read my file, Lopez. I was a paranoid guy before all the shit that came down in the last few years. Now? Ghosting me is like stalking an insomniac deer with six eyes. Close to impossible."

Lopez laughed then, and I smiled in spite of myself. She turned in the passenger seat to face me fully, and the neon lit one side of her face. The smile dropped.

"You arrogant fucking jackass. You think some phony spook is big game for us? The goddamned overtime for your ignorant—"

"Use your head muscle, Agent Martinez," I snapped.

"Lopez."

"Whatever. Agent Lopez, roll with me on this. So far, every move I've made up the food chain in Old Town has caught the attention of a monster. It's what I do. And that makes me federal bait. Have you talked to Dessel? I mean, actually listened to him?"

She said nothing.

"What we have here is the new bad thing, and I'm hoping that 'third time is the charm' shit is just another dumbass bumper sticker. So yeah. I tipped you guys off.

And you should be happy I did, too. Dessel wants to be the next J. Edgar Hoover by the time he's old enough to drink and I keep scaring his big scores away."

Lopez snorted at the Hoover thing, but soured fast at the end.

"We think you killed Nicholas Dong Ju." She watched my reaction carefully. I grimaced.

"I never killed anybody, dummy." I was on a roll because she blinked first.

"We still don't know how you made Oleg Turganov return to Russia."

"Maybe I drew him a really convincing fake treasure map. With my art skills." I'd airmailed him in a transmission box after I rufied him.

"He died in prison. Five months ago. Never talked."

"Good for him." We were back to a staring match.

"The Russians would have killed you to pieces by now if this was some kind of retaliation." She shrugged with her eyebrows. "Since you and me are friends now, why don't you tell me who it is you pissed off this time. Save us all some trouble."

"That's the thing!" I was genuinely exasperated. "I don't know. No fucking idea, lady. What we do know is that I'm being ghosted and you can't figure out who it is and neither can I. That's a fact all by itself. Agent Dessel is way fucking smart. So is my Delia. I can see someone getting past one of them, but both?"

Lopez thought about that. I watched her do it. Finally, she crushed out her cigarette and put her seatbelt on.

"Drive."

"Where to?" I started the engine.

"Who cares. I just don't want to stare at this dump."

I took a left and headed for the freeway. Lopez stayed quiet as she went over her impressions and added to the list of shit to be used against me, sorted and catalogued and filed. I almost turned on the radio, didn't. When I finally hit I-84, I drove toward the airport.

"I needed to talk to you for all kinds of reasons," she confessed after a while. "Pressman and Dessel, they have this raging boy boner for you. Never seen anything quite like it. Right now you're red hot in so many ways. Money, but no one can figure out where it is. Prosperity, even, but the foundation is like a mirror. You look at it, all you see is yourself looking. It's driving them crazy, and with Bob set to retire and me taking his place? They want you on the shelf before the band breaks up." She made a *tsk*ing sound. "You're their last gig as Tenacious D."

"I so love that band." I took the airport exit.

"I knew you were going to say that." Lopez sighed. "Your profile suggests that you're the type who would go for a rainy drive at night with a curious fed to feed your own intuition. That you'll read me like a comic book, and that it will make you more confident as you move forward."

I didn't say anything. I took the airport exit and turned into the cell phone waiting area and parked. Two other cars. The distant maintenance runways were lit up. A squat little cube of engine with tiny wheels was towing a plane. Slow. I turned to Agent Lopez, who was watching me.

"Lopez, look into my eyes. Do it like you're trying to

read my mind." She did. "Now, you try this kind of shit with me one more time, ever, and I will shut you out. You don't get back in. In my book you're already one step in on the bad side of the equation, so I'm being really, really nice here. There are motherfuckers in this world so goddamned awful that even breathing their air is unhealthy, and yet here you sit, playing games. With me. If you were worth half a shit you would be out there kneecapping human traffickers, the shithead dog fighters and all the rest, but you're not. And you're not even very smart. We're all alone in the loneliest place in the entire city. Together. In the dark."

Her hand didn't move to her gun. I'd forced her to measure my threat level, and in that instant we really did read each other's minds. When her hand didn't move, we both noticed. Her eyes flashed in awareness. I smiled thinly.

"You fucker—" she began.

"Yes," I interrupted. "I just dug around in your head. Just like my profile said I would, so thanks for the idea 'cause I'm not really that enterprising unless I get a few hints. You already know I'm not the bad guy, and now I know you know. You're welcome. And I say that because what I mean is that I find you to be one rung lower on the fed ladder than your new buddies, and that's a ladder no one should be climbing. Says something about you."

Agent Lopez didn't say anything. We sat there, eyes locked, until she finally cocked her head, but it marked a conclusion.

"You're a bad man, Holland. Just not in the way people think. You come in tomorrow and talk to the guys, understand? Tomorrow. They have a line on something and they want you to connect the dots. You don't? I find you again and drag you downtown."

I started the engine.

By the time I finally got home it was after midnight again. I expected another note, or even Dessel himself, sitting on my porch and drinking one of my beers, petting one of my traitorous cats, but the street was quiet. The house was dark and there was no one waiting. I didn't even have any mail. I let myself in and turned on the lights, cringing inwardly, but there was no blood sprayed all over the walls, no body in the middle of the floor. I was greeted by the cats instead. They blinked at me and then went back to napping, waiting for the sound of the can opener.

I fed them and then sat down on the couch with a pint of tap water. A late dinner would have been nice, but I was too tired to chew. Too wiped out to get drunk. I took my boots off before I was too tired for that, too. Then I lay back and looked at the ceiling.

Surveillance had pulled way back on my house, so they had either dropped it or they'd found something and they knew it wasn't right on top of me. Neither scenario was particularly good. Connect the dots could mean anything, but it most likely meant identifying a photo of Oleander, the Mineral Man, Chester G. Goodwin, Robert Gold. Trevor Connor, late of room 7119. The guy with all the names Santos and I had buried at the edge of the party field. I didn't feel like doing that. If I didn't know who the guy's boss was yet, I doubted Dessel did either. He'd always been two or three steps behind me and there was no reason to think that had changed, especially with Pressman halfway out the door and the new chick on the fence about everything.

So I'd put them off until I needed them to do something else. It was as simple as that. That left me free to think about Suzanne. I drank the water and went and refilled the glass, drank the second pint right there at the sink. I didn't even want to consider it at the moment, but I forced myself to try.

Move to the magical land of wherever at long last. It sounded good, but there was a catch, of course. She wasn't asking me to move as much as she was asking me to change. Suzanne had been trying to transform me into the perfect guy since the morning after the night we met. If I was honest with myself, I'd tried to do the same thing in some way to her, but I'd given up almost instantly. She hadn't. I knew what she wanted, and what she wanted was in no way a bad thing, either. She thought I'd be happier if I was happy, and that's a very, very confusing notion.

I carried the water back to the couch and sat hard. My legs felt like clay bags. I closed my eyes and pictured Suzanne's face. She was frowning.

What made her happy, content even, was fixed in her marrow. Suzanne liked nature, travel, immersing herself in the interior definition of giant buzz words like "culture" and "philosophy." Which made her a tourist in almost every single way imaginable. And there was nothing wrong with that. I just wasn't willing to get in the cruise boat and wear the shorts and sunglasses. Her version of the American Dream had much in the way of dreaming about it, and as delusional as it sounded, even to me, my way of life was closer to the ground and seemed more real to me because of it.

The truth was I didn't know what the hell to do. Life was one crisis after another, and while it was true that I kept winning as far as the bank was concerned, only the worst sort of cretin defined success in life with numbers. The daily bread, the Art of the Moment, that was more my speed, and I wasn't any good at it anymore. Now I was bluffing. I'd spent one too many nights drinking in an alcove in front of a shoe repair place.

Still, it was possible. What Suzanne proposed was flexible in many ways. If she could get used to the fact that in *my* marrow I was a criminal, and accept that I didn't have a problem with her obedience dilemma, then there was a good chance that shit could work out, long term.

The lies I tell myself never go down without booze, and at that moment I was too tired to get up. But I did have the juice left for one last thing. I took my phone out and dialed.

"What's up? I was just getting into my Underoos. Batgirl."

"You dipstick. Hank there?"

"In the bathroom. What in the world would you—no way! Operation Tuxedo!"

"It's a go. Can he meet me at the shop at eleven? In the morning, just so we're clear."

"You bet. Gomez was asking for you earlier, so you can kill two birds with one stone." Delia sounded relieved. Happy. Bubbly.

"Know what? That might take a while, hate to get Hank all tangled up in shop shit. On your way to work tomorrow, drop him off at the Commodore. We can grab a quick beer, then hit the tuxedo place. By then it'll be lunchtime. We can hit up the taco cart row on Second."

"Thank you, Darby. Don't screw this up, I mean. Remember the penis skinning, wiping my parts speech."

"How could I forget? And don't call me every ten minutes. And text me the address of the tuxedo place."

"You're the best." She was yelling the good news at Hank as she hung up.

Fury. It gave me just enough energy for a nightcap after all.

In the morning the Alfa wouldn't start, so I pulled it into the garage and hooked it up to the charger. It was raining and the windows had leaked, so the car smelled like mildew and motor oil. The Prius tail was nowhere to be seen. I smoked and waited a few minutes, then started the engine. The cats watched from the window, saddened by their grounded status, as I pulled out and revved the engine to build the charge a little more. Then I was off to deal with Hank Dildo.

Meeting at a bar was a good idea, I thought. I'd slept in till nine, and after eight hours of sleep and breakfast, the morning workout, I wanted to beat him to death without preamble. But in a bar setting we both stood a chance. I'd been banned from the Commodore once already, for a period of five long years, and I wasn't keen on getting back on the 86 list. Plus, the first few beers usually had a mollifying effect on me. Sometimes they didn't, and that was a chance Hank was just going to have to take.

I still had an hour and a half to kill, so I drove to O'Reilly's and traded in the old battery for a new one. It would still bleed out, but it would take more than a week. I swapped them out in the rain with a wrench they loaned me, and by then I was ready.

Hank was alone at the bar when I walked in. A hundred and ten pounds, five seven and change, wearing diseased-looking combat boots and jeans held together with duct tape, an orange T-shirt under a black Levi's jacket festooned with band patches. Bleached white crew cut. He was regaling the bartender, Tom, with a comic exploit. They both turned when I came in and the happy vibe evaporated. Hank clammed up because I had that effect on him. Tom just plain didn't like me.

"Darby," Hank said. He glanced nervously at Tom. "I, ah, I started a tab, man. Delia said it would be okay."

"Darby Holland," Tom drawled. "Just walked in and you already owe me ten bucks and a tip."

I sat down on a stool next to Hank. We didn't shake hands.

"Dildo," I said, by way of greeting. "Tom. I'll have a draft, shot of well bourbon."

"You remember the rules, Holland?" Tom asked. He poured anyway. He knew I did. I turned to Hank.

"We can't play pool. In case you wanted to."

"Holland here can never play pool at the Commodore again," Tom said. He set the glass down in front of me and picked up the plastic bottle of well bourbon. "Ever. We do let him in, but not into the back room where the tables are. Ever. Isn't that right, Holland?"

Hank looked on expectantly.

"Don't ask," I said. Tom sat my shot down and I gestured at Hank. "He wants a shot too."

"Holland here was banned for five years," Tom continued. "And he got the pool room ban indefinitely. Wanna know why?"

"Tom," I began, "we took care—"

"It's educational," Tom interrupted. "The kid here needs to know these kinds of things. Right, kid?" He looked at Hank, who had the presence of mind to shrug.

"Sometimes," Hank said, "when, I mean. There was this one time—"

"Darby here, he's in one night playing pool with this fat guy with beady eyes, this Big Mike. Ever met him?"

Hank nodded.

"What a pussy, but there they were, drinking beer like they had hollow legs and playing pool. Holland here? He's kind of a pool shark, and the fat dude is getting his ass handed to him. Pitiful. It was like watching a barracuda eat a sofa cushion. Anyway, the big skinhead at the next table over, you know the kind, with a trashy mall girlfriend, he decides he's gonna get in on the action, starts making fun of Holland's pet dumbass."

"Here we go," I said.

"Yep. The place is packed but I had my eye on 'em. This great big skinhead? He has his flight jacket draped over that stool right there at the end of the bar, saving it for himself." Tom pointed. "I let him. Real monster, this guy. No point in fucking with him, if you're *rational*. If you *think* about it." He glared at me. Beside me, Hank giggled nervously.

"So the guy comes out for another pitcher of beer and sits down to wait while I pour," Tom continued. Incredibly, just telling the story was making him mad all over again. "I look up and what do I see? This Big Mike guy, red faced, headed for the door. I look over at the poolroom and here comes Holland, smiling to himself with this shitty evil smile, and as he passes the big skinhead guy? Guess what he does?"

Hank opened his mouth and closed it.

"He grabs the back of the guy's shirt and yanks. Pulls this giant off his stool and it was like watching a tree fall over. His big bald head? That great big fucking cannonball hit the edge of the table behind him and it catapulted every last drink on that table right into the bar! That's right! In one move Holland here used a guy's head to destroy three thousand dollars' worth of booze on a Friday fucking night!" Spit flew out of Tom's mouth.

I turned to Hank. "True story."

Tom glared at me, mute with rage, just as he always was when he told the story of that night. Hank squirmed, and then finally asked the burning question.

"Why do they let you in?"

"Tom?" I asked, redirecting the question.

"My daughter is a stripper." It came out in a strangled whisper. "She works for the Mexican Conan."

"His daughter Destiny," I clarified, "is a private contractor at the fine nudist establishment I have part ownership of. Santiago manages it. We, ah, we keep an eye on her."

"Ready when you are." Hank downed his shot and drained his beer. I did the same and tossed a couple of twenties on the bar. Tom glared at me without glancing at the money. Outside, Hank and I lit cigarettes. It was misting rain, but it didn't seem to bother him. I didn't mind, either.

"You're, ah, you were kinda mean to that dude," Hank commented. He tried to sound casual, but I could tell the whole thing had rattled him.

"Tom," I said. "He's on my permanent shit list. The bully kind of bartender. Scowls at everyone. Saw him card an old lady one time, freaked her out. Not a wino old lady, either, just this old gal out with her daughter. He didn't card the younger gal. Plus, you know what kind of dad has his baby girl wind up on the pole?" I squinted over at him. Hank shrugged.

"Dunno. Depends, I guess."

"On what?"

"Dance lessons." He looked at me and smiled. I sighed.

"Delia texted me the address of the tux place," I said. I pointed at my dirty little Italian car. "That's me. Let's get through it without freaking the guy out and then maybe grab some lunch."

"What happened to your other ride?"

"Fire."

"Ah."

We got in and I started the engine. Already not as robust as a new battery should be, I could tell. The problem was getting worse. Hank marveled at the antique dials, very retro, especially for a brain-damaged ten-year-old, and seemed to get a little more excited about the prospect of spending the afternoon with me.

"Can I drive?"

"No."

I pulled out. We smoked in silence. I thought about Delia, who was at the Lucky mopping and checking the messages, her art supplies out on the light board in back with her first design of the day. I thought about Suzanne, of how proud she would be if she knew what I was doing, that I was actually taking Hank to the tuxedo place instead of an abandoned building with a human shaped hole in the foundation. That made me smile. Hank took it as his cue to start talking.

"You know, man, I sometimes feel like we got off on the wrong foot, me and you."

"Why's that?" I tried to make it sound casual.

"When I first started dating Delia, you were all fucked up, man. Your face—" He trailed off, looking for the right words. "You got in a fight with those dudes, and then the whole hiring my band to help you with, the ah, the—"

"Remember the deal," I cautioned. "We never, ever, ever talk about that, even with each other."

Hank was referring to the incident where I hired his band Empire of Shit to help me rufie the real estate developer,

Oleg Turganov, and Santiago. Hank himself had put the crushed-up pill in Turganov's drink, had in fact given him an almost fatal overdose because he'd been too stupid to follow instructions. In the aftermath, when we thought the guy might die, they'd all helped me transport the bodies and they'd well and truly lost their collective shit as they did. Per our deal, I paid for their first and only 45, Empire of Shit's epic sonic assault entitled "Vomitorium."

"I remember," he said, a little too quietly. "I mean, I remember that I don't remember anything. Whatever. My point is that it was a gnarly time all around. We didn't know each other real well and we still don't. Delia says you're a private sort of dude, but you and her are tight, I know that. So let's try to maybe get a good thing going here, you and me. Whaddya say?"

"Sure." I smiled when I said it. Hank nodded.

"Good. Make her happy. She's been all bummed out with her family lately. You know about that?"

"What, her dickhead dad and her country club mom? The bitchy Stepford sisters?"

"Delia's family. Shit. You ever met any of them, before I came around?"

"Nah."

Hank glanced at me. Dude could lie so well he should have gone into politics. "None of them have ever even been here. And mine, well, pretty much the same thing. It bums her out."

"I can imagine."

"She tells me that you don't have any kind of family either. Guess that puts all of us in the same boat."

"I hope not. She deserves better." We came to a stop-light and I turned a little to face him. "Know what I do when she starts in on the whole family business?"

"What?" He squirmed a little. It was an unconscious thing.

"I don't say anything at all. I tell you this, Hank, not to be a dick or anything, but because I've been handing out advice like M&Ms the last few days and I'm on a roll. I don't say anything because whatever I do say will make it worse somehow. So I just listen. Maybe try that. Listen to her without coming down on one side or another. Delia is an amazing creature if you can get past her broken glass and nails routine. See what I'm sayin'?"

"I guess." He looked away. The guy had no idea what I was talking about. I patted him on the knee. To his credit, he didn't jump.

"You just listen. Bet you'll appreciate her even more than you already do."

That provoked no reaction at all. Instead, he took his cell phone out and a few clicks later he was checking his Facebook page. I drove on and at the next stoplight I glanced over again. Still looking, smiling now.

"Delia tells me you're starting a country band."

"Yeah." Distracted. He scrolled.

"What about Empire? You gonna do both?"

He looked up to see why we'd stopped, then at me. "We broke up."

"Ah. I see. This country band have a name?"

"Solo project. So Hank something-or-other."

The light turned green. I realized for the first time that

all my CDs were gone. Every last one of them, the sum total of all the music I had purchased in my adult life, was burned.

"Lost ten CDs when my car went up," I said ruefully.

"Bummer, dude."

I stopped talking. Hank's shift from weasely and fearful to arrogant, now that I was trying to be polite, had him close to the edge. One wrong word at this point and I wasn't going to even try to stop hitting him. We were quiet when we pulled into the parking lot of Tuxedorama.

"Door to door service," I announced. He looked up and pocketed his phone.

"Rad. Let's make this snappy, man. I'm fuckin' starved."

I started to reach for him as he got out, jerking like I had rabies, and he didn't even notice. He ducked under the awning of the place and lit up a pre-fitting smoke. I blinked rapidly, willing the bile back down, and got out, giving him a chipper smile as I joined him. Behind us, the lone Tuxedorama clerk looked out on us with dread.

"You have specific orders?" I asked.

"What?"

"The kind of tuxedo you're supposed to get."

Hank shrugged. "I don't think there's more than one kind. The James Bond type, I guess. You know, the one with the little bowtie."

"Right. They have more than one kind, Hank."

"They do?" He turned and glanced inside. I did, too. The clerk stepped back and turned, headed for the cash register.

"Yeah, dog. Gray ones, even green ones. Blue. Tails. Frills. Old-fashioned, weirdo super modern David Bowie."

"Well fuckin' hell." That seemed to confuse him. He looked at me, and we were close enough for me to see the crust in his eyes. "What kind are you getting?"

"I already have a tux," I lied smoothly. "Black. The funeral kind, but it works for all tuxedo events."

He nodded. "Maybe let's take a sec to check it out. I'm supposed to buy mine, not rent it. Delia wants me to have one for all the other shit I might need one for."

"Expensive."

He flicked his hand. "She's picking it up. You know how much money she makes." He laughed, like he was saying something good about her behind her back. I dropped my cigarette and ground it out, gave him a dead clown smile.

"Shall we?"

He looked at my glassy eyes and his smile faded a little, so I opened the door and held it for him so the moment wouldn't stretch. He slipped inside and I followed.

"Jesus," I said to myself.

A horrific party disco was bubbling at volume one from a broken speaker somewhere and the place smelled like plastic, nervous sweat, and men's cologne. There were mannequins everywhere, all of them with blank ovoid faces, and a ghastly orange and lime green piñata was lying on the gray shag carpet to the side of the register counter. Hank threw his arms wide and spun around like he was on camera, in a documentary where he had just summited Mount Everest.

"I love this place!" he declared gleefully.

Something gurgled in my guts then, and I felt a clammy wave of sickness. I glared at the clerk, who winced at my face.

"C-c-c-can I help you gentlemen?" he stammered. I pointed at Hank.

"Dildo here needs a tux. He's buying, so let's not sell him the Mercedes of matrimonial whatever, got me?"

The guy nodded.

"They *do* have different kinds!" Hank held up an old Rhett Butler affair, beaming. "Holy shit. I thought you were just fuckin' with me, man."

I snapped my fingers at the clerk and rubbed my fingers together in the international sign for money. He jerked into action.

"Let's get you measured first Mr . . ."

"Dildo. Hank Dildo." Hank gave the clerk his best smile and handed him the Butler. "Put this on the maybe list."

The clerk took it and looked my way, terrified, and I shook my head.

"G-good, sir. Now, if I can just get you to step over here, I'll take your measurements and then we can see what we have for sale that fits you."

"These aren't all for sale?" Hank looked confused. The clerk glanced my way again and I squinted.

"No, sir. Certainly not. This is primarily a rental outlet. All tuxedo establishments have that in common."

"Ah man." Hank deflated and held his arms out. "Measure away. But that's a bummer, dude. I mean, what happens if you rent a tux and fuck it up? *Then* is it for sale? I bet it is. One more example of the system shankin' it to the little guy. And when he's getting married too, no less. Fuckin' raw, dog. R.A.W. Raw."

"I'm gonna sit," I said. I looked around and realized there were no chairs. The clerk began to hurry in earnest.

"Just one moment." He zipped his tape over Hank's bored, crucified posture and stepped back. "This way, sir. You're unfortunately much smaller than American Standard, so—"

"Meaning I'm not fat," Hank snapped. "Jesus. Let's see what you have in the boy's section. Christ."

Less than five minutes later we walked out with a cheap tuxedo wrapped in plastic.

"That wasn't bad," Hank said. "Fast anyway."

"Regular turnstile." It was raining a little harder. "What you in the mood for, foodwise?"

"Delia usually makes banana pancakes."

"I don't know where to get those, dude." I fired up a cigarette to keep my mouth busy.

"What do you usually have for breakfast, Darby? You're a physical fitness kinda guy, right? Some kind of smoothie action?"

"Tacos. Sometimes beer."

"Delia is so into smoothies, man."

I didn't want to talk to Hank anymore, and right then I realized why Suzanne was so mad at me all the time. I was terrible at faking it. I just sucked when it came down to eating my daily ration of shit. This was a perfect example. All I had to do, at this moment, was play it cool. Don't punch this foul little grease bag in the throat. Don't even menace him. Do what everyone else would do and be nice until I had a rational, measured way of dealing with the situation. I took a deep breath and looked at him.

"What's your least favorite horror movie, Hank?"

"Dude!" He laughed, still deep in his own headspace. He hadn't heard me. "I just realized the best possible solution! Let's go to the food cart cluster on Hawthorne, down by Twelfth. They got tacos and they have the Belgian french fry place! Crepes right across from that! And they have a beer wagon!" He turned to me and winked. "I can try to eat like a tough guy! Grow an extra load of jizz, yo."

I resolved right then, at that very instant, that this would be the first and last time I would ever roll with "tempered and even" as a description of my behavior. It felt good, so I smiled. Hank smiled, too.

"You'll need your strength," I said. "For the coming storm."

He looked up at the sky. Unbelievable.

The food court Hank was talking about was one of the older ones, in my estimation, or at least one of the more well known. Ten or twelve colorful food carts were arranged in a ring around a collection of wooden picnic tables. People were coming and going as noon approached, and there was a low-key midway feel to it. Hank peeled off toward the Potato Champion wagon, where he loudly ordered the chili cheese fries, for all the world a celebrity of some kind briefly walking the earth before the paparazzi drove him back into the heavens. I went straight to the nearest source of beer, which turned out to be a BBQ place.

"Pint of—" I looked at the selection.

"You gotta order food, too," the girl said. "Sorry. OLCC."

"Okay, I'll have the ribs, mustard greens, cornbread, pint of your World Famous Brawnier."

"Mini pitcher's two dollars off."

"Deal."

She gave me a ticket and the mini pitcher, which was distressingly miniature, just over a pint, and I went and sat down under one of the umbrellas on a wet bench and watched Hank work his magic. He had the poor woman at the potato wagon under his spell, chatting her up and flexing his mighty charisma, and for an instant I could see what Delia saw. Hank was a charming guy, there was no doubt. It was a natural charm, too. He did it without even trying. When he was done he gave the woman his name and then looked around, spotted me and did a little Irish jig in my direction.

"Calm," I said to myself. I sipped and smiled his way. "Easy. Be a unicorn on a unicycle."

"I told her I was suuuuuper hungry," Hank said. He dropped on to the bench across from me. "She might have gotten the wrong idea. Women."

"You got quite a way about you, Hank," I admitted. He shrugged.

"Tell me more about the band," I continued. "You say you guys broke up?"

"Long time coming," he replied. "Long time. Band like Empire of Shit was pretty much made to break up. It's, like, a design flaw built into all punk bands. Here today, gone tomorrow."

"The guys sticking around when you and Delia split for Austin?"

"Moving to somewhere, I forget. Fresno. Bakersfield. Somewhere apocalyptic. Kinda hard news when you get right down to it." A flash of real sadness went across his face and he glanced at my beer. "Those guys, damn, dude. We had some very fuckin' good times." He looked up at me and I knew what was coming. "Bad ones, too."

"What about work?"

He frowned and looked away. After a moment, he smiled. "Sure as fuck ain't working at a Tuxedorama. Dude, you see that piñata? What the fuck was in that thing? Mice?"

I had to laugh.

"And that dude," Hank went on. "Man, dude was wilted. Crushed by the system and life at the same time. Minimum wage job, but shit, dude had no wedding ring. Can you imagine that? Selling wedding crap to chumps all day. Forever the bridesmaid but never the groom or whatever? Post gnarly."

I laughed again, surprising us both.

"Glad you're finally warming up," Hank said. "You're a scary dude, man. I always get the feeling you don't like me all that much."

"Don't take it personally. Me and the world have problems in general."

"I can dig it. You and Delia, you two are both kinda that way. You ever, I mean, you know." He made an "O" with his thumb and index finger and stuck his other index finger through it, making the pokey-pokey sign.

"Nah."

"Suzanne." He changed the subject that fast. "Tall. Sorta bossy. How's that going? She's in Seattle?"

"It mostly sucks," I admitted.

"What'd she move there for?"

"A brighter future. Same as Delia and Austin."

"Huh." He looked away.

"Yeah, man. Cool that you're so supportive of Delia. Guy has to stand by his gal. Sometimes right behind her. She isn't as tough as she lets on. This career change, it won't be easy for her, but she's worked so hard for it, for years, long as I've known her."

"Yeah." A little darkness came into him, so subtle that I wouldn't have noticed it if I didn't know all about it. "Yeah. Good to stand by your gal. But it's a two-way street."

"How do you mean?"

"Dunno. I guess—" He took a deep breath. "She's pretty focused, dude."

"You mean bossy, like Suze. Get real, kid."

"There it is again." Hank's eyes flashed anger. "That tone."

I scowled and finished the beer, plonked the empty down, and gave him my best fake smile, the one I usually aimed at Dessel. Hank looked bewildered.

"I've had the longest fuckin' week," I began. "I mean, long long." I had to play it cool until I decided what to do, I reminded myself again. Cool, cool, too cool for school. "Let's get more beer. I think part of my problem is this hangover."

"Delia says you've been hitting it especially hard."

"I have. But the Lord hates a quitter."

The Potato gal began calling for Hank, so we both went back to our respective windows. I ordered another beer, and while I waited my ribs and sides came up, suspiciously like they were done already and just sitting there. When I met Hank back at the table it was clear he had gotten the royal treatment. His steaming pile of chili cheese fries was enormous, overflowing with everything, and he'd doused it with hot sauce.

"She called me Emperor Dildo," he confirmed. "Believe that?"

I picked at my non-steaming ribs and stale cornbread. Hank ate like a starving dingo, snorting, dry hacking, farting, and vocalizing a range of custom sound effects. His abdomen made an incredible amount of noise too, like whale song. He actually got food in one of his eyebrows. He saw me watching about halfway through and gestured.

"Wanna get down on this?"

"Thanks, no."

He shrugged and continued his circus of consumption. I sometimes ate like that, I realized, but without the sound effects. Hank was full of revelations for me, because I decided to maybe not do that anymore.

"Hank, where the hell did you learn to eat like that?"

"I seen you eat," he said around a mouthful of food. He glanced at my slippery ribs. "When it's good, I mean."

I shrugged with my face.

"S'part of the problem, no lie," he went on. "Name was Rose. My second foster mother. The one with the food." He took a breath and stopped eating, picked a chunk of something out of the back of his teeth and inspected it before flicking it away. "Rose is in county right now, so Delia is bummed. No wedding mama on the Dildo side of the family either. She thinks it makes us look like total losers, no family in the chapel. I keep telling her it doesn't matter, but it does." He belched and frowned. "Rose, she was good people. Eleven kids under her roof. Fed us all on state money, which is about enough to feed a small dog. Hence my manners."

"Rose," I repeated. I felt a twinge of sympathy for him.

"I'm still fucking skinny." He laughed bitterly. "Ate all my fat cells growing up."

"I can relate, unfortunately."

"Delia told me that about you. Said you came up the hard way. Born old, Rose called it."

"Wasn't so bad," I lied.

"Where to next?"

"The shop. I'll drop you off and you can store your tux there with Delia. I've got to talk to Gomez."

"Cool."

"Aw yeah." It was my turn to stare into space. "Aw yeah."

We were both quiet on the drive into Old Town. Hank was high on his speedy victory at Tuxedorama, no doubt, and having eaten was likely thinking about scoring some dope and hitting up his one true love to unload some of his surplus man juice while Delia was at work. I was busy con-cocting a lie to feed to Gomez and multitasking by mon-itoring the engine, which didn't sound right. No matter how I turned it, there was nothing I could tell Gomez short of the truth that would explain the situation. That wasn't going to be easy, but worst of all, Gomez was a violent man of deep feelings. His reaction would be unpredictable.

There was parking across the street, so I took it. Hank must have texted Delia at some point because she was expecting us, and darted from the shop before I cut the engine. Hank and I watched as she held up traffic. Today she was wearing a lurid pink mini tee and shiny red pants, her Banksy boots. She leaned in with her tiny butt cocked out, classic streetwalker pose, and gave me a wink.

"Thanks."

"Hey baby," Hank purred. She winked at him too, then tossed her head at me.

"He gave you a pass, did he?" She glanced at the plastic-wrapped tux.

"We got along famously," I said quickly. "Tux was no big deal, practically free."

"Goody. Gomez is looking for you." She inspected my hornet sting. "He was really, really insistent. You beat up the kid or what?"

"No, no," I lied, wincing. "I, ah, did he look mad?" I must have made a pained expression because Delia laughed in my face. She smelled like bubble gum and Chapstick.

"You ding-dong! You're his landlord and you just gave questionable advice to his troubled nephew! Of course he looked mad!" Then she made a mock zombie street samurai face and said in a deep voice, "He also looked very Gomez. 'You tell Darby I lookin' for him, no? Good chica, *buuuenooooo.*'"

"Later," Hank said, seizing the call to abandon ship. He hopped out and yanked his tux out of the back, slammed the door. "C'mere, little chica. I was just telling Darby how I was growing something for you."

Delia circled the car and slid into Hank's arms, looked up into his sleazy smile.

"Mold?" she asked prettily.

"Guess again."

"Mildew? A shroom of some kind? Right behind your gonads?"

"Warmer. Warmer."

"An unguent." She raised one foot, making dainty. I couldn't stand any more so I got out and slammed the door, heading for the Rooster Rocket for a drink and fistfight with a possible knifing crescendo.

The inside of the Rocket was dark as ever. And cold, too. I let out the breath I'd been holding as the door closed behind me and drew in a deep breath of bar smell through my nose. Cherry was behind the bar and she gave me a curious look. My hackles went up.

"Gomez around?"

She flicked her eyes in the direction of the booth across from her. Gomez leaned out and looked down at me, took his reading glasses off. He was sitting there doing paperwork, waiting for me.

"Darby," he called in that way he had, of being loud without raising his voice. "C'mere, *vato*. Sit with me."

I walked toward him with my head down. I couldn't help it.

"Cherry, sweetheart," Gomez rumbled again, "how about a round here. Christian thimbles."

I slid into the booth across from him. Gomez set his glasses down and stared at me. In front of him was a spreadsheet, the ordering forms, and a Dollar Store calculator. Coffee. I looked up from all of it into his eyes. Gomez didn't have brown eyes like most Mexicans. His were close to black, a single shade away from his actual pupil, and right then they looked like the eyes of a serial killer on a movie poster. He'd come close to hypnotizing me in the past with his impressive ozone glare. I smiled nervously.

"Hey, dude," I began lamely, "I, ah, I wanted—"

"Hold your tongue," he commanded softly. "First, we will drink."

I swallowed. He stared at me while we waited for Cherry. I tried not to squirm. After ten hours, she set our drinks down and drifted back into the bar gloom. Gomez took his tiny glass in his scarred fingers and raised it. I took mine and raised it as well.

"To family," he breathed.

"Cheers." It came out of me almost like a question. We drank.

"Gomez," I began again, "there are times in a man's life when—"

"Stand up," he directed. He slid out of the booth and gestured for me to rise with both hands. I did. Reluctantly. We looked at each other. Gomez was a seasoned street fighter, swinging before I was born, so there would be no rookie telegraph messaging. His strike would be blind and fast, to a wet place like my eyes or the roof of my mouth if it was open, or the neck. He might even try to pull my lip or an ear off. He spread his arms wide and my eyes went wide too.

Gomez hugged me.

"I owe you, homie," he whispered. "We always had each other's backs, but now you are a brother to me. I have no idea how you saved the boy. He will not tell me. But"—he stopped and sniffed, continued in a hoarse voice—"he is a changed man." He drew back and shook me by the shoulders, then raised his voice. "Cherry! Sweetheart, bring us real drinks! The top shelf! Bourbon!" Then he drew back and gestured for me to sit.

"This is welcome news," I said, amazed that I didn't stutter. "Santos is, where is he? I mean right now?"

"At work." Gomez leaned back. "Preparing."

"Ah." I nodded, like this made sense. "Good."

"What did you say to him?" Gomez smiled and leaned forward, glanced in Cherry's direction. "He said it was private, that he did not want to violate your trust. But if you tell me?" He spread his hands, palms up.

"We had an interesting day." I nodded and considered. Cherry gave me a moment's reprieve by delivering our drinks just then, so I picked up my glass and gave her a smile, waited until she was back at the bar before I addressed him. "What did he tell you, Gomez? I mean, when did he get back?"

"Last night. Late. I don't know what time. He called me this morning and said he was on his way to work. We talked." Gomez picked up his drink. "He told me that he had cash. Him and his brother, they had made some. It was money I didn't know about. He told me he had it because . . . I don't know why he told me, not really. But it had something to do with you. Santos wants to be more honest about who and what he is. He won't work for the government, but he will not ever run for office either, he says. He intends to exist outside the system, which is good, but he means all the way out."

"And these preparations . . ."

"The new start." Gomez lowered his voice. "Santos does not believe he can beat the game if he plays by the rules."

"Right." I had no idea what that meant. "Right. Good."

"This new car of his." Gomez frowned. "He says it is, what was his word, a relic of yours, left over from something you did?"

I said nothing.

"Darby, I used my car connection to run the VIN on that ride. Santos already did, but I had to make sure. That car was never manufactured. It never rolled off the line. No one ever owned it. It never existed." His voice went all the way down to a whisper. "Priceless, *vato*."

A chill went up my back. A phantom with a phantom car. I should have expected as much. I shrugged.

"Oh! Your piece of shit minivan! It's in a parking garage over by the convention center. The one across from the bank plaza."

"Drop the keys off when you can, no rush." He sipped his drink and nodded appreciatively. "So, homie. You. How are you? How is Suzanne?"

"I'm okay," I said. "Suze is still up north. She's coming down to visit this weekend."

"Good. The feds?"

"One of them has colitis."

"Good!" Gomez brightened, then abruptly glowered. "You still being stalked by a renegade stripper?"

"Nah. I think I still got a pretty big problem there, but I don't know what to do about it just yet."

"You need help, you got my number. The family thing,

no shit, Darby. Santos has a chance now. You two gonna stay friends?"

"Sure we are. Tell him to call me, in fact. I got a couple coats I think would fit him. Snappy vintage, hard to find."

"Will do. Flaco wants to see you too, man. Free tacos for a while."

We drank in companionable silence after that. My initial relief on the matter of Santos had faded, giving way to low level alarm. He'd come back, resumed his old life, and he was preparing for something. Whatever it was would no doubt be blamed on me, so it was in my best interest to find out what the hell he was up to. But for the time being, it was one less thing to worry about. When I was done, Gomez and I said our goodbyes with a fist bump, same as always, but he smiled this time.

On the way out, I stopped at Flaco's window. The old man looked up from chopping onions with tears in his eyes.

"Darby!" he howled. "My friend! I must tell you—"

"Tell me while you cook, man," I interrupted. "Fuckin' starved. Four juniors, and two more on the side. If I don't eat, I'm going to drown."

"Six of the best juniors! One fire!"

"I'll be right back," I said. "Gotta poke my head in the Lucky and yell at Delia."

"I will bring them over!"

That gave me pause. In two decades, the closest Flaco had come to delivery was throwing a taco out the window into the street. I nodded uneasily and ducked into the tattoo shop.

Delia was alone, kicked back at her station reading a trashy magazine, a pair of scissors in one hand. She'd been cutting out random words to use in the border of a piece of flash. The new kids wouldn't get there until early afternoon. The Nordic death metal was cranked so loud it was hard to tell who it actually was. I went to the stereo and turned it down.

"Hank was bummed you were mean to him," she said immediately. "He didn't go on and on about it like a baby, but all he had to do was mention it for me to know it bothered him."

I held my hand up for silence.

"I wish you two could somehow get along," she continued, ignoring me. "You have to think, Darby. Hank and me, this is real, like wedding real. I don't think the big picture has really sunk in all the way with you somehow."

"I watched him eat," I began, "and this was after I watched him drink."

"You're serious?" She put her scissors down and stood, folded her arms. "Unbelievable. Be nice to my man, Darby Holland. Period."

I deflated.

"And no shit-talking about him either." Delia stepped closer to me and the look on her face was sincere. "From now on we gotta have a rule, man. Play nice and stay nice or no dice."

"Like the three monkeys in the Chinese postcard," I ventured weakly.

"My god. You two have so much in common."

"I'm only a dick because I care," I said firmly. "Quit being such a bully."

"Fine. This means I can talk all the shit I want about that phony bitch Suzanne, right?"

I sighed. She did, too.

"You look cute today," I ventured.

"Hank thinks so."

I sat down in one of the customer chairs. Delia remained standing. We were at a crossroads and I was the one with the map.

"Let's agree to not be critical of our questionable choice of mates," I proposed. "At least for now. A diplomatic truce until the smoke clears."

Someone kicked the front door open and we both turned, fast. Flaco came through with a red plastic serving tray in his hands and a giant smile on his face.

"Delivery, for the one and only Darby Holland! Six deluxe juniors! Extra sauce! Extra meat! Extra everything that makes a taco great!"

"What the—" Delia began.

Flaco set everything on the counter and unfurled a white paper napkin with a flourish, took a bow.

"Thanks, dude," I said, rising swiftly.

"What the hell is this?" Delia asked. Flaco pointed his smile at her.

"Darby worked a miracle with young Santos."

Delia looked at me. "What kind of miracle." It didn't come out as a question.

"The hardest kind," Flaco replied. "Santos, he is a criminal. We all are criminals these days to some degree I suppose, but it is in his blood. His bones." Flaco frowned then. "We were all sure he was headed back to lock up. His soul, it was"—he looked for the right word—"like bad meat. Old before it could be cooked. Spoiled. But Darby gave him something we couldn't that will keep him free. Something rare and precious."

Delia and I both looked on, waiting for whatever it was. Flaco looked up with tears in his eyes.

"Hope," he said. "Hope is how the bird flies. It is a thing of the heart." He gestured at the tacos as if they were too simple now, bowed his head, and walked out slower than he'd come in. I walked over to the counter and looked at the juniors. He'd arranged them in a perfect little row. I picked up the first one and bit into it, then glanced at Delia.

"Amazing," she said.

"What?" I managed. I was eating as fast as I could, and at that moment I must have reminded her of Hank. She cocked her head.

"You bond with a young Mexican criminal, and you even change his life in some way so profound that Flaco is delivering tacos, and yet you spend the morning with Hank and I get the impression that he's lucky to be alive."

I plowed into taco number three at speed. Delia's face was wrinkled in disgust when I looked over. I swallowed.

"It was an accident. Me and the kid, I dunno. Maybe I was the first guy to treat him like an adult." I thought for a second. "That can't be it. But maybe I was the first real fuck-up he'd ever met who had some real level of commitment to it. You buy that?"

"Jesus." She looked away. I gestured at the tacos.

"Delia, eat one of these. He wasn't bullshitting about the extra deluxe. C'mon."

She slowly walked over and picked one up, took a bite. Her eyes were especially huge when she looked up at me.

"Good, right?"

She nodded. I patted her bony shoulder.

"You did the same thing for me," she said when she swallowed.

"What?"

"Hope. Gave it to me like you were giving away feathers. I told you that a million times, man. I just can't see why you don't have the same effect on Hank."

Shit.

"How's it feel to be right about everything?" I asked. "Every single time, without fail, all the fucking time."

"Pretty good." Delia took another bite and smiled as she chewed. "S'why I do it."

"Spaz."

"Weenis hole."

"Harpy."

"Knob."

"Knobber."

"I got something to show you," she said. She wiped her hands on the presentation napkin. "You'll actually like it."

"Where is it? If it's a bump or a rash of some kind . . ."

"In the back room, dummy. On the drawing table."

She watched as I finished the last taco. When I was done, I followed her into the back. There, spread out for review, was a sample T-shirt, screen printed with a design that could only be one of hers. I stood before it in awe, Delia beside me. I put my arm around her shoulder.

It was a three-color graphic. King Kong, hanging from the side of Big Pink, the Portland skyline's lurid salmon flesh skyscraper. The King was in his classic movie pose, depending from one hand, but in his free hand he held an enormous revolver, smoke and fire curling from the barrel. His eyes were wild and crazy, and his lips were pulled back to reveal teeth capped with gold and inscribed with Satanic symbols. Below, Burnside and Sixth was littered with upside-down police cars and screaming yuppie pedestrians, many of whom were on fire. LUCKY SUPREME TATTOO was on a banner being dragged across the story sky by an old-fashioned biplane. Our phone number and address went across the bottom in the reflection of an oil slick.

"It's a masterpiece," I whispered. My voice caught in my throat.

"One of my parting gifts," she said. She put her arm around my waist. "I'm glad you like it, Darby. The boxes arrive next Wednesday. Hoodies, too."

"Awesome."

"All right," she said finally. She went to the lounge couch across from my desk and fell into it. "Chase Manhattan, employee evaluation. How you think he did on his first Black Op?"

I lit a post-taco cigarette and sat down on the edge of my desk. Chase Manhattan. She still didn't know about the car bombing. I had to tell her, of course, but the evaluation of Chase was important, especially now.

Some people are at their best when the music is deafening,

the lights are blinding, all the fevers are contagious, when the car is going way too fast and the tires just blew. The joy comes from being the lone minnow who shot the gap, who flitted through the fiery chaos untouched. On the opposite end of the spectrum are monks, who have no variables at all. Sometimes you can tell where a person falls in between those two poles. Delia watched me consider, patient. She belonged nowhere on that scale, maybe above it.

"Not bad," I said finally. "He talk to you yet?"

"Called this morning, said he'd be on time, shit went down but it worked out."

"Huh. It went down all right. Someone blew up my car. Almost killed him."

She didn't seem surprised, which surprised me.

"I picked him up in that van. Dessel and Pressman are eager to talk about it. I was busy."

"I'll miss this," she said. "All the madness." She meant it, too. I went and sat down next to her, patted her knee.

"Careful what you wish for."

"Never. So, Chase."

"He's Nigel's replacement, if you see what I mean. We give him opportunity and a little safety, as in back his outside plays, and we'll get results. Most of the time."

"Darby, if having money has somehow compelled you to understand people in the same way people understand mutual funds, I will consider it the most polluted irony of all time."

"Huh? My point is this. Chase rolls with whatever, no questions asked. You think that's a good thing?"

"I see your point. He's been around way too long to

be a dummy. Guy like Chase stayed in the game because he knows how to move. Look at our old guys. Big Mike. Cracked, went pussy, and that was that. Nige got busted because he played a little too fast and a little too loose for a little too long. My guess is that Chase is a little more like we are," she said.

"So *that's* a good thing."

"I think so. He probably won't burn us, for one thing. I'm smarter than he is and he knows it. You'll beat him to death and he knows that too. But that isn't it. I think Chase is the guy we've been looking for. Old School is a foul fuckin' concept in the tattoo world, 'cause you're talking nasty old perverts who were big on the con, but in the broader sense of it, like in how it's applied everywhere else, Chase has it. He's solid. Guy isn't turn-n-burn, isn't a prima donna either. He's set on glide."

I thought about that.

"He totally freaked out someone blew your wheels?"

"Just the opposite. He wants in."

"In what? Like *in* in?"

"Yep. He says he noticed that the Lucky keeps going no matter what happens, and the people here either crack and go down or they get rich. He wants to try his luck."

"Interesting."

"Yeah. He asked me right after the whole thing. Gotta admit, I was impressed. With you on the way out, I'll need him. He pointed that out, too."

"He's right." Delia looked down at her hands. "You've been wondering how all the pieces will fall into place once I'm gone. Picture's coming together. I'm glad." I looked sideways at her. She didn't sound all that glad. I patted her knee again.

"I know why you have to go, sweetie. We've been over this. Your art . . . grew. It kept getting bigger. I get that. What I'm wrestling with, if there is anything, if you really want to know . . ." I trailed off. She gave me a wry smile.

"I know. Mikey gone off to nowhere, traded his boots for Birkenstocks, Nige in the slammer. Now this new shit. Your car. And here I am, movin' on up like *The Jeffersons*. You're wondering if the fear got me at long last, or if common sense did." She shrugged. "I'm wondering something, too, if you really want to know. I'm gone, it'll be just you. Sure, you'll have Chase now. Flaco. Gomez. My backup emergency dildo, Santiago. That's a life. But Suzanne isn't coming back, and Old Town is part of the *Portlandia* set now. So I'm wondering why you still think you can hold on to your old life. I mean, don't you?"

I didn't say anything.

"That long road," she continued. "So romantic, really. You're on it for life. I always wanted to be, too. Just keep on walking and walking, until you become fearsome and fearless, and I swear, right then is when you want to stop and smell the roses. I can see it in you these days, Darby." It was her turn to pat my knee. "But the road never ends, and now, here in the City of Roses? All the roses come from Safeway and they smell like fabric softener."

"Fuck. You're depressing today, Delia."

"Yeah." She crossed her hands behind her head. "Maybe. But back to you. I don't know what you should do, Darby. I don't think you do, either. But you have to do something.

What I do know is that no matter what it is, you ever need me, I'll be there." Then she looked over at me and winked.

"That was the worst pep talk ever."

"But you listened to the whole thing now, didn't you?"

Before I left the Lucky, we were able to find out where the remains of my car had been towed. It turned out that having your car bombed was enormously expensive. Almost five grand already, and the bill was rising. Other cars had been damaged in the explosion, from cracked windshields to blistered paint, and there was also the matter of my insurance, which had almost certainly been canceled. I had no idea how that angle would shake out, but it was sure to be bad.

On the plus side, I was half drunk and in a reasonably good mood when I got in the drippy Alfa and it failed to start. I locked it up and struck out on foot, headed for nowhere in particular. The afternoon and evening were blank in many ways, as in I was making it up as I went along, but it had a promising feel to it. On foot, it was easy to peel off anyone behind me, so there was that. I was five moves away from clear. Or I could lead my little parade around and give them time to catch each other. Productive. But more than all that, I had a rare lightness in my chest.

Even Delia thought I was due for a new tune. She would have spontaneously spit out a toad or a roach if I told her

Suzanne had said the same thing, but it was good to know. The tacos had cleared my head a little and the wet wind was cold and clean. On impulse, I decided to visit Santiago and display my relative cheer.

Alcott was in the twilight between lunch and the early dinner rush. Table presentations were being changed, the menu was being printed (a different one every night) and busy prep work was steaming away in the kitchen. Santiago was drinking an espresso at the bar and looking at something on his laptop. He smiled when I came in and I returned it.

"Heard you got stung by a bee," he said. "Flaco." He scrutinized my chin when I sat down next to him. "Not bad. Not bad. Not good, but it could be worse."

"The kid got it worse," I replied. "But he's tough."

"You two hit it off, Flaco tells me." Santiago chuckled. "Knew you had it in you."

"The kid did most of the heavy lifting. He, ah, he mentioned that he might like some restaurant work. He was talking about Idaho right then, but—"

"Mentioned?" Santiago's giant face darkened. "Idaho? Darby, there was some prevarication in that statement."

"Can't help it." I looked at the bartender. He was doing inventory and checking a wine shipment. Santiago followed my eyes.

"Let's grab a table. I have a few minutes."

He went around the bar and had a quick word with the bartender while the espresso machine burped and sputtered, then we carried our cups over to a two top by the windows.

"So the kid. Santos is his name?" Santiago watched my face carefully.

"Yeah, man. Dark shit happened out in the woods. Hard to put it all together just yet, but my stalker guy showed. He wanted to take me for a ride in the trunk of his car, I had other plans, shit got out of control, the kid got involved. Anyway, done. But here's the deal. The kid took the guy's car, which is *clean* clean, FYI, as in no record of it exists, and he was headed to Idaho to start a new life. He changed his mind, which happens, but part of that new life was doing something better than pushing a mop at a hospital."

"I see." Santiago sipped. "I'll offer a tentative no." He raised his hand before I could object. "Darby, do you and this young man have anything in common other than a shared experience in the woods, where, I quote, 'dark shit went down'?"

"We do." I sat back. He nodded.

"Then absolutely not." Santiago gave me a curious look. "You make a good partner, Darby. Loyal, trustworthy, insightful at the strangest times. Brave. But you're also reckless, barely housebroken, and you fight too much. Be honest. Would you hire you?"

"Fuck you," I said, offended. The bartender glanced our way, so I lowered my voice. "Fuck you," I whispered. Santiago laughed.

"You make my point for me!" He shook his head. "I'm glad you're who you are, my good friend. But you keep the young lunatic. Bring him around and I'll feed him. The best possible use for a protégé of yours would be to get him a job at the bistro I hear is opening down the street. Let him fuck all the waitresses and drink all the booze. Beat the shit out of the owner for a social injustice or a matter of honor."

"There's another bistro opening down the street? Who in the fuck are they?" I glared out the window and Santiago laughed again.

"Attaboy."

"All right. And he's not my protégé, dude."

"How's the wedding?" He changed the subject before I could try a different angle.

"Ah, man. Dark shit there, too. But it's still going down. I took that piece of shit Hank to get his tux earlier."

"Ah, Hank." He frowned. Hank had rufied Santiago when we were working on opposite sides. "I'll always owe him. If you ever decide to mail him anywhere, I'd love to help." He looked up at me and squinted. "You know that little fucking zit actually winked at me? If it weren't for Delia, well . . ." He trailed off and looked out at the rain.

"Interesting."

He glanced at me and said nothing. I nodded and rose.

"I'm outta here. Thanks for nothing."

He smiled. "You hungry?"

"Nah. Full of tacos." I stretched. "I think I'm gonna go fuck around down on the waterfront till dinnertime. Lead my tail around."

"Party on."

My phone rang almost the moment I stepped out on the sidewalk. Private number. I answered.

"Speak."

"Darby," Dessel began, "before you hang up, listen for two minutes."

"Talk fast, dude. I'm still pissed you blew your cover to bum smokes off me."

"Good for you." He sounded tired. "I understand you had a chat with Agent Lopez."

"She hates you, little guy."

"We have news. You're coming in today, right?"

"Just tell me. I don't like your office." I took a left and headed for the bus mall, sticking under the awnings.

"No can do. We have photos for you to look at, names to run past you, all kinds of shit. Did something change? I mean, you still want to know who's following you, right?"

"You're fishing, Dessel. You want to know what I've already figured out, and you want it for free. Is that right?"

"Trade. I'm proposing a trade."

"Interesting. But just barely. Dessel, I always figure this shit out without you. We both know it. I'm using you to flush out another tail and we both know that, too. You found out enough about whoever is after me to become interested. All that means is that, just as we both guessed right from the start, we have another scumbag with a big plan that involves fucking up my world. Show some cards or I'm hanging up."

"Fine." He paused, and I heard part of a muffled conversation. Then he was back. "Darby, we've never seen anything like this." He cleared his throat, like he was about to say something of great importance. "It appears that you're in a play of some kind."

"*What?*"

"A play. You're an unwitting actor in a drama. It's unfolding right now."

"Are you, are you speaking metaphorically? Dude! We're all actors in a play all the time, you fucking idiot! That's it, I'm—"

"Someone is filming you right now, Holland," Dessel said soberly. "They have been for we don't know how long. I'm talking about an actual play, you cretin. You have been cast as a player. You have a role. You're acting out a part. We're trying to figure out who the playwright is, and we need to locate the main character before the play is over. The last act is not something we want to happen."

I stopped walking.

"You just stopped walking," Dessel said. "You don't have a physical tail while you're downtown more than half the time. I'm watching you on the city center traffic camera system."

I looked up at the nearest light pole. The Old Town nightworld had been aware of the cameras for the last year, but word was that the PPD needed a warrant to track you with them. Anything they saw at random was inadmissible. I raised my middle finger. The pedestrians around me reflexively added a foot to my personal space.

"Someone else has been using the system," Dessel continued. "That same someone might be able to hack your phone. So come and look at the pictures, idiot." He hung up or the line went dead. I looked at the phone and then broke it in half, walked to the nearest trashcan, and dropped it in. Then I stood there in the rain, thinking.

I had been cast in a play.

The strange horror in Dessel's voice, the impossibly odd nature of the notion, had combined to freeze me in my tracks, and I wondered then if that was part of the script, so I unfroze and headed for the first bus. I paid and took my ticket, then went to the back and sat down. My mind was racing. I stared out the window at the rainy streets that had become a stage, and the haunted feeling washed over me in a great, gripping pulse of cold.

The hair on my scalp felt like it was full of static. A play. I had been cast in a play.

In the last few years, I'd dealt with terrible men with terrible agendas. First there was Nicholas Dong Ju, an art collector, pimp, and criminal of the highest order, who had come for some of the Lucky Supreme's oldest artwork. The flash of Roland Norton had been used to smuggle treasury bills, property deeds, bearer bonds, and assorted other financial tools through Panama after the Second World War, and all the remaining pieces, the ones that had vanished when Norton died unexpectedly, were still loaded. We never knew until Dong Ju came for them.

Dong Ju was a genius. He played several games of chess in his head. His servants claimed he owned their souls. In the end, I'd killed him in a fight to the death on the underside of the Steel Bridge. The whole experience had changed me in many ways, all of them bad. Dong Ju's body was in the river, wrapped in rotten concrete and fencing, and the entire ordeal had made Dessel and me enemies for life. He knew I'd killed Dong Ju, but he'd never be able to prove it.

Then came Oleg Turganov, the Russian real estate developer who blew up part of Old Town, the Lucky Supreme with it. Dessel and Pressman had tried to pin the blame on me, and in the hunt for the truth I'd gotten the scar on my face and another one on my ass. Santiago had worked for Turganov, and in the end I'd mailed the Russian back where he came from in a transmission box. In the aftermath of that, I'd become rich.

Now this. I had a terrible feeling that whoever had sent Oleander, the Mineral Man, to collect me was not like Dong Ju or Turganov. He or she was worse. I played back everything that had happened, and as I did, the color drained from the world around me.

The city passed and I didn't really see any of it. I had no idea where the bus was going, but it was time for emergency maneuvers.

By six, I was deep in Beaverton.

Traffic was terrible, which worked in my favor. I hopped off the 4 bus and went into action. The first thing I did was duck into a Radio Shack and buy a flip phone and a card with a hundred minutes. Once I was outside, I called the Rooster Rocket. They'd had the same phone number for twenty years and it was one of the only numbers I could remember. Many of the rest were in a tiny three-page phone book I kept in my wallet for these occasions, but it wasn't very up to date.

"Rooster Rocket." Short, clipped, male, hard to tell who it was.

"This is Darby Holland from the Lucky next door. Gomez around?"

"Nah. This is Kenny. What up, dog?"

Kenny was a night hipster, new. "What about Cherry?"

"Hang on." The phone was bumped around and then I listened to what sounded like the Ramones for three or four minutes.

"Darby?"

"Cherry! You got a pen?"

"Sure. What's up?"

"Can you do me a solid? I lost my phone. I'm in a great

big rush and the number at the Lucky has been busy for a fuckin' hour. Copy this down and maybe shoot it next door real quick?"

"Sure. Give it to me."

I read the number off the back of the box and she repeated it back.

"Thanks," I said. "If Delia is there, tell her to call me from her cell. Best if she calls from her cell."

"Her cell." Cherry repeated.

"Yep. Don't ask. But only her cell."

"Mum's the word, Trouble."

Suzanne's number was at home in one of my sketchbooks. It didn't matter for the moment, but it would be important later. I put the phone in my pocket and threw all the plastic trash away, then headed for the MAX. I had to get to my storage unit and get some cash out of the safe. If someone was watching me move around Old Town and Dessel was worried that the same person had hacked my phone, then it was time to switch back to cash. I had several grand in nasty currency tucked away and it was time to get some.

The storage space was a last resort. It had been left to me by a customer who had paid it up for a year, then moved a giant antique gun safe into it, then left town and sold it all to me. I used it to store junk, mostly, but a few years ago it had turned into the secret repository of all the cash that kept coming my way. It was all stolen, and that was bad, and worse, it was all stolen from criminals, so the numbers might be on some kind of radar. Worse than worse, many of the bills had dried blood on them and some of that blood was from dead people. So I hadn't been there in a long time. I'd gotten into the habit of never going there at all, which was good.

There was a crowd at the MAX stop, clustered under the shelters. My new phone rang as I walked up and I answered off to the side, sticking to the shadows.

"Delia?"

"Yo dude, it's Chase." He sounded chipper, even happy. "Delia was gone by the time Cherry dropped off this number and the cryptic message of 'use cell only.' Is the phone tapped?"

"Probably," I replied, relieved. "Just got a call from one of the feds I tricked into trailing me around. I'm using this Radio Shack burner for the moment."

"Got it. What can I do?"

"Post this number in the back in case anyone needs it. Delia with Hank when she left?"

"Yep. She waited almost an hour for him so they were fighting on the way out. Kid's kinda shitty, you ask me, keeping her waiting like that, but whatever. I do worse all the time. But not to a woman like that."

"Great. Okay, leave her be for the time being." I thought. The train was just visible through the rain.

"Flaco came in a few minutes ago. He asked about Cherry's message."

"Flaco! Good. I might need help a little later on. Can you duck out for a sec and give him a message for me? Tell him I want to talk to Santos and give him this number. Let on that it's nothing, I lost my phone or dropped it somewhere, that kind of thing."

"Easy."

"Right on, man. We're heading into the shade."

"Ready steady, boss."

"Thanks."

I boarded the MAX headed for the city center and sat in a clump of commuters. I was deep in thought and close to the lights of the skyscrapers when the phone rang. I looked at the number and tried to memorize it, then answered.

"Darby?" It was Santos.

"Hey, man. You're back."

"Eh. Changed my mind." He sounded bored.

"Wanna make some money?"

"What kind?" Still bored, but incrementally less so.

"The kind with dried blood on it."

"Huh. This is, like, a recurring motif, no?"

"I guess. But first, tell me what changed your mind. Your uncle thinks I had something to do with it."

"Maybe. Maybe not. I forget."

"Fine. So listen, I'm gonna go pick up some cash. Then I have a short sequence of moves to make. I gotta visit this waitress and give her a stack of it, encourage her to split town. That's step number one."

"Sounds sticky, yo."

"It will be. Then I need a ride to Seattle."

"Sounds boring."

"It will be. It all has to happen tonight, too."

He sighed. "I was gonna hook up with Cherry later. Get some. I bought flowers, dude."

"An even grand. You can buy her a small tree."

"She might like that," he allowed. I rolled my eyes.

"Fuckin' thank god. When the hell did it get so hard to give people money?" A couple people glanced my way.

"What time? Do you want to give me this money, I mean."

"Stay by your phone," I replied. "I'll call you in maybe an hour, little more if I hit a snag."

"I'll be here." Santos yawned and hung up.

It is possible, I've learned, to move about the City of Roses in secret. If you're willing to get muddy, brave the brambles (which are impressive to the point of being actually dangerous), and endure tremendous discomfort. It helps to be impervious to cold, and to be able to see in the dark. Failing that, cursing helps.

I got off the MAX at the first stop on the east side, then went to the nearest bar, a place called Mex's, and called a cab. While I waited, I drank coffee and prepared myself for what was to come. The rain was coming down a little harder and I didn't have gloves. An umbrella would have been useless, but I wanted one anyway.

"Where to?" the driver asked when I hopped in.

"The Montage."

"You got it. Oyster shooters? The alligator?"

"You bet. Someone's birthday party."

I watched the city go by as he droned on and on about food. The Montage was a barn of a French place under the Morrison Bridge. The original owners were a couple of cool guys who hit the grand prize in the early Portland food scene by serving two-dollar bowls of mac and cheese alongside bigger ticket items like blackened oyster salad and alligator fritters. It was open seriously late too, and soaked up the boozy after-hours crowd.

I got out and looked through the windows. Packed. The dinner rush was on, but as a solo diner I had a shot at the bar. I smoked a cigarette out front and admired the view. The Montage was close to the train tracks. A block down, they ran under the bridge between the restaurant and the water. The place was at the edge of industrial no man's land and that was a huge part of its charm. Above, the underside of the Morrison Bridge sheltered anyone standing out front, but it dripped.

Just after nine I ducked in and went to the bar, grabbed one of the vacant stools. It was loud inside, and steamy. I ordered a beer and the mac and cheese and ate and drank slowly, killing time. Then I had one more slow beer for good measure. Then a few more to blend in. Just shy of eleven I paid and left.

It was colder, and I could see the rain was coming down harder. Like a sated diner having an after-dinner smoke, I drifted a little closer to the train tracks. Still empty, and across from them, after a two-block stretch, the river began, a dark thing shimmering with the lights from downtown. I drifted a little closer. A low rumble filled the night followed by the bleat of a whistle. I moved closer still.

The train was headed north, the direction I was going, and it was moving slow as it passed through the city. It would begin to speed up as it passed under the Burnside Bridge, and somewhere between there and the Steel Bridge, where my storage unit was, it accelerated even further, becoming too fast to jump off of without risking your skeleton.

I turned and looked back at the Montage as the train hove into view. A small cluster of people stood chatting by the door, none them looking my way. The engine passed and I waited until it had curved away, far enough so that the conductor couldn't see me, and then I ducked under the traffic arm and ran up to it, then alongside until I came close to matching its speed. A ladder passed, one of the metal ones welded to the side, and I grabbed a rung and pulled myself up. Then I looked back to make sure no one was following me.

I was clear.

The wind and rain whipped at me and the ladder was slimy with oily grime, but I felt like I always did when I was dangling from the outside of a moving train. Like dogs feel when they have their head outside a speeding car's window. Free and elated, for reasons I didn't care to understand. I tilted my head back and let the rain smack my eyelids.

I couldn't kill Hank. But I could bribe his junkie girl-friend. Then I could take a "vacation." Split town until whatever was going on blew over. Hang out with Suzanne and read books while she was at work, cook food in her little kitchen. Watch old movies. Drink. It was giving up in a way, but this time I wanted to. There was no reason to fight anymore, no reason to keep on fighting. I didn't even want to open my eyes.

When I finally did open them, it was because the sound of the train had changed. The rhythmic surge was louder and faster, the knocking of the rails more intense. We had passed underneath the Broadway Bridge and were headed for the Steel Bridge, then after that, the long hard pull into the east. I looked down at the passing rock and gravel. The longer I stayed on the shorter the walk to the Steel Bridge would be, but the train was a swinging hammer now, getting faster by the minute.

I passed a giant metal box with unknown train crap inside it, and it marked the farthest I'd ever made it when I figured out how to get to my storage unit from the Montage over a year ago. We were really moving by then and the gravel had given way entirely to jagged rocks interspersed with flattened trash and patches of rusty metal. I looked up and I could see the lights of the bridge a quarter of a mile away. I closed my eyes again.

I was going to ride it out. If it looked like certain death when I opened my eyes again, I'd just keep going and live out the dream I'd been having, of going anonymous and starting over from scratch, free of every last connection in the world. If I could survive it, I'd jump and fight for one last night. An image of Suzanne, laughing and reaching out to touch my face, slammed into my guts and in that instant, in the hurricane of cold wind, I could smell her perfume.

I blinked and looked down into the blur of gray and shadow. Then I took a breath and gritted my teeth, flexed, and dropped silently into it.

The impact almost tore my boots off. I was tumbling, end over end, once and then twice and then I was on my feet, skidding to a halt. The train roared past and I stepped away from it and the fearful sucking wind around it. It was so loud at ground level, so much louder than it had been when I hung from the side, that I could barely think. I staggered, then began my limp. I raised my hand to my face and saw in the dim light that it came away red. My nose was bleeding. Something warm touched my neck and I probed my scalp with my other hand. It came away red, too. I wiped my hands on my pants and lurched into the lee of a brick wall, slunk along it until I found an opening, and then went through.

In that dark alley I lit up a smoke and took stock. The tumble hadn't broken anything, but I was going to feel it in the morning. I clamped my smoke in my teeth and rinsed my hands off in the spill of a nearby rain gutter, then peeked out at the rails. The train passed and then it was gone, some kind of crazy hope with it. The lights of the Steel Bridge were less than a quarter mile away. I started walking.

The river in this stretch smelled like eggs and abandoned bird nests. The rain was reasonably bad, but I was already soaked and freezing so it didn't matter. When I finally got to the underside of the Steel Bridge I almost breathed a sigh of relief. It was lit with orange municipal halogen, and the muddy stretch hadn't changed much. I walked past clumps of rusted metal machinery and piles of rotted concrete and came to a point where I could see the garage doors of the storage units on the far side of a hurricane fence.

It was dead quiet.

I paused. I couldn't tell what it was, but something inspired me to crouch down and watch. Once, I had been inspecting some old flash inside my unit when a car pulled up and I was trapped inside. It wouldn't do to have anything like that happen again. I listened then, straining my senses, and willed my breath to slow.

There.

Someone was standing on the other side of the fence, just outside the edge of the halogen, a dark, motionless figure. It was a profile shot. A man. Tall. Facing the road.

Riley Wharton.

I was sure of it. He knew I was coming here, and that meant he also knew why. But he'd expected me to drive or take a cab. Holding my breath, I backed away into the shadows. The figure didn't move. I considered, my heartbeat loud in my ears. I'd been so paranoid since the whole mess began that it was hard to make a call and not second-guess it instantly. I could, possibly, circle up behind him and maybe take him out. If he didn't have a gun. Which he certainly did. Then again, I might get lucky and carry out a successful assault on a stranger who was waiting for his ride. The odds were high that it was him, however. The guy had my number. I'd need to make another attempt in any case. I couldn't make a late-night withdrawal in front of a witness. I started back down the tracks. An hour later, I had Santos pick me up in front of a 7-Eleven on Broadway. He didn't wish me luck when he dropped me off in front of the Federal Building. He just shook his head.

Dessel looked up at me in genuine shock. Pressman grunted and spun his clipboard into the cluttered mess on the table. There was a tidy window of space and a third chair where Lopez would be, but no sign of her. The meeting table had the foul aura of an all-nighter, just as it always did, and Pressman and Dessel looked like the guys who'd pulled it. But there was something worse in the air than usual. They looked especially terrible. Dessel looked like he needed to shave, possibly for the first time in his life. Pressman looked like he'd died and been electrocuted back to life in the last ten minutes.

"Where's what's-her-name?" I crashed down in her chair.

"Darby, I've been calling and calling." Dessel blasted me with his smile, huge as always, but it did nothing for his eyes this time. "You either found your way here out of habit or you're drunk. Maybe both." He sniffed. "Bob, check the drunk box. Now, what happened to your face this time, and"—he laughed and leaned back—"what happened to your head! This has to be good."

"Got in a hornet fight." I picked up the lukewarm coffee in front of me and drained it, smacked my lips. "Then I was riding around on a train. But that's not why I'm here. I got a lead."

Pressman whistled. Dessel's eyes went impossibly wide and he crowed with a hollow delight.

"The clouds have parted! The bees have finally told their secrets!" Dessel clapped his hands together. "What did they say? Ooh, make the buzzing sound, too! And the choo-choo whistle! Please. I—I need that."

"Let's talk about your information first." I lit a cigarette and stabbed it at him. "Then maybe you get your buzz."

They looked at each other. I waited. Pressman took point.

"Not the way it works, Holland." Pressman got slowly to his feet and walked to the window, opened it. Slower than usual. Arthritic. "You tell us your shithead theory about Martians or cavemen tracking you with a butt probe and then we decide if we tell you a goddamned thing." He lit a cigarette of his own. "I think calling you in was a mistake and you fucking showed up anyway. Not my day. Night. Morning. Whatever."

"Bob also has colitis, as I mentioned," Dessel said primly. He pointed a sympathetic expression at his partner. "Maybe you should go first, Darby."

"Fine." I blew smoke. "I was right about my stalker with that fishing story. Most gnarly monster in the history of bad news. Genius, and we're talking your high school chess club-level genius here, Dessel. Tougher than I am, too. Faster. Meaner. The iron will of an Olympic distance runner and the resources to get anything from a vial of plague to an endangered spider on a Tuesday night."

"Putin," Dessel breathed. "You've done it at long last."

"Nah." Pressman turned away from the window. "Bigger. He's talking Wells Fargo."

"Wrong on both counts." I dropped my butt in Lopez's cup. "Cokehead stripper. I might have pissed her off, we just don't know. But my people are terrified. You guys are barking up the wrong tree with your wacko reality TV theory."

Pressman turned back to the window. Dessel stared at me. I looked at the new dirt under my fingernails. Dessel was trying to read my mind, and he was so bright that it sometimes seemed like he could. Eventually he caught a glimmer of something and rooted through the papers in front of him, came up with a page of glossy photo print and showed me the back. Watching my eyes, he snapped it around. It was a photo of Oleander, the Mineral Man.

"I bet you killed this man. Recently."

I leaned forward and studied the picture. He was in front of the insurance office across the street from my drinking alcove in front of the shoe shop, facing the neon. Watching me. It was on a different night than when he'd visited disguised as a hobo. In this picture, he was dressed as a passing office grunt.

"No," I said slowly. "No. I'd remember if I killed that guy." I looked up at Dessel. "He owes you money, I'd flash your badge. But don't shave. You almost look like a grownup right now."

"Amazing." Dessel set the photo down without taking his eyes off mine. "You're my natural enemy, Darby. Nature designed us to oppose each other. You ever think about that?"

"Get out." Pressman said it without turning. "Just get out. Walk out that door and don't look back."

Interesting. Bad interesting. I changed tactics.

"Arrest me."

Pressman turned and glared at me, a red stare of murder. Dessel finally looked down. His eyes refocused on the photo in his hands. He stared at the dead man whose body he would never, ever find, knowing exactly what he was looking at.

"No," Dessel said softly.

"Then how about if I straight up beat the shit out of you guys? Then you'd arrest me. You'd have to. I got better odds doing time for beating on pussies than I do walking like you want me to, right?"

Dessel put the photo down, then wiped his hands on his pants like he regretted ever touching it. Disgusted, and not with me. I'd never seen him like this.

"He's an animal. Midnight Rider Productions. They make a kind of . . . pornography, maybe. We're not sure what to call it."

"Dark web." Pressman said it like his mouth was giving birth to a lamprey.

They let that sink in. It did.

"I'm being chased by a porno guy?"

Pressman shuffled back to the table. His gray face was even more gray than it had been when I walked in. He looked ill, in a profoundly real way.

"We don't know," Pressman continued. He looked at Dessel. "Holland is a piece of shit, but not this kind."

Dessel evidently agreed. He lit a cigarette and when he did his mask dropped a little more. He was as bad off as his partner. Worn. He got up and started pacing, slower than usual, and the spring, that characteristic tight pop that ran from his calves to his boyish butt was flat.

"The man in that photo actually has no name," Agent Dessel began. "His teeth are implants. Fingerprints chemically removed at some point along the line. No DNA on file, which is amazing. Amazing." He said it the second time like he was suddenly talking to himself. "He takes on the name of a flower, sometimes. More often than minerals, but there's that, too. He's the, ah, he's the meat." He stopped talking, searching for the right words.

"The guy with the dick," Pressman intoned.

"Right." Dessel rubbed his eyes. "Midnight is for hire. The case came to us with a thousand question marks and redacted pages. Cold and lost and rambling, just a collection of half-mad bullshit from Quantico and Homeland, some rookie crap out of Scranton PD." He took a breath. "Midnight has a market angle, I guess you call it. Shame. This last one, the one we downloaded last night, on my personal fucking computer!" His voice had risen sharply. He controlled himself. "Which I will have to burn now. It was a housewife. They, ah, it's a montage? Series of vignettes? Help me, Bob."

"Episodic documentary."

"Right," Dessel said lifelessly. "They have her on camera. Maybe three months of it. See . . . they destroyed her life, this woman. Followed her while they did it, so it was really clear what was happening. Got her fired from a good job. Then evicted. Fucked up her bank account. Isolated her, very carefully." He stopped talking. Pressman picked it up.

"The camera footage from the bank, we have no idea how they did that. Lots of it came from security cameras. That's what tipped us off to the street cam system."

"Such perfect evil," Dessel said then. "In the end she was ruined. Made hopeless. She went from person to animal and they filmed the entire transformation." It was Dessel's turn to sit by the window. He talked as if to himself again. "Last clip is of her in this shitty motel. Alone, like . . . alone. Desperate. So confused at it all, too, and so sad there at the end. Blows her brains out. God knows where she got the gun. They probably arranged that, too."

"That's when the Mineral Flower Man enters," Pressman said, his voice the voice of a ghost. "Wrapped in clear plastic, but it's him. He . . . does things to her then." He pointed at my place at the table, the empty coffee cup. "Agent Lopez is in the bathroom puking."

No one said anything as Dessel returned to his chair. He sorted through the mess in front of him and came up with a second photo, stared at it.

"There is one shot of the Mineral Flower Man's employer," he began. "From the Scranton PD." He turned it around in. Two men, talking in front of a warehouse. One of them was their mineral flower monster, dead from Santos's shovel. "You recognize the other guy?"

Riley Wharton. Alive.

"Shit." It just came out of me. Pressman and Dessel were stunned.

"Who is this, Darby?" Dessel leaned in. "Please, please don't lie. Not this time. This is the nightmare man. The animal after midnight. We can show you this video, but

233

you'll never sleep with the light off again for the rest of your life. This one time, no shit. This time tell the truth." He leaned back. Pressman put his hands flat on the table. He was trembling. I watched as he reached under the table and clicked something. The recorder.

"No shit, Holland. These guys need to die." Pressman's vice was a low growl. "This isn't about the law anymore. This isn't even about right and wrong. We're past that."

"Who is this?" Dessel hissed. Abruptly, he dropped the photograph and started wiping his hands on his pants again, rhythmically, like a broken toy.

"Off the record? I mean all the way off?"

They both nodded without looking at each other.

"The new lady," I said. "I mean her, too. This goes no further than the three of us."

This gave them pause. What I was asking would officially put us in bed together as conspirators. It was a pension wrecker for Pressman and a career-ending move for Dessel if they followed me into the dark and got caught in it.

"No DA would give a shit what happened to these guys if he saw one of the videos, Holland." Pressman rubbed the patch of chest over his heart. "You give us this and we will take it to the wall. But if you pull one of your vanishing acts, where this guy is never seen again and no one can ever find anything, keep in mind the woman in the video we told you about. There are almost a hundred of them that we know of. People hire Midnight Rider Productions to do this horror shit and it's all done via encryption. The names are in their heads. We need that list."

"We need every single name of everyone who ever hired

them," Dessel said emphatically. "This isn't about my career or having Bob land a promotion on his way out. This shit is real. Everyone has to go down, every last one of them, every single motherfucker who ever got involved."

I got up and looked at the door. Then I looked back at them. It amazed me, but I was going to tell them. The truth, too. It was every bit as ugly as it could be.

"Bob," I began. "Gimme your flask."

Pressman didn't even flinch at my use of his first name. Without missing a beat, he reached into his suit coat and took out the flask we all knew was there, tossed it to me. I spun the cap and took a big pull, set it on the table so I could finish the rest as I ratted out the devil. There was a camera high on the wall, so I walked over and unplugged it. I didn't know if it was recording, or even if it worked, but I'd seen people do it in the movies. Then I picked up the photograph of the Mineral Flower Man and showed it to them.

"This sack of shit is already dead." I tossed the photo back on the table, face down.

"How?" Dessel was not fazed, relieved, or irate. Neither was Pressman.

"Followed me earlier. Long story I'm not going to tell so don't even ask, but essentially he was going to abduct me and the gangster I was babysitting killed him with a shovel."

Pressman closed his eyes. Dessel nodded and looked at the back of the photo, reached for it, changed his mind.

"He have a computer?" Dessel asked. "Cell phone? What happened to his personal effects?"

"Gone. For good kinda gone."

"Fuck. What about his boss? The other guy in photo number two?"

"He was called Riley Wharton when I knew him." The name caught in my throat. It all came back in a gutty heave when the sound of it left my head. The fire. The screaming howl of sirens. All the blood. The train tracks and the rusted tire iron. A lone tooth, glinting in the moonlight.

"Darby," Dessel prompted softly.

"It was after the last foster home," I continued. "I was fifteen." I drained the last of Pressman's booze. The crap whiskey tasted like weed killer. "Denver. This one night, God it was cold. I was so broke and so hungry. Neither of you guys have ever been there. I mean right on the edge of where the body gives out and you sit down and you feel warm. Right there at the end. I could see it."

I stopped talking. I'd never told anyone what I was about to tell them, not even Delia. It came out of me like broken light bulb glass.

"Denver. Two a.m. I—I wanted to find a warm place to look at the stars. Can you believe that? Like an air vent or a patch of roof with a hot pipe sticking out of it. I could see them as I walked but it was too cold to stop." My hand went out at the memory. All my memories changed after that night, but in some bitter paradox I could still remember the difference. "So many stars! Oh, and they were so bright. That was the night I met Riley, and I was young enough to still believe in something. I thought he'd been sent to save me." I laughed. "One thing led to another, and a couple hours later we were at some rich guy's house.

That's where Riley brought the street kids. Rich guy had a thing for 'em."

I stopped. Pressman and Dessel were frozen.

"They made the mistake of giving me food. I got away that night, but two, maybe three nights later this boy Owen tells me a story. Owen, he ran away from a foster home in Boston. Fourteen years old. Loved the Grateful Dead. Owen didn't get away when Riley picked him up. They threw him out three days later. He could hardly walk."

I finished the bug poison and lit a cigarette.

"A week later I had nine kids together in this crappy coin-op laundromat. We met Riley there and told him what was up. The rich guy was gonna pay and we were all gonna leave."

I smoked. It was Dessel who finally said it.

"Riley killed them all, didn't he?"

"Pretty much," I replied. "The rich guy hired two killers, pros, and they worked the neighborhood. One by one they all went down. Hard, too. No bullets. All of them died bad hard deaths. Except for me."

I could still see their faces. We were all so dirty.

"Tell us the rest," Dessel said softly. "I'm sorry, but we have to know."

"Riley took pictures of the carnage with one of those old Polaroids. He knew everything. He had all the cards. I was hiding out when the two hit men vanished. Then Riley went to ground. I knew something was going down. Rich guy was named Roberto Montoya. I figured if I could get them together. I dunno. Maybe I could kill them." I looked up. Pressman was unreadable. Dessel licked his lips.

"But you didn't." Dessel clearly wished I had. I shook my head.

"No. But I put it all together. They were going to meet in front of this place by the university. Riley was going to hand over his photos in exchange for ten grand." I laughed. "Ten grand."

"Jesus," Pressman growled. "That's where it all started. Those photos. They were his first documentary."

"I followed Riley after the exchange. The hit men were waiting for him, but he didn't go home. He went straight from the blackmail meet to the train tracks."

I smoked the rest of the cigarette in silence and tried to calm down. They let me try. It didn't work.

"What happened then?" Dessel asked. "That was a long time ago, Darby. A different life."

"A train was coming and I knew what he was going to do. He had a backpack stashed in the junk and the weeds. He'd get on that train and no one would ever see him again. So I stopped him. Or maybe that's when he saw me. I can't remember. But I asked him the only thing I could think of, the only thing that could stop for a second what was about to happen. I asked him, 'Why did you do that?'" I dropped my cigarette on the floor and ground it out. The flask was empty. I took a deep breath.

"He told me he knew everything. He knew I'd find him at the tracks. He laughed and took my picture with the same camera." I stopped talking. I could see it so clearly, the look on his face, the logic of it, how he believed he was a hero of some kind. The lights of the train spilling over my shoulder, the sound of the horn.

"What, ah—what then?" Dessel's voice was barely audible. I focused and looked at him, back in the room again, and for the first time in all the long nights I'd been grilled by them, in all those hours, Dessel looked sad. I didn't know his face could do it, but I could tell in that instant that it was his default expression. Dessel was sad all the time.

"I beat him to death. Or I thought I did. Took his backpack and the money and hopped the first freight train, went into hiding after that because so much shit had gone so crazy fuckin' wrong. And I just stayed hid. Until you guys."

They were quiet for a solid minute. Pressman spoke first.

"And he's been looking for you all these years. And all these years you've been hiding because of crimes he committed." Pressman looked like he was going to vomit. Dessel's lips were blue.

"Then the big question is how did this fucking guy find you? If we can understand that, then we can maybe catch some part of a trail." Dessel stared into space then, listening to his impressive brain as the wheels spun him out to nowhere.

"I think I know." I took my phone out and dialed Delia. While it rang I looked at them. "Go get the new chick's head out of the toilet. Shit just went from bad to worse."

Delia got there ten minutes later. She was angry.

"Now you've gone and done it," she spat at me. Dessel unconsciously recoiled at her fury. Pressman folded his arms. Agent Lopez opened her mouth. "You went and let them play with your Legos, didn't you?" Delia tossed her thumb at Lopez. "Who's this bitch?"

"Easy." I raised my hands. "We're on the same side tonight."

"Have a seat, Ms. Ashmore," Dessel said, rising. "We have a few questions if—"

"Lawyer," Delia said. She pulled out a chair and plopped into it. "I'll wait till she gets here."

I sat, too. Then Dessel. When no one moved to make a call, Delia took her phone out and began doing it herself.

"Sweetie," I said. "The, ah, don't do that. All the cameras are off. This meeting is off the books."

"Wait a minute," Lopez said, turning to Dessel. "What the fuck is he talking about? If this shit—"

"Everyone shut up," Dessel snapped, suddenly furious. He glared at me. "Darby. Tell her."

"Delia. You told me that before you left you were going to drag the Lucky and me into the twenty-first century. Explain."

"Now?" she asked incredulously. "What the fuck, man? Me and Hank were just getting ready to—"

"He's asking if any of this upgrade, or whatever you call it, involved any mention of Darby and his past on any websites or social media," Dessel said. "Any mention of Denver."

Delia looked from them to me and back again.

"Someone from Denver found me," I said. "If we can figure out how, it might help."

"Shit," she said, clearly thinking fast. "Shit shit shit. Who?"

"The worst fucking guy I've ever known."

All four of us watched Delia think. She was wearing a wet black raincoat, a black bra, and bright red pants, but even Lopez could tell some impressive calculation was going down. Eventually, Delia looked right at Lopez, whose eyes widened.

"Name," Delia demanded.

Lopez frowned. Delia didn't let her say anything, just raised her hand and turned to me.

"Let's roll."

Everyone rose, me last.

"Delia," I said, close to pleading, "if you can just calm the fuck down—"

"Not gonna happen," she snapped. "You talk to me first. In private. Then I decide who gets to know what."

"This is a crisis—" Dessel began. Delia stopped him with a finger.

"Get the new chick up to speed," she said, "or out of the picture. If it's a crisis I'd hurry the fuck up."

She took my arm and pulled me from the room. I looked back. Pressman had turned to Lopez and the two were about to get into it, I could tell, but Dessel was staring right at me. The door closed.

"Delia."

"Not here," she whispered. "Not yet. Fill me in while they get their shit straightened out." She pulled and I went with it. "I don't know what kind of deal you were striking with the Boy Wonder and Bat Cow but the chick wasn't in on it. So no dice. Keep quiet until we get out of this fucking bug-infested building."

"Christ."

We silently made our way down the empty hall to the elevator, then out through the lobby. It was still raining. Delia had her arm through mine, and I allowed her to guide me down the steps to the sidewalk. Her car was parked across the street but we weren't headed that way. At the corner we stopped. When she didn't say anything, I realized she was waiting for me to take the lead.

"Denver," I began. "I told you I came from Denver."

"Something bad happened," she replied. "You came here. It was a long time ago."

I blew out a breath. "Not long enough. It will never be long enough. Let's walk."

Over the next hour, I told her everything. We wandered all the way up to the edge of the Pearl and then headed back. I started to wrap it up as we got back to her car.

"Squarespace," she said when I finished. "I started a Lucky Supreme website. Your name and some pics of your work. A little bit of your story but not much." She looked at me then. "After all this time I don't really know that much."

"Any mention of Denver?"

"I didn't think it would be a big deal."

I wiped my face. I was soaked. She must have been cold, the way she was dressed. We stood under a streetlight looking at each other.

"I'm surprised, too," I said. I looked up. "I . . . I thought . . . fuck. That night all those years ago changed my life. Now it seems like, like, like—"

"Darby."

I looked down at her. She reached up and cupped my cheek with one cold hand.

"You didn't kill those kids. Turns out you didn't even kill this guy Riley."

"What now?"

"Depends." She put her hand back in her pocket. "Let's go back to your place. If Dessel and Pressman have the new gal on the same page, we need to give them everything and then lend them a hand. If they don't"—she shrugged—"we still give them everything and help out, but we get an immunity deal. But before we do anything, we need food. You need a drink. I need to think."

"What about Hank?"

"He's asleep," she said. "If he isn't he's off with one of the idiots from the band. I'll be glad when I can have his nights to myself."

On the drive back to my place, we were quiet. Surrounded by monsters. Again. I looked over at Delia. Her wet hair was plastered to her skull and her makeup was a mess. She was thinking. Thinking about the feds, about Riley, about the sick video business, about me, about how I was going to get out of it. If I was going to get out of it. What Suzanne would think when some awful thing bubbled up from my sketchy past and tried to eat me alive.

She wasn't thinking about Hank.

So I was.

Delia made migas without asking. Scrambled eggs, chilies, tortilla strips. We ate at the table. I'd changed into dry jeans and a T-shirt. She was wearing my Ramones hoodie and my best black pants, the ones I reserved for court, rolled up and tied at the waist. She looked like a hobo from an old black-and-white movie.

"You look vintage hobo in those pants," I said around a mouthful of food.

"Your pants, dumbass." She chewed. "This Riley guy, they said he was able to hack bank security cams, traffic cams and the like?"

"Yep."

"And he has a photo of you from Denver."

"Yep. And he was taking them the whole time he was setting us up. So yeah, he has quite a few now."

"Facial recognition." Delia put her fork down. "Tie that in with any mention of Denver and there you go."

"How long has this site been running?"

"Six, seven weeks. I've been loading photos, profiles on the new guys, that kind of shit. Content wise, I started with you. So about that long. It all adds up. This guy has been looking for you for a long, long time. Any way he could have guessed you'd wind up here in Portland?"

"I never mentioned it. I almost went to Boulder."

"That must be why he sent the dead mineral dude first. To make sure it really was you. You say Santos came back?"

"That's what Gomez told me. Turned over a new leaf, based on my bullshit. I should warn him how bad an idea that is."

She didn't say anything. I got up and went into the kitchen. It was closing on five a.m., so last call. I poured myself a glass of scotch and carried it back out. She eyed it but stayed quiet once again.

"You think Dessel can figure out how he found me and trace him based on the website deal?" I drank a little. Delia finished eating and put her fork on her plate.

"No. My guess is he's here, in Portland. They can find out all kinds of things looking at the Lucky site, but the damage is done. Once he found you? Shit. He'll never look at that site again. Too risky for one thing, but now he can look through your bedroom window."

It was my turn to be quiet.

"He wants money, Darby. That's all."

I looked up, confused. There was no way she could have misjudged the situation so badly. She'd lost a shade of pink in the last thirty seconds. Her eyes narrowed. The knuckles on her hands were white.

"Delia," I began, shaking my head, "I—"

"Dessel might have already figured this out," she continued softly, "but if he hasn't, I'll clue him in. You, ah, you wanna take a bath with me?"

I was stunned. Delia winked, but she wasn't smiling.

"A bath?"

"Yeah, dude. You, me, bathtub. C'mon. Bring the hooch."

Delia got up and walked into the kitchen without another word. I stared after her. A moment later, I heard the faucet running. The tub was filling. I got up. I finished my drink. Then I walked slowly after her.

She was sitting on the toilet, fully dressed. When I came in, she motioned for me to close the bathroom door. When I did, she motioned me in. I knelt next to her and she whispered into my ear.

"Darby, I think there's a mic in your house somewhere. He wasn't watching you through your bedroom window. He was filming. This Riley guy is making a video of you."

I drew back. We stared into each other's eyes. Delia reached out and took my hands, and I realized they were shaking. We sat like that as the steam rose around us. Finally, she let go and turned the tap off. I watched as she reached into the hot water and splashed it around a little.

"Quit staring at my ass," she said loudly. "I got a pimple? What the fuck?"

"No, it's not that," I said. "I mean you do, but, lemme take a better look."

"This better not be going where I think it's going."

"I'm not a doctor," I went on, "but I think I can tell the difference between a McDonald's ass blister and a Doritos brand butt volcano. Just, hold still! Something's coming out!"

She slapped my arm. I grabbed her wrist and pulled her close, whispered, "I'm gonna kill this fucker way better this time."

Delia whispered back to me, a hot gust of chili. "I can help."

Riley was listening. I knew it. I could feel it. I'd known it for weeks. I reached out and splashed the water around. It was amazing, but I could feel all of the bones in my hand. Delia watched me. Watching me think must have been fun for her, like watching a dog play fetch with a Rubik's Cube. I tried to catch up.

"Fuck those feds," I said, conversationally.

"No shit," she said, relieved. "They dangle you out as bait every chance they get. They think they got shit on this guy, good for them. Go get him. Since they can't even find their own car keys it doesn't matter one fuck. We find the guy and we pay him. End of story." She splashed the water around. "Mmm. That feels good. Shame it's so small. I read about these implants they got in Thailand, supposed to be just the bomb diggity."

"Right. Maybe you can get some titties while we're there. A caboose."

"I honestly don't know what we see in each other, Holland." She flicked some water in my face. I smiled.

"No one else can stand us."

I played with the water a little more. The windows were still cloudy with steam when she pulled the plug, and as the water drained we went through the motions and chatter associated with getting dressed. When we were done, I realized how tired I was. I drank two pints of water at the kitchen sink and then went into the bedroom. Delia was lying in Suzanne's place, her eyes closed. I took the blanket from the edge of the bed and gently draped it over her. I was about to go out to the couch and sleep there when I realized how it would play to our one-man audience, so I lay down next to her.

Rain hit the window. Chops and Buttons came in from the couch and jumped up on the bed. Chops curled up on Delia's pillow in the crook of her cheek and shoulder and Buttons stretched out on her stomach. I realized then that the cats hadn't slept on the bed for a long time. Not since Suzanne left. I was just getting back to it myself.

I lit a last cigarette and smoked. As I did, Delia's breathing changed, from waking to sleep. She snored a little. I thought over the events of the last twenty-four hours. Riley, back from the dead. My hiding in Old Town, ending all this long while, since the day I took ownership of the shop, was done. The cat was out of the bag. With the help of a complete psychopath, I'd taken the last step toward being a real person, a citizen, and it didn't feel good at all.

In the morning we split up, fast. Delia went to the closest 7-Eleven and called Dessel, told him to meet me in an hour at the place where we swap fishing stories. It was raining, because it's always raining when shit goes down. I took a succession of cabs to the bad café. I was an hour late, but I doubted anyone could have followed me.

"You dicks," I hissed, sitting down across from them. "You're using me as bait again."

Pressman looked a little surprised, but it was hard to tell because he was so exhausted. Dessel was apologetic.

"Delia, right?" He shook his head. "I knew she'd figure it out."

"Fuck. How the hell am I supposed to trust you guys?" I took Dessel's coffee and gulped it down. He motioned at the waitress for more. Dessel put his hands on the table.

"Darby," Dessel began, "we went back and forth about it. About if we could rely on your acting chops. The jury is still out. Put yourself in my position, just one time. Yes, we think he's making another one of his videos, and this time the star of the show is you. Now, all three of us want to catch this guy and put him away or put him down. Either or. Right?"

I glared.

"For the moment, you're safe. He's still filming. How

250

do we know? At the end of every video, the star has lost everything. This is a project that just entered the last phase of production. While he's filming, we have a chance of catching him, but only if your performance rings true. The minute you go bad actor, the narrative changes. Get it? We couldn't tell you."

"Plus we figured you'd kill this guy at some point," Pressman said. He tapped his temple. "Do your whole psycho thing."

I sat back.

"What happened last night?" Dessel asked. "You and Delia went back to your place. Then what?"

"She started a website," I said. I took out a piece of paper and slid it across the table. Dessel took it and put it in his coat without looking. "All the information is there. It's live, but hardly any visitors yet. It's like a store with no sign and paper on the windows."

"And?"

"Delia figures there's a mic in my place. Some kind of bug."

They looked at each other.

"You feed this bug a false trail?" Pressman asked. "You did, didn't you."

"Delia's idea. We were talking about Riley before she put it all together. Story goes now that we think he wants money. Knows I have it, knows he wants it. I'll try to pay him off and steer clear of you guys at the same time."

They were relieved. Dessel rubbed his face.

"Where's Lopez?"

"Small problem there," Dessel said from behind his

hands. "She really hates me, for one thing. Finds Bob here disgusting." He lowered his hands and gave me a red stare. "Wants you in the electric chair."

"Great." The waitress refilled Dessel's coffee and gave me one. We all nodded and smiled and she moved off.

"What are you guys gonna do?"

"She's at a computer lab, tied up for the moment. Figuratively, I mean. But she filed a protest."

"Your problem," I said. I sipped my terrible coffee.

"Our problem, Holland," Pressman said. "We're in this together, remember?"

"Right. So what now?"

"The question of the hour." Dessel poured sugar into his coffee. Dumped. Then he stirred. "Me and Bob are gonna go fuck with this hacker we know. Guy actually lives in his mother's basement, if you can believe that. Totally cliché. Feed him this website data and set him loose. You?"

"Dunno." I had to go get money out of the U-Store-It, and that was going to be a super huge problem with so many people following me. There was a good chance that Riley wouldn't be waiting this time. I was going to telegraph a different plan, and I'd already learned he wasn't watching the rail lines. They watched me brood. "I, ah, I have some personal shit to take care of."

They looked at each other, then me.

"Darby, I have to call my dad later and check to see if the new meds are making him dizzy. Bob here has a colonoscopy at three. My sister is in the middle of a divorce. Bob's youngest daughter is in rehab. What personal shit are you talking about?"

"Fucking Delia," I growled. "She's marrying a musician."

They laughed, like it was the first time they'd laughed in weeks. People turned at the other tables and smiled at the joy of it, the sincere delight. I smiled, too. Dessel finally wiped his eye.

"Do tell," he managed.

"Hank Dildo." I shook my head. "Thing is, she's so smart! You know that. But-but—"

"My daughter is the same way," Pressman said, his smile turning a little. "So much talent. Started with pills, just like they always do. But there were a couple boys in the mix she could have done without."

"I sort of pictured Delia with another artist," Dessel said, shaking his head. "But a real one, like a painter or something."

"Me too," I said, "but noooo. Dude sniffs glue. I mean, that's a real thing. He spray paints his hair. Why? Because he has lots of spray paint. He inhales it."

"That isn't good." Dessel sipped. "You want us to look the other way while you kick his ass? Say the word. We admire Delia."

"Nah. Thanks, though. No, I was thinking I should just bribe him. Money talks. I have a little cash. I give it to him and tell him to fuck off until she comes to her senses. He says no, then maybe you guys look the other way."

"Think he'll go for it?"

I shrugged. "Maybe. He has this other chick. Maybe the two of them can run off together."

"I wish I'd thought of that," Pressman said thoughtfully. "This one guy, I knew he was trouble. But every time

I tried to talk my daughter into going one way, she went the other."

"Okay then," Dessel said, trying to wrap it up. "Darby. What do you need from us?"

"Not much for the moment. I'm going to lose my tail as soon as the sun goes down. From here I go to the shop, but after dark I'll be off the radar for a few hours." I still hadn't told them that I thought I'd seen Riley at my storage space. I wasn't completely sure I had, for one thing, not in the light of day. But I couldn't risk Lopez finding out about the place. There was too much evidence inside. There was more. Riley must have been watching me on the traffic cams, and putting that together with the equipment in my house, he'd known where I was going. For whatever reason, his surveillance didn't cover the outside of the Montage or the train tracks. I had to go back, and now I could.

"Fine." Dessel leaned to the side and took his wallet out, put a ten on the table. "Bob, let's go torment our geek for an hour and get him rolling, then I'll drop you off at the clinic."

We all rose.

"When I'm done tonight I'll head back to the Lucky and pick up my tail again there," I said.

"Should be me and Bob this evening. Bob will have recovered from his afternoon of getting scoped. Maybe Lopez or the basement wizard will have something for us by then."

"What are you guys gonna do about her?"

"Walk with us," Dessel said.

The three of us went outside. All three of us lit cigarettes. Pressman coughed and turned up his collar at the wet wind. Dessel seemed to find it refreshing.

"Darby, this brings us back to the performance part of things," Dessel began.

"Your performance," Pressman added. "Sorry, man."

"See." Dessel searched for the right words. "When we first came after you, shit. You were just another chump. A guy we needed to lock up. That's what Lopez sees. She reads your file and she sees criminal. Black and white, no in-between."

"They all come out of the chute that way," Pressman said. He made a pained expression and rubbed his stomach.

"You talked to her the other night," Dessel continued. "You went for a drive, she said."

"Yeah. That was maybe not good."

"It actually was." Dessel smoked. "See, it was the second time I talked to you, maybe the third, I don't know exactly how or exactly why, but I started to like you."

I laughed.

"Seriously! You don't know what this job is like, Holland. Me and Bob, we actually signed up to catch guys like you. But it turns out that your garden variety criminal is fucking awful. No sense of humor. They're stupid. Tacky. They smell bad."

"He's saying that we, ah, we like chasing you, Darby. You're a cut above."

"Jesus," I said wonderingly. "Thanks, guys."

"We told her that just this once we're working with you." Pressman said. "One-time deal."

"And that we trust you," Dessel said. "This one time."

"And she isn't buying it?"

"Nope." Dessel messed up his hair a little more. "A file is just a file. You read about a guy and you still never get to know the real man. You are a criminal, Darby. All three of us know that. But right now we need one. You're our criminal."

"What you have to do is convince her," Pressman said. "Convince her that you have standards. Morals and ethics. Get to know her a little and she'll get to know you. We need her to know you like we do. She wants Riley in a body bag but she won't come out and say it. She doesn't know us either. Not like that. You're our way in."

The Lucky Supreme was in a late afternoon slump when I got there. Chase was sitting at his station tinkering with a machine. One of the new guys, Larry or Barry, was gloved up and scrubbing down his station. Chase smiled when I walked through the door. The new guy didn't.

"Boss," Chase called by way of greeting. "How's it hangin'?"

"Darby," the new guy mumbled.

"Dudes," I said. "What day is it?"

"Weekday," Chase replied. He returned to his machine.

"It's, ah, Thursday, man." New guy's confidence was falling already.

"Groovy. Calls?"

"A few. People asking about names. Gomez is looking for you."

I sat down in Delia's station. Chase put his machine down and smiled at me. The new guy vanished into the back and then I could hear water running.

"You aren't working today, are you?" He asked like he knew the answer.

"Nah. Killing time."

"Feds still following you? What happened to your face?"

"Yeah. No biggie."

257

Chase looked at the back and then leaned in fast.

"New guys are set to freak out," he whispered. "Somehow they found out about Nigel."

"And?" I could already see where he was headed.

"Dude," Chase hissed. "He might be in jail because of you. Indirectly, but still. It was your personal feds who took him down."

"You think the new kids are up to shady shit? Afraid of what might turn up?"

Chase rolled his eyes. "Of course they are! Jesus, man!"

He sat back and so did I. The door to the employee lounge opened and closed.

"What about you? Getting cold feet?"

"Nah." He put his arms behind his head. "I make bank here. I'm cool. Figure I get busted for anything it'll be drunk and disorderly. I kinda like the thought of being followed around by guys in suits. Makes me feel like a somebody." He laughed, not a care in the world. Guy was hiding something, I knew, but so was I. We all were. I reached out and slapped his knee.

"Attaboy. Chill that new guy out. Tell him whatever he needs to hear, but send out a few feelers, too. Might need to import some talent out of Cali. People who know the name but not the game."

"Fans of the Lucky abound, my brother," Chase said. "I can make a few calls. Sacramento is brimming with A-grade tattooers who would do anything to get the fuck out of that town."

"Good." I stood up. "Think I'll go see Gomez."

Late afternoon at the Rooster Rocket was my favorite

time to be there. I smiled at Cherry and Gomez and went to my favorite booth in back. A minute later, Gomez joined me with two Christian thimbles and a clipboard.

"This rain, man," he said. "Five months to go, no?"

"Roof leaking?"

"Not bad. What'd you do to your face?"

"Took a grater to it."

Gomez raised an eyebrow, but said nothing. We drank and soaked in the vibe. There were a few day drinkers and the first few local office types had just come in. Bob Seger on the jukebox. He took a breath to tell me something, then he didn't.

"Santos okay?"

"He has a lot of money now, Darby."

"Ah."

"Yeah."

Gomez would never ask me to rat anyone out, that wasn't what this was about. I thought about it.

"What's he doing with it?" I asked.

"Shit." There it was. "Fuckin' kid sold that ride and bought a Monte Carlo, so now he has even more money. He could fix his place up, maybe go to community college and get his GED, but no. No, he wants to run Oregon weed. Few pounds at a time. Take it south and make a few bucks. That's the plan he came up with."

"Good for him."

"I know, right?" Gomez fingered his moustache. "But there has to be something better. I like the idea of him maybe getting into the food industry."

"How so?"

"Well, he likes to cook. Worked in the kitchen in juvie. Flaco says the boy has chops for a kid who never used a real knife. But I'm just dreaming out loud. He's a bright young man."

"I asked Santiago if there was any openings at Frond. He said no. He draw?"

"Sure. Cholo shit. Pretty girls with big tits and clown makeup. Lowriders."

"Huh."

"So, I know . . . shit. Whatever he decides, maybe . . . I hope you keep talking to him. We went over this already, me and you, but this was before I knew about the cash being as long as it is." He shrugged.

"Easy. I got so much difficult shit to do right now, talking to the kid will be a relief."

"Right on." Gomez tried to project neutral cool, but inside he was doing backflips.

"I might need a favor too, now that I think of it."

"Of course. I owe you bigtime and thousand times over, homie. What is it?"

"Hank Dildo."

"Ah, the darling little Mr. Dildo. Si." Gomez smiled sadly. Then he sighed and looked at me expectantly. I looked over my shoulder to make sure Cherry was out of earshot.

"Tomorrow, maybe the next day, I'm going to give him some money. Enough to get started somewhere else. He has a mistress, Gomez."

Gomez's face hardened. "He does now, does he?"

"Yep. Nigel told me when I visited him. I went and talked to her."

"Motherfucker." Gomez made a fist.

"Right. Now, this other chick, I don't think she knows about Delia. But that isn't my problem. Hank is."

"What can I do?" There was murder in his eyes.

"We can't kill him, Gomez. But we can make sure he leaves and never comes back. Without Delia's money."

"How?"

"How," I repeated. "This is where Delia usually comes in. But this time it's just us."

"Not good, amigo." He leaned back and raised his hand. "Cherry! Dos? Gracias." Then he turned to me. "What if we hold the other woman hostage? Then we—no, no, wait. That's stupid."

"Maybe we set Hank up for a crime. Get his fingerprints on something. People try to do that to me all the time."

"He wouldn't believe it. Too thin. Too much wiggle room."

Cherry set down new thimbles for us. We sipped. A new song came on, Roy Orbison this time.

"Cars," Gomez said. "We have lots of cars."

I looked up and watched him think.

"One time, Darby, we gave this car, another Monte Carlo, to this woman Maria. She loved that ride. But as long as we knew where that car was, we knew where Maria was."

"Huh. We give Hank money and a car. And we hate him."

"That or we put him in the field with Bella."

"Okay then. Can you get me some wheels? The kind of thing Hank won't get rid of too fast."

Gomez narrowed his eyes. "I can."

It was an hour before full dark and I had two kinds of tail to lose.

The feds would be easy. Traffic was terrible and they knew I was scraping them off already. Pressman and Dessel would make a brief show of it and then sit on the shop until I came back, mostly to keep Lopez in check. But Riley was a different matter. He could use traffic cameras. So I had to move in a strange new way.

Fortunately, I knew just what to do.

Back at the Lucky, I closed the door to the lounge/office and took stock. First, I put on an extra Lucky Supreme hoodie from the merch cabinet. It was going to be cold as fuck, just like last time. Then I got some old leather gloves I used for impromptu construction and stowed them in my pockets. Last, I needed a bag of some kind for the money. I was thinking ten grand would do it, so I didn't need a big one. One of the white trash bags for the small station can was perfect.

Then I was off. I was going back to the U-Store-It, this time alone.

Dessel and Pressman were parked a block down. I ducked around the corner, moving fast, and they followed. Two blocks down at the Chinatown gate I lost them in a snarl of delivery trucks. From there, I zipped long under awnings, making my way to the river. I had to cross. I had to change the way I looked, too. It helped to have money.

First, I ducked into a convenience store with two entrances. I bought a bright blue umbrella and went out the other way. From there, I crossed the street and did the same thing, this time tossing the umbrella as I entered. Two more umbrella changes later I boarded the MAX in Chinatown. As I got on, I ditched the last umbrella and donned my new hat.

On the far side, I got off at the first stop and started walking. It was dark by then, and darker still by the time I got to the train tracks. On the off chance that Riley was James Bond, I took the battery out of my cell phone. Then I walked.

I was thinking about the Hank problem when the U-Store-It came into view.

Approaching from the train tracks again was just as long and bad as before, full of wind and rain, but I wasn't as cold this time around. Riding the rails through the city at night was something I might have enjoyed even a month ago. Now, I was just glad the train was a little slower the second time around. I lit a cigarette when I stepped into the yellow field of light spilling out of the lone halogen security lamp, then started across the mud to the fence. There was no one on the other side this time. I looked up and paused. The access plank was up there in the darkness.

"You're thinking of Nicky, aren't you?" came a disembodied male voice.

I dropped into a crouch.

"Don't run! I have something to show you." Laughter. "Time we talked. *Mister Holland.*"

"Riley!" I yelled. I stood up. If he was going to shoot, I'd already be dead. "Come on out! Last time I saw you I beat the unholy fuck out of your ugly head. I'd kinda like to see what you look like now."

"Quite a little life you made for yourself." I scanned the

underside of the bridge. The voice was coming from some-where high to my right, where an access ladder led up to the undercarriage causeway. "'Little' sums it up entirely."

"You want money? Fuck you. Want a piece of my little life? Back to fuck you. Why don't you come on out and I'll show you what I mean by that."

"I know all of your secrets." The voice was playful now. "This is where you killed the art dealer Dong Ju. His body is probably less than a hundred meters from where you're standing, out there in the river, weighed down by concrete. Am I right?"

I flipped the bird to the darkness.

"That's the spirit! But you got the money in the end. So clever. So very very clever. Your new friends Dessel and Pressman got so close! So much time, wasted! Dong Ju's people never talked to them. But they did talk to me."

That wasn't good. I didn't say anything.

"Then the bomber. The Lucky Supreme and half a city block, blown up to make room for the real world. You found the bomber, didn't you? Ralston? Oh, he loved talking about you, too. He was never the same after you found him. But that did lead me to a pimp named Cheeks. You killed him, too. And you stole his car. Shame on you!"

"What do you want?" I yelled. Tittering laughter came back.

"So many crimes! Why, I could send one email, one! And away you go. Life. You and your old friend Nigel could be cellmates. He's mad at you, but he'll get over it. If not, I guess you can kill him too!"

"Here's an idea," I called. "Why don't I tell the feds

every last thing I know about you. Then we'll actually get to meet each other in jail!"

"You killed Oleander, too."

"Sure as fuck did. Kinda. I mean, I was going to. It's a long story."

"Your life is crumbling." Now he was a judge, handing down my sentence. "Your life is unraveling, coming apart at the seams. I love it."

"Why?" It was all I could think of.

"You're the one who got away!" The answer came instantly. "You! The only one who ever got away. I looked and I looked, but there was never a sign you were alive. But I always knew you were. You were somewhere out there."

It was my turn to laugh and I did, loud and long.

"I thought you were dead, you moron! I was wrong. And now guess what, you sick fucking lunatic! I am going to kill you! I know you're filming me right now and I don't even care! You should have believed what those people say about me, Riley! Because now that I know you're alive you are DEAD DEAD DEAD!"

Nothing. Quiet.

The U-Store-It blew up with enough force to throw me ten feet backward. I landed in the mud and tried to breathe. The ringing in my ears was deafening. I crawled away from the heat, gasping. Even at that distance I could feel it burning me. After ten feet I managed to get to my feet and staggered to the edge of the train tracks. Then I turned and looked back.

The inferno was huge. Riley must have been unable to figure out which unit was mine, so he'd blown them all.

The cash. My safety net.

I ran.

"So this is how you kept getting in and out of your place when you were under surveillance last year," Dessel marveled. "Cut through all the backyards and then, voila, enter the shithole." He looked around, admiring. The four of us were in the only dive bar close to my house, affectionately known in Portland as the Fart Club.

"You look better without eyebrows," Delia said. "Sort of *Blade Runner*-ish."

"He does," Pressman agreed. "Like Roy Batty's, I dunno, vat mate."

I'd showered and changed my clothes when I got home, then painfully made my way through late-night backyards to the club before I called them. By the time they got there, I was into well whiskey number four.

"Fuck you," I said in a generalized way.

"We knew you had a storage unit somewhere out there," Dessel said. He scrutinized his dirty beer glass, drank anyway. "But we could never pin it down."

"Riley did," I said. "Hence—"

"Hence another explosion, yes." Dessel frowned. "We tipped off the fire marshal and said someone was filming it. They found two cameras and a speaker system rigged to an iPhone. He was never even there. You must have tripped an alarm of some kind."

"Ah. What a dick." So he'd found out that I had more

than one way to get there. I was having no luck outsmarting him.

"What about Agent Lopez?" Delia asked. "She going to try to pin this on Darby?"

"Normally she would," Pressman said. "We all would. But those cameras finally brought her all the way around. This Riley character is technologically sophisticated. We can't tell at this time how many inroads he has into the department's computer system, so the investigation has gone off the books entirely. She's taking the iPhone out to our geek now. So maybe a lead, but I'm not hopeful."

"Me neither," Dessel agreed. "We don't have any choice but to continue to use Darby as bait."

"Means I'm bait, too." Delia ordered tea, but the cup had lipstick on it. She worked at the red patch with her thumbnail.

"So is the Lucky," Dessel said. "The bar. The restaurant. Pretty much all of it."

"We have to try to anticipate his next move," I said. "We know he's here, in town. We know he's filming me. We also know his MO. He's going to try to isolate me. Turn my friends into rats. Burn my money. Make it so that I'm broken and desperate and crushed. Right?"

Everyone looked grim.

"So who's next?" Dessel drained his glass and scowled. "That's the question. What relationship will he try to destroy? What, what—what accomplishment will he undo? What dream can he steal and twist and try to give back?"

I looked at Delia. She looked back at me. If she knew, if

any of them knew, if Riley knew that I'd found out about Hank, then Delia was next.

"I'm getting another drink," I said, rising. "Anybody?"

Dessel raised his empty and nodded. Pressman and Delia shook their heads. I went to the bar and stood in the short line. Around me, sweaty young punks and trashed-out glam girls were yammering and having a good time. The vibe wasn't contagious. I looked over and watched Delia talking to Pressman and Dessel. She said something funny and both of them laughed. Pressman shot something back and Delia laughed, too. They were actually getting along.

"What?"

I snapped into focus. The rude little bartender glared at me and forced a smile.

"Well whiskey, two pints of PBR."

"Who're the suits?" she snapped, pouring. "You make new friends?"

I wasn't in the mood for chitchat, so I didn't say anything.

"Darby Holland, king of the jungle," she snarled, "hanging out after midnight with two G-men. Gotta be a story there."

I drew a breath.

"Not that I want to hear it," she went on. "But keep it cool, okay? You hear me? I don't—"

"Keep the change," I interrupted. I was too burned out to fight back. She shut down and snatched up the ten I tossed on the wet bar. I carried the warm beers and the shot back to the table. Nobody said anything until my shot glass was empty.

"We think we know what will happen next," Delia said.

"Oh goody."

"Darby," Dessel began painfully. "You didn't come right out and say it, but this guy has dirt on you. My kind of dirt. The kind me and Bob here have been looking for. Am I right?"

I glowered.

"Right." Dessel looked at his beer. "Now, if it was bad enough, he might try to trade it in, for partial immunity. Is, ah, is any of the dirt that bad?"

"Nah. He's a different kind of scumbag and several sizes bigger to boot. We aren't even the same species."

"I told them," Delia said. "That means he'll go for the Lucky. Not me."

"Why?"

"It's the weak spot. Gomez is too old school. He'll never turn on you. So is Santiago. So am I. But the Lucky is weak. I have one foot out the door. Chase is Chase. The new guys have probably already quit. And it's the center of everything in your world. He takes that down, he scores."

"Even if it's a purely psychological score," Dessel said. "Like counting coup. That place, it's been your life for so many years, right? Take that away and it's like he took part of your soul."

I thought about that. I didn't tell them about my recurring fantasy every time I passed the train station. But what they were getting at was true. I was still there. I never did take that train. I sighed.

"There are a million ways to bring a weak shop to its knees," I said.

"Like what?" This from Pressman. He seemed genuinely curious. I shrugged. Delia took point.

"The easiest way is from the inside. Turn a guy. Make him your own. Take Chase. He has so many secrets that he calls himself Chase Manhattan. That's common enough in tattoo land, but it also marks him. You find out what some of those secrets are, he's like putty in your hands. Guy's already shady, so there's no telling what he could get up to."

"The new guys," I said. "They might be a better bet."

"What else?" Dessel asked.

"So many ways. Health Department can shut a place down, but that never sticks. But if it gets shut down and then something else happens, like a drug raid? Different story." I sipped my terrible beer.

"Destroying the Lucky outright is hard," Delia said. "It already happened and we came back. The second time would be easier to recover from. We have practice now."

"Food for thought," Dessel said. "Okay. In the meantime, Darby, you watch your bank accounts. You too, Delia. We'll take that phone apart and see what we see. Find out where the cameras were purchased, might get lucky there, no pun intended. But it's a start."

"I gotta split," Delia said. "Hank." She got up.

"Me too," Dessel said. "Get some sleep." He patted Pressman's shoulder. "Ready, old man?"

"Let's boogie." They got up too. Pressman looked down on me. "Gonna get home okay? You're wasted."

"I'm fine."

"Agent Conover is supposed to be sitting on your place," Pressman said. "Sleep good."

I saluted with my beer. Pressman and Dessel left. Delia lingered.

"You think the gun safe survived the explosion?" she asked.

"No idea. But it'll be weeks before we find out."

"Shit."

"Yep." I looked up at her. "I'm gonna finish this beer and head home. Go get some rest."

"Darby. Just so you know, I'm looking, too. We'll find him."

"I wish you wouldn't."

Delia smiled sadly and left.

I was too tired to cut through any backyards to get home, so I went the front way. Something told me that my days in my old place were numbered. The landlord was a weird old law office clerk, and one or two well-placed calls from Riley would inspire him to evict me and raise the rent to the current Portland standard, almost double what I was paying now. Agent Lopez was sitting on the bench outside my front door waiting for me. I staggered up the steps and crashed down next to her. We looked at each other.

"Hey," I said.

"Hey yourself. I sent Conover home."

"Right on." I took my smokes out and offered her one. She took it.

"Your storage space got torched tonight." She lit her cigarette and then lit mine.

"It happens."

"Happens to you a lot." She blew smoke into the night.

"Not a competition, lady. You just need to try harder." I gestured at the night with my smoke. "Pick up a few solid enemies. Plenty to choose from out there. You'll catch up."

"The iPhone was a dead end. Cameras, too. We got nothing." She looked at me.

"Bait. You got the perfect bait."

"Pressman and Dessel want me to work with you on this. The whole thing has already gone black because they're afraid he's hacking us, but there's black and then there's Black. You follow me?"

I shrugged.

"The Law, Darby, is something I don't think you really understand. Riley Wharton is going down. But he's going down by the letter of the law. He's going to sing for a chance at parole and we're going to get names. That's the way the system works."

"I know how your system works, Lopez."

"Then you know why I can't condone any kind of vigilante bullshit, Holland! Dessel says you can survive anything. Know what that means to me? It means that as soon as they have an in, as soon as they can find those names and those lists, they're going to let you kill him."

"Let me kill him?" I turned to her. "That guy is a murderer a hundred times over."

"Indirectly. We have no proof that he personally pulled the trigger on anyone."

"Listen to yourself, Lopez. You're brainwashed. Take a huge step back and open your eyes. Riley Wharton is a monster. He knows the rules of your 'system,' so he's a certain type of monster. A smart one. I don't know if it's because I'm drunk or because you're stupid, but we aren't speaking the same language."

"You are a criminal, Holland." She enunciated every word clearly. "A criminal."

"Let me break this down." I smoked and we glared at each other. "Okay. For one second, just look at me. Not like you read my file. Not like you know anything about me. What do you see?"

"A criminal," she said instantly.

"A human being!"

"A man, then. Fine."

"Right. Now, what is that exactly?"

"Flesh, blood, bone, teeth, hair—"

"No no no." I put my cigarette out. "A person is . . . a person is memories. Dreams. Feelings. A person eats and sleeps. A person has friends and lovers and jobs. You take all that away? It isn't a person anymore. It's just an animal. That's what Wharton does. When person goes to animal? That's what he's interested in. It's the animal he likes to play with, not the person. Now, look at me one more time. Now what do you see?"

"Darby—"

"I worked so hard to be a person, Lopez. I'll fight to the death before I give it away."

She sat back. I did too. Eventually she cleared her throat.

"That bar still open? The one you were hanging out in just now with Pressman and Dessel?"

"Maybe. Why? You want a drink?"

She looked at me. I smiled first.

"I was just wondering if you were heading back out," she replied. "I'm your tail for the rest of the night." She stood up. "I'll work with you in a limited way, Holland, but I wouldn't have a drink with you if you were the last man on earth."

"Yes you would," I said easily. "Don't be like that."

I watched her go down the stairs. The rain was steady,

just as it would be for the next several months. I closed my eyes and considered my place in the world.

I wouldn't be able to bribe Hank to get out of town. I was out of cash and the feds would be eyeing my accounts. A big withdrawal would raise too many questions.

Riley Wharton was closing in. The next move he made would be the last one. Whatever it was was going to be his checkmate play.

The players on my side of the board were already becoming divided. Delia, my genius Delia, was about to get married to the wrong man, and her inner turbulence had dulled her edge. Nigel in prison. A long-distance girlfriend I could never even tell about this. I still had Gomez and Santiago and Flaco, but endangering them was a terrible idea, and someone had to attend my funeral. Dessel and Pressman, my unlikely new allies, had a snitch on top of them and were hobbled because of it. I was already alone.

Riley's plan was unfolding.

I woke up on the couch with my phone on my chest. It was ringing.

"Oh my god," I answered.

"Darby." Suzanne said it like she regretted calling. "Jesus, man. Let me guess. You were asleep on the couch. You got plastered last night."

"No, no," I said, struggling into a sitting position. Chops and Buttons were staring at me, amazed that I was lying the instant I awoke. "I was, ah, shit you know what, I—what's up?"

"What are you doing!?" Already mad.

"What am I doing?" I got up and staggered toward the kitchen. "Making coffee. Getting ready for a fun-filled day of wedding crap."

"The Halloween goat wedding."

"Chickens," I clarified helpfully.

She sighed with voice in it, extra dramatic. "Alright. Good. So we were talking about the weekend."

"Right!" I took the coffee down. "This is gonna be so great."

"I was thinking maybe we could go to the Gorge. I need some photos for something that just came across my desk. Then we can go to the railroad museum in Hood River."

"A working vacation," I admired. "You multitasker, you."

"Is that gonna be a problem?" Probing now. This was all beginning to follow a set pattern. For the moment, even the phone call was a bad idea.

"Nah. I think about trains all the time anymore."

"I figure the lighting in the Gorge will be about right at—"

I put the phone on the counter and let her drone on while I made coffee. Old grounds into the compost, rinse out the filter, put it back. Add new coffee. Rinse out the pot. Add water. Hit the little red button. Then I wiped my hands on my pants and took my bent smokes out of my pocket, fired one up. It was cold in the house. The cats wanted breakfast, so I popped a can and put it on a dinner plate for them. While they ate, I picked up the phone again.

"—second time. And then no one said anything at all. If the entire presentation hinges on a live feed, if there are more than five people in five time zones, then—"

"That sounds fuckin' terrible, baby," I interrupted. "They don't pay you enough for this shit. Fuck those guys. You should move back home and get your old job back."

Silence. Then: "*What did you just say?*"

Oops. "Chase was looking at fully furnished apartments in Barcelona on Craigslist yesterday. Unreal, Suzanne. We should think about something like that. We both dig pork. Olives and whatnot."

We listened to each other say nothing. It was hard to tell where she was calling from. I couldn't hear any office sounds in the background. I poured coffee and leaned up against the counter. "Suze?"

"Sometimes I think you're not listening to me. That you just tune me out."

"What can I say to that. I hate your new job." I put my cup down and massaged my eyes. "I kinda hate my job, too. I just wish we could go somewhere. Anywhere, as long as it was far enough away. Like we were talking about."

"We'll talk about it more tomorrow. But you can't run from your problems."

"Yes you can," I snapped. "Don't quote bumper stickers and expect me to bite."

"All we do is fight."

"All *I* do is fight," I said clearly. "And I'm tired of it." I hung up.

I was counting on Riley listening in. Taking Suzanne off the menu was critical. It was a shame she'd made it so easy. I plugged my phone in and took a shower, then put on my Beating-Up-Hank clothes: construction boots, sturdy jeans I wouldn't mind burning, nondescript black T-shirt, and my backup bomber jacket. Dessel and Pressman were parked a block down, so I headed their way.

"'Sup, dudes," I said as I got in the back. Their car was remarkably tidy. Dessel's short hair was still wet from the shower he still smelled like. They were freshly on duty. Pressman handed me a coffee.

"Finally got a ping," Dessel reported. He turned around in his seat. He'd shaved. "One of the cameras we found was different from the others. Purchased locally. We ran down the credit card number and it was a dead end, no surprise there, but we did get a list of the other crap Riley bought at the same place."

"And? Tell me it's some shit you can track."

"It is. Bob, get us out of here."

Pressman started the Prius and took a left, headed for Burnside. Dessel continued.

"Three other phones. All burners. Lopez figures it's possible to track each one of them for about thirty seconds, right when they're activated. It's complicated, but when you light a burner up for the first time, it shows up in the system while it comes online as a new number. How many phones with that make and model pop into the system in the Portland metro area every day? Dozens. But not hundreds."

"Anything else?"

"Little things," Dessel said, thinking. "The reason why it was always so hard to figure out what you were doing, Darby, is that apparently you were making it up as you went along. That makes you super fucking unpredictable."

Pressman snorted. "You wouldn't even believe how much we've talked about this."

"Normal people aren't like that," Dessel said. "Don't be offended. When I say 'normal,' I mean, well, you see—"

"I get it."

"Right. So the U-Store-It. Cameras everywhere down there. Thousands in a twenty-block radius if you go wide. Riley covered his tracks extremely well. No footage of anyone planting bombs, putting cameras in place, that kind of thing. But we think it took more than one trip to get all that shit done."

"Maybe three," Pressman added. "I'm thinking three is the magic number."

"Right," Dessel agreed, his enthusiasm ramping up. "Simple enough to track all movement in and out of the area over the last month. Thousands of cars. Ton of them local. But late at night? In and out at one, maybe two-hour intervals?"

"No wonder you guys could never catch me," I marveled.

"I know," Dessel agreed. Pressman looked in the rearview.

"How would *you* catch this guy, Darby? I mean, you know. Think like a criminal out loud for us."

I did.

"First, think fury. The cold kind. This guy has had all these years to stew. Rage like that goes from fire to dead sludge in the guts after all that time. So—"

"Let me interrupt," Dessel chirped, "that's way disgusting, I love it. Go on."

"And then, then . . ." I looked out the window. "Then consider the difference between a psycho and a lunatic. Now, I'm not talking your fancy textbook bullshit. I'm talking about the popular understanding of the words. Dudeboy fits into the psycho camp. Lunatics are too sloppy. This guy is up there on the *Mission Impossible* Tom Cruise end of things."

"Riiiight . . ." Dessel drew it out. "You totally lost me."

"Me too," Pressman said.

"I was just lecturing Lopez on something like this last night. She was waiting on the porch for me when I got home, by the way. But I chatted her up."

"That's what happened," Dessel marveled. Pressman snorted.

"She's warming to you," Dessel agreed. "This morning she told us we should arrange for you to give a lecture at PSU in the humanities. A convincing portrayal of where not to go. But she smiled."

"Whatever. The point of my drunk-ass yammering had something to do with people. There's a person in Riley Wharton. Somewhere."

"Still lost," Dessel said.

"Still lost," Pressman echoed.

"Right. Now, let's go back to your pictures. The photos of the Mineral guy."

The mood darkened. Neither of them said anything.

"It was contact. These guys like to *see* what's happening with their own eyes. It's important to them."

"You think he's going to brush up against you before the end?" Dessel was worried now.

"I think the end is super close, dudes. I think he's going to be there in person, too. He won't be watching my final moments on camera. He'll be filming it in person."

Silence. I didn't believe they could catch Riley before he made his big move and now they knew it. When they had nothing to say to that, I realized they'd been thinking along the same lines. I'd just been the first one of us to say it out loud.

"Where to?" Dessel asked. His morning pep was gone.

"Drop me at the Lucky. This is going to be one weird fuckin' day."

Chase and one of the new guys were cleaning when I walked in. New Guy was on the mop, Chase on vacuum. The music, early reggae, was close to deafening. Fitting, because they were both unforgivably stoned. I nodded and went straight to the office lounge.

It was noon, so early by Hank's standards. I called Delia and it rang five times before it went to voicemail, so I sent her a text, something I try to never do. SOS. Suitably emergency. My phone rang almost instantly.

"Caught it in your zipper again?"

"Where are you?" I tried to sound casual, like I wasn't about to go tell her fiancé to leave town or die.

"Just woke up. Hank is making eggs. Everything okay?"

"Yeah. Dessel and Pressman think they have a lead or two."

"Good. So strange talking to them last night, wasn't it?"

"Yep. Those guys have been after me for two years. And now, I mean. I don't know. But my instinct is that we can trust them until this is over. They're truly pissed."

"Speaks well of them, doesn't it? That they can stop trying to claw you back into the gutter for long enough to catch this guy?"

"Talked to Suzanne this morning."

Delia giggled. "Eww, neato! What's my favorite Amazon up to? She go on about the romantic side of prime interest rates and the latest Google office fashion?"

"Not sure. You got the day off, right?"

"Why? Need a babysitter?"

"Nah. Gonna help Gomez with this car thing. Commune with the kid again and impart more of my stellar wisdom."

"I got an appointment in about an hour." She grunted as she got up. "Have to get all this material measured and then pick up some new dye samples, then more excellent stuff you don't care about."

"Rad. Call me when you're done.

"Dealio."

I hung up and went over to the Rooster Rocket. Flaco's was busy so I made it past without getting slowed down. Gomez was waiting for me, car keys in hand.

"You got a plan?" he asked as he handed them over.

"I already feel bad, so I got a good one. Where's the car?"

"The Dildo's new ride is in your parking lot. '77 Town Car, black. No way a sane man would give it away. But for Delia, I make an exception."

I looked at the keys. Three, with dice on the ring.

"Flaco has a line," I said quietly. "Can you get me five juniors to go? I gotta go do bad shit."

"No problemo!" Gomez said brightly.

An hour and a half later, Delia and Hank walked out of her house and got in Delia's car. They were laughing about something. Delia was dressed professional, in a little power suit. Hank was braving the cold in skintight jeans, no shirt, and a red denim jacket, hanging open. I'd finished the juniors while I waited.

The Town Car drove like a dream, I thought. They headed for I-5 and I stayed back. Dessel and Pressman had let me slide out without them and were off doing their own thing, so I was tailing her without a tail of my own. It was easier than I thought it would be. The rain and the heavier traffic helped. She dropped Hank off at the corner of 30th and Alberta in front of a music store. He blew her a kiss as she drove away, and then he lit a cigarette. When she was gone, he went past the store and took a right, headed into the residential area. I got out of the Town Car and followed on foot.

Becky lived three blocks down. She greeted Hank on the porch and they hugged. Then he kissed her long and hard and grabbed her ass like he was digging for gold. She laughed and threw her head back, shaking her hair out. Damn, she was beautiful. They went inside.

I walked back to the corner. There was a little Mexican convenience store, with cigarettes and candles and canned food. I went into the back and got a six pack of Hamm's in a can, carried it up to the register. The tiny old woman looked at the beer, then me, then rang it up. The whole transaction was silent.

Becky's house had an okay porch to drink beer on. Not as good as mine, but passable. A freeloader like Hank couldn't bitch too much. There were five mismatched wooden chairs and a moldering green recliner. I sat to the side of the living room window and listened. I couldn't make out words. The rain was too loud, the hiss of passing cars. But the laughter rang through, clean and clear. Halfway through beer number three, Hank put a record on. Twangy country.

It was go time.

Hank was holding a beer, standing by the record player, when I walked in without knocking. Becky was at the kitchen sink wearing an apron. The place was cheap but tidy, retro garage sale mixed with movie posters. I focused on Hank and ignored the startled woman.

"What up, Dildo."

Hank dropped his beer. I gestured at him with mine.

"I have a proposition for you," I went on. "Have a seat."

"How the, how the fuck, what the—" he stammered. I dropped my beer, too. Then I flexed my hands. They popped.

"Sit."

"I'm callin' the cops!" Becky yelled without moving.

"No you aren't," I shot back. "Be cool, Becky. No one is here to cause trouble for you. I'm here for Hank." I pointed at the couch. "And he needs a new beer."

Hank sat down. He was shaking, which made me feel a little better. He could fight, for a wiry little bastard, but it didn't look like he was going to. Not yet. Becky brought him a beer while I watched. She scowled at me, but not like she meant it. She knew they were busted for something, and even though she didn't know what it was, she knew it was real.

"I need you to leave town, Hank," I said. "Tonight."

"Not gonna happen, man." His eyes were wide. He sat up a little, tensing, expecting the beating to begin right then. I sighed instead.

"Why? You're busted, kid. I know about all this." I gestured at the house in general. "I tell Delia and you're shit out of luck, dumbass. So go. Get outta Dodge and don't look back."

"We're broke," Becky said.

"Yeah, about that. I was gonna give you a little cash, but it's all tied up at the moment. I got maybe a grand. And I got you a car. Get where you're going, I'll send a little more. But for right now, I need to see people packing bags."

"Or what?" Hank barked out a fake laugh. "Or what, Darby? What the hell do you think is happening here? You think you can just show up and tell me to leave town? Are you fuckin' crazy?"

"Yep."

"Fuck you!" he screamed. He stood up. "I run this show, you piece of shit! Me! If you think for one second—"

My first punch knocked him out. It had only happened three or four times and it always surprised me. I looked up from his twitching body at Becky, who looked up at me at the same time. We stared at each other.

"Okay, now you sit," I said, pointing to where Hank had been. "I hope you're a little more reasonable."

She sat.

"What's this about? Hank rip you off?" Her big eyes were sad and tired. "We don't have shit, man." Then she focused on me. "You're the guy came into the diner the other night."

"Sorry."

"Jesus. I lead you here? You follow me that night?"

"Nah." I sat down next to her. "Listen to me. Hank got mixed up in some serious bad news. He stays here in Portland, well. He's dead. But you know how he gets. Hardheaded. Guy thinks he knows the score. But not this time."

"What'd he do?"

"Set up a friend of mine. It won't work. The jig is up."

"I wasn't lying when I told you we were moving," Becky said. Her eyes welled up with tears. "We gotta get the fuck outta this place."

"He never told you where the money was coming from, did he?"

"Music," she whispered. "He said he made it in the music world. But I knew it was bullshit."

"It is. He ever mention me? I'm Darby Holland."

"No way." Her teary eyes widened. "Y-y-y-you're the guy, you, you fuckin' broke up the band!"

"What?"

"Empire of Shit, man! You got them mixed up in some kind of robbery at a Mexican food restaurant! They've been fighting ever since!" Becky folded her arms. I couldn't help it, but the sudden pout was endearing.

"Well. I don't know what they would fight about. I mean, I paid them. I even bankrolled the record."

"And did you think about what that was gonna do to

them? Having dirt on each other?" She sniffed and narrowed her eyes. "Did you?"

"No."

"Every time they get in a fight about the dumb shit a band gets in a fight about, that night comes up. 'You did this' and 'you did that.' You wouldn't even believe how bad it gets."

Hank moaned and stirred. We both looked.

"I'd believe it."

"Shit." She shook her head.

"Why don't you take the car and the money?" It came to me suddenly. "Just go. I'll tie up the dumbass and gag him. You pack. Call my cell when you run out of dough and I'll send you more. You gone, Hank has no reason to try to run his burn."

"Nothin' is ever that easy." She said it like she wished it was. "We're in love."

"Maybe. Sure. But love comes and goes. You love him enough to let him die for trying to get together enough money for a new life? Or do you love him enough to split so he can live? Only two choices."

Becky stared at me for a long time.

"You motherfucker," she whispered.

I shrugged.

Twenty minutes later, Becky was gone, with the understanding that if she ever showed up in the Pacific Northwest again, I'd kill Hank personally. She was to call from a bank in California tomorrow. I'd call the bank back to verify where she was and then I'd wire more dough if I had any. I took her phone, too, so that Hank wouldn't be able to coax her back in the near future.

Hank snored while she packed. I left him like that, with her goodbye letter taped to his forehead.

I left the with confusing feeling that I was on a winning streak. The shit had hit the fan in a massive way. Delia was going to—I had no idea what she was going to do. Before I left Hank's, I found his phone and broke it into ten tiny pieces. Becky took all their dope and the two hundred bucks they had in a sock. So one part of the huge mess I was in was officially on fire.

Things were moving.

There were no cabs on Alberta, so I took the bus downtown. Midday it was mostly empty. I sat in the back and looked at my phone. On impulse, I called Santos.

"*Hola,*" he answered suspiciously.

"Hey, dude. It's Darby."

"What up, white man." He didn't ask about the feds. Too cool.

"I wanted to talk to you about the car you stole."

"Oh." Sudden darkness. "What about it? I sold it."

"I know. I was wondering if you found anything in it before you did. We searched it, but we didn't use a microscope. Guy who bought it? I bet he did."

"Maybe," he agreed. "I can ask, but the answer might cost money. And I don't mean my money."

"Knew you'd say that."

"Well, now I did."

"Okay. One more little thing. My friend Delia."

"The lady with the mouth?"

"That's her. I was wondering if you can find a way to waste some of her time today."

"No fuckin' way, man." Now he was irritated.

"It's important. Maybe take her to the car guy and they can talk. Anything."

"Dude." I could almost hear the wheels spinning in his head. "Dude. Gimme the whole juice. You send me off on a babysitting gig with half the facts and I will fuck shit up."

I thought. The bus made it to Interstate and took a left. We were down to me and the driver.

"Okay. Santos, I gotta trust you here. Delia's fiancé is a wad named Hank. He's going to exit the scene. Most likely. But it's like this. He shows up? The shit will hit every green light rolling through Crazytown. She's busy, there's a chance he'll cool off and consider his options. But a twenty-four-hour window of Delia running down a dead-end road would help me out in a big way."

"What did you do? Out with it."

I sighed. "Fiancé is having an affair. I convinced the woman to leave town. Gave her money and a car. Plus, I kinda kicked the guy's ass. I only hit him once, but . . . ah shit. You had to be there."

"Ah!" Now he was delighted. "You want me to act a chaperone! I'm flattered, man. Really." He yawned. "Like, really."

"Good. I'll text you her number. Call her now and set it up fast. She's doing shit at the moment, but the minute she's done, Operation Goose Chase, charming Santos at the wheel. I owe you one."

I hung up and sent him Delia's number. It was an emergency solution, but there was a slim chance Delia would find out something. If Riley was going for her instead of the Lucky, he'd have mean little Santos to deal with too. I had a window of maybe five hours before roads began to converge. The Hank and Delia collision was imminent, and Santos as referee/bodyguard was maybe not the best play. Dessel and Pressman and the loose cannon Agent Lopez had something cooking, and the crosshairs on my back were palpable. My next best play was to pay a visit to my banker and business partner.

The bus let me out in the transit chute on Sixth. I tried to stay dry under the awnings and made my way to Alcott Frond. The sidewalks were thick with the early edge of commuter foot traffic. When I got to the restaurant, I looked for the Prius but it was nowhere to be seen. Pressman and Dessel had abandoned their post.

Santiago was in his office. I nodded to the bartender and followed his eyes to the door. The restaurant was in perfect shape for dinner. Tables set, three waiters and two waitresses going over something with the kitchen staff, and a few early drinkers already at the bar. I knocked on the office door and Santiago let me in, a troubled expression on his face.

"Sit," he directed. I did. He went around his desk and sat as well, tapped at his computer.

"Gimme the weird news."

"Most of your accounts are frozen. That's the good news. The feds froze two of them and then I froze the rest when I heard about the U-Store-It. The bad news is that your cards are dead. All of them."

"And I just gave all of my money to a junkie."

He looked up and raised an eyebrow.

"Long story. How do I get my hands on some cash?"

"You're still rich, but right now? You can't."

"Loan me some money?"

"Course. How much you need?" He took his wallet out.

"Couple hundred. In case I meet a wino or something."

He gave me four, everything he had. "For now we'll have to do it like this. You have money coming in from the shop, but don't deposit it anymore. Keep records, but for now, until I can figure out how to open these channels again, that's your personal operating capital. You need more, come ask me. Cool?"

"I guess."

"Hungry? I am." He got up. "Something you have to try." He went out and closed the door behind him. I took my phone out and steeled myself, dialed Delia. Straight to voicemail. Relieved, I called Dessel.

"Darby," he answered. "I hope this doesn't mean our psychic connection is becoming stronger. I was just about to call you."

"My accounts are frozen, there's no eyes on the Lucky, and I just knocked out Delia's fiancé."

"Sweet Jesus."

"Yep."

"The wedding is, Darby, it's in less than three weeks, right?" In the background I heard Pressman say "Aw shit, he did what?"

"No wedding now."

"Ah. Well." Dessel's prude kicked in. "Hmm. Your accounts. That was Lopez. Standard procedure in a flight risk situation, did it before we could stop her. It's a formality, but for the next forty-eight, the microscope is on. I can try to get her to back down, but we're thinking that she's not going to give too much more. You're a scumbag, in the best possible way, don't get me wrong, and me and Bob are dicks. She isn't keen on any of us."

"S'okay for the moment, but this is Riley's dream. I'm almost broke. One of his key ingredients."

"It's temporary, but I sympathize. If it's any consolation, we think this is almost over. In the, ah, the videos, dealing the subject a crippling financial blow always came right before the end." He paused. "That didn't come out right. Sorry." And he was sorry. I could hear it in his voice. "You've been broke before. And his shit is backfiring in an unexpected way on another level. No way he could have predicted we'd be on the same side."

"Hmm. Where'd you guys go?"

"Lopez came up with a list. The cell at the U-Store-It was calling back and forth to the industrial shit zone out by the steel mill. The signal scattered into the entire peninsula, but there were eleven new rentals out there in the past five months. We're pitching in. Off the books means low manpower. As in the three of us."

"Happy hunting."

"It's so lovely out here, Darby. All this tin shining in the rain, the dark fields of mud, the smokestacks. Where are you, as in why aren't you out here helping us?"

Santiago entered and kicked the door closed behind him. He was carrying two plates. Oregon chanterelles with shaved truffle piled over what looked like one large ravioli in the center of each dish.

"Lamb," Santiago mouthed.

"Dessel, I'm neck deep in the shit, amigo. Grueling action on my front too. You find anything, call me right away."

"Roger that."

I put my phone away. Santiago was already eating.

"What's the plan?" he asked.

I told him about Hank. He listened while I ate and talked. When I was done, he pushed his empty plate back and put his giant arms behind his head.

"So, what's the plan?" he asked again.

"This whole thing is set to blow on every side," I confessed. "I'm going to try to survive."

"Ah."

"Yeah."

"Wine?"

"Sure."

He went and got a bottle of something red and expensive and we drank from expensive glasses. After he poured, he saluted me.

"Darby, I've gotten the feeling that it was the last time I was ever going to see you more often than with everyone else I've ever known combined."

"Hear, hear." I saluted him back. "Be on the lookout, man." I drained the glass. "Terrible time for this place to be blown up or for you to catch a bullet. I might need more money."

From Frond I went to the shop. Flaco stuck his head out and stopped me as I passed the taco alcove.

"You get the car?" He looked both ways. "What happened to it?"

"Gone."

"Figures. You hungry?"

"Nah." Then I thought about Dessel and Pressman, out there chasing down my phantom. Another long night in the Prius for them, and all to check the "no" box on a list of addresses. "Know what? Can I get ten juniors in a go bag? And two lime sodas."

"Bring it over?"

"I'll pick 'em up in five."

He nodded and ducked back in. I skipped from his awning into the shop. Chase was talking on his cell, and one of the new guys was tattooing a stoned hipster kid. I smiled pleasantly at both of them and gestured for Chase to join me in the back. I went and sat down at the chair behind my desk and tried Delia again. Straight to voicemail. Santos had her doing something interesting. So interesting that she'd turned her phone off.

Or Hank had found her, and she wasn't taking any calls.

"Boss," Chase said. He closed the door behind him and sat down on the red couch.

"Delia come in tonight?"

"Yep. She was all dressed up, too. Like, for court. She watched the feds for a while, bitched about one thing or another. Got something out of her station, bag of weed I think. I dunno. Why?"

"No reason. What about Hank?"

"Nope."

"Right on. For the time being, I need everyone to start making daily deposits, top drawer of my desk." I patted my desk. "I'll pick them up in the mornings. Fuckin' feds have my accounts locked up for the next little bit."

"Happens." He shrugged. "How goes the war? You find your shithead?"

"Not yet. He's gonna make his move and I'll nab him in the confusion. New guys still freaking out?"

"Aw yeah." He made a dismissive gesture. "I told them that shit was crazy right now because of the wedding, this and that, bullshitted them back down to zero. They're okay for the moment."

"Thanks."

He shrugged again.

"Your feelers turn up anything?"

"I was just talking to a guy, actually. Used to tattoo with him in New York. He's game to come and slay ass if people jump ship. Marko Sloan."

Another tattoo guy with a phony name. "One less thing to worry about."

We chatted for another minute, then I called Dessel again.

"Darby. Tell me you're bringing us coffee."

"Tacos," I said. "Where you at?"

He gave me an address. "Lopez thinks this is the most likely place, though even she isn't hopeful. Empty warehouse but the power is on. She's watching it to see if anyone shows and we're watching her."

"You guys are sitting in different cars?"

"Bad blood at this point."

"Should I bring her tacos, too?"

"I don't think that'd be a good idea. In fact, as good as those tacos sound, maybe you should hang back for now. Bob agrees. I'll call if we sight Santa or the Tooth Fairy." He hung up.

"Taco night!" I called out.

Chase made a yipping call back. The new guy didn't.

"You gave the car to a woman you barely know." Flaco shook his head. "Darby, following this line of reasoning, I must ask you. May I have some money? As much as you feel comfortable with. Not a loan. I mean a gift. Like the gift you gave to the heroin waitress with the pretty eyes."

"I'm broke." I raised my lime soda to him. He looked started.

"You owe me thirteen dollars! Tacos don't grow up on trees!" He tried to snatch the bag back. I grabbed it and stepped away.

"You still owe me. Besides, this is for the guys. Chase will pay you later."

Flaco narrowed his eyes. I was about to lecture him about the dog Bella and having to buy the shovel myself when my phone chimed. I took it out and flipped it open. A short text from Dessel.

"Lopez gone. Bring tacos."

I rolled my eyes.

"I'll pay you tomorrow," I said. "I have to deliver these after all. Fuckin' hundred-dollar cab ride, too."

"You gave away your car too?"

I hailed the first cab and hopped in with the tacos and a

single soda. I gave the driver the address and took out my phone.

"You sure about that?" he asked after he punched it into his deck. "That's way out there in total nowhere, man."

"I'm sure."

He shrugged and away we went. I tried Delia again and it went straight to voicemail. Then I called Santos. He answered on the first ring.

"You get her?" I asked.

"No, dog. We talked and she told me to meet her at this woman Biji's house. We're chillin' and watching Netflix. No Delia." He lowered his voice. "But Biji is rad, dude. I mean, she's like, I mean—"

"Shit."

"I know, man. You call her, ah, the dude, the ah—" He couldn't talk in front of Biji. Good. He hadn't spilled anything.

"Broke his phone. So no calls there? No nothing?"

"We're waiting, man. S'all I got."

"Call me as soon as she shows up."

Then I stared out the window. Delia had gone from her appointment to the shop, talked to Santos, then gone radio silent. A nervous tingle radiated from my stomach. She knew. Hank had whipped up some bullshit story. He might have told her he wanted to elope. There was an outside chance she was in the trunk of Riley's car. I rubbed my face.

"You goin' to work or something?"

"What?" I looked at the driver's eyes in the mirror. He pointed at the phone mounted on his dash.

"Steel mill. Couple factories out there. Just wondering."

"Ah. No, I'm dropping off dinner for a friend." The second the word "friend" left my mouth an electric jolt went through me. The driver nodded.

"Gonna take us maybe another twenty-five to get all the way out there. Mind if I DJ some tunes for us?"

"Go ahead."

He went with Nick Cave. I took my phone out and stared at it. Time to kill. I knew what I should do, but I didn't want to do it. But soon I'd have Dessel and Pressman breathing my air, so I took my little phone book out and dialed.

"Hey baby," I said.

"Baby, is it?" Suzanne made her disappointed cluck. "What's shakin'? This your one call from county? Or did your old phone get lost in a bar?"

"Nope. I'm in a cab. Thought I'd call. I was wondering if you were in the bath."

"Where you going?"

"Have to drop off tacos. Then, I dunno. Shit went down with Hank and Delia that might not be good."

"Bummer." She wasn't even faking it. She really didn't care.

"It happens. Greedy guy that I am, I wanted to make sure we weren't breaking up too. Sort of all I can think about and I really have tons of other shit to think about."

"Is that supposed to be charming in some way?"

"Let me try again. I know I've been a handful. Ton of shit going on and me and you always reach this point where I don't feel like I can communicate without judgment. But

I still want this to work. I still totally love you. You're my super tall woman. Sorry I hung up on you. I didn't want you to come, but I changed my mind. We can leave as soon as you get here. I'll meet you at the airport. You won't even have to go through security. Just, like, one plane to the next."

The driver glanced in the rearview, back to the road. Suzanne didn't say anything, so I tried again.

"Remember the first time we went to the movies? Like on a corny date that had nothing to with anything?"

"I don't remember what we saw," she said. "We snuck in beers in my purse."

"We didn't really watch the movie. It was January. Cold as fuck. You were wearing a green scarf and your nose was red."

"You groped me."

"You groped me, lady. Let's get it straight."

She sighed. "Why can't we get that back?"

"We can."

We drove. The driver was uneasy. He didn't want to turn the music up and drown me out, because then I wouldn't be able to talk. So he was forced to listen to my version of pillow talk.

"We can't argue anymore, Suze. Neither of us ever wins. We have to shoot for a balance, a middle ground. And there's enough room in that middle ground for both of us."

"You're right," she said. "But don't take that as a concession. I'm simply stating my understanding of the obvious."

"I have to get out of this place," I said. I stared out the

window. We'd left the pretty New Portland behind and gone into the environs of yesterday's industry. "I have to."

"We can go away together, right? You said it yourself."

"I hope so." I tried to hear her background but the music was too loud. It occurred to me that it would be great for us to go away somewhere together. On the off chance that Riley knew where she was and had a plan to mess with her head. "Remember that first weekend? We went out to the coast? Got a little grill and put it out on the balcony?"

"We didn't put pants on for three days."

"Let's go there again. Say yes. The wedding fiasco has reached the boiling point. I have to take a break from all this and we need the time. Just me and you. The wind and rain and no people. We can figure out what to do and then do it right."

Silence. Then, "Okay. When?"

"Meet you at the airport tomorrow night? We roll straight from there in a rental? My car is in the shop."

"You got a date, Darby Holland. You better bring me flowers."

"Oh, I will. I will." I made a kissing sound and hung up. Then I looked at the driver's eyes in the rearview. "Can I help you?"

"N-no," he stammered.

It was the best play, I realized. Vanish completely for a few days while the rabid Agent Lopez and Dessel and Pressman did their thing. Subtract Suzanne and guard her myself. It they didn't have a bead on Riley Wharton by the time I was supposed to come back, then I wouldn't come back at all. I'd come clean to Suzanne and turn over a new leaf. As soon as my accounts were free, we'd move to somewhere she could make a living in and I could do whatever. Hide more. I'd always been hiding.

Shit had a way of working out. Now all I had to do was make it happen. Riley was obsessed with the whole notion of "the one who got away." It had driven him for years, for as long as I'd been driven to hang out in Old Town. Times change. I was finally going to change with them.

Riley was going to hate this plan. They all were. Except for me.

The driver let me off under a lone street lamp by the Prius.

I tipped him extra for the long ride to nowhere. When he was gone, I waited by the car. They were off taking a leak or doing their peeping Tom routine, but if they'd found anything the entire empty street would be full of cop cars. After a few minutes I was wet enough to seek shelter, so I drifted over to the nearest building and stood in the entryway. It was an electroplating place. Another few minutes went by and I got a sudden sinking feeling that they'd joined up with Lopez and headed off to a Denny's. I took my phone out and dialed Dessel. Nothing. Then I tried Delia again. Nothing there, either.

The taco bag was wet. I put it down in front of the electroplating place and headed out into the rain in search of Lopez's car. It was one block down, a bland black two-door Taurus, and the only way I knew it was hers was because of the four coffee cups and the ashtray. I looked around. From where the car was parked, the driver would have a good view of the empty parking lot of a lone metal building that looked like a hangar. I walked over to it. Old, weathered aluminum, easily three stories tall, and dirty. The entry was in an alcove full of dead leaves and old newspaper.

The plexiglass window in the dented metal door was

scratched and filthy, but I put my face up to it and shaded my eyes to get the streetlight glare off. Black inside. Then, just as I was about to pull away, there was a faint flash of blue. I tested the door.

It was unlocked.

I slowly opened it and slipped into the darkness inside, closed it silently behind me. Ahead, I could hear voices, too soft to make out. I crept forward. As my eyes adjusted I could make out some of the crap around me. A forklift with a tarp over it. Barrels. The voices were coming from a doorway about fifty feet away. I moved toward the sound, my arms out, silent as a ghost. Halfway there I stopped and dropped into a crouch.

The voice coming from the room ahead was mine.

I took my phone out and flipped it open. In the dim glow from the screen I could see maybe five feet around me. I kept it pointed away from the sound of my voice as I searched for a weapon. Nothing. Nothing. Then an open toolkit filled with rusty junk. I took out an old screwdriver.

"*Darby, don't ask me to lie to a friend of mine.*" Jane the bartender's voice.

"*—like your friend Darby, owner of the Lucky Supreme Tattoo Parlor in Old Town, co-owner of Racy, and big investor in Alcott Frond, is being stalked by the guy in this photo. Even hundred for you for asking. Even hundred for him for asking his pals. Even five for whoever gets me a room number in the next hour, plus free dinner at Alcott for you, Barry, and the lucky concierge.*" Me, talking my way into finding the hotel room.

"*Barry likes blow.*" Jane again.

I peered around the corner.

Dessel and Pressman were sitting in chairs, looking at the screen, their arms tied behind them. In the flickering light I could see that they'd both been beaten. Dessel was bleeding heavily on the left side of his face and his eye was swollen shut. There was a pool of blood under Pressman's chair and he was listing to one side. Lopez was facedown in front of them, contorted at an unnatural angle. She was dead, half her head blown away.

"And a gram of blow for Barry. I can have some delivered in the next ten minutes by bike messenger." Me again. Making a drug deal.

"Just in time," Riley boomed from somewhere out of sight. "Sit, Darby, sit! They were just watching the opening credits!"

Shaking, Dessel turned his head in my direction. He mouthed the words "kill him" and then his head sagged to the side.

"What the fuck, psycho!" I roared. I took a step toward Dessel and something loud ratcheted, like a shotgun attached to a contact mic.

"Stop."

I stopped.

"Look at the screen."

"No." I dropped the screwdriver. "Not unless we look at it together, Riley. You have a gun. I don't. We watch whatever sick thing you made together. And then you kill me. Or you kill me now and I never see your Oscar-winning final film."

Riley Wharton stepped out of the shadows, a shotgun

in his hands. He smiled. I squinted and studied his face. There was a long, old scar trailing from his hairline to his right ear. I smiled.

"My scar is way cooler than yours," I said. I stepped closer to him, my hands raised. "Still can't pull off cool, eh, boy?"

"Keep it coming," Riley prompted. "Let it all out."

I gestured at the feds. "You think these people were my friends? You jackass. I hate these fuckin' dudes. They hate me. Your best play was to watch them work my case to the end and then do a prison flick with shankings and what-not, but you're not even that creative."

"I'm not going to kill them because they're your friends, Darby." Riley grinned. "I'm not going to kill them at all. You are. You already did. I have your fingerprints, and they're all over all kinds of interesting things."

"Ah." I nodded. "Framed. Interesting. It's been tried before."

"And then there's the movie." He kept the shotgun on me one-handed, finger on the trigger, and took a remote from his pocket. Then he tossed his head at the screen. "Watch. Watch or I shoot Dessel in the hip. I already showed them the first few minutes and they loved it. I don't think they'll mind if we rewind."

The screen was a tattered plain of off-white plastic, streaked with soot at the edges. It was big, though. I looked at it. It flashed, and then the movie played.

MIDNIGHT RIDER PRODUCTIONS PRESENTS

DARBY HOLLAND

CRIMINAL WITH A CRAYON

The opening shot was Suzanne. She was on the front porch of my house. I guess I wasn't there. It's night. Raining. She makes a call on her phone. A cab comes and she gets in.

Suzanne standing over me, looking down. I'm in the alcove in front of Ming's Shoe and Boot Repair. Passed out. Another sleeping bum. She nudges my foot. I don't wake up. Cut to Suzanne at the airport at sunrise. I can tell she's been crying all night. She looks so tired. I can also tell that it happened at the very beginning of fall. In the last month.

She'd come to see me and I never even knew.

Cut to me and Hank outside the tuxedo place. He's laughing and I'm glaring at him. The camera slides to Agent Lopez, who is taking pictures of us a half a block away.

Cut to me sitting across from Pressman and Dessel in the café where I told them the fishing story. My face is moving at faster than triple speed as I talk. Then I get up and leave and the footage drops back into real time. Dessel and Pressman stare at the door, then look at each other.

"My God, he's crazy," Dessel says. Pressman shrugs.

"I say we kill him. Game over. Darby's gone where you don't come back from."

They look out the window again.

Smash cut to me in the bar downtown, talking to Paco the bike messenger/drug dealer. Both of us are smiling. Then cut to me going to the elevator. Me in the hallway, going into Oleander's room. Then me lying on the bed, staring at the ceiling.

Cut to Paco in the same hallway with his girlfriend. They knock on the door and it opens. They go in.

Cut to them with duct tape on their mouths. She's already dead. Someone wearing a coat just like mine is drilling into Paco's head with a Makita. The entire hotel room is enshrouded in plastic.

I closed my eyes.

"Open your eyes!" Riley thundered. "We're just about to get to the best part!"

I turned to him. I shook my head. The movie kept going, but we were watching each other now. Riley turned the shotgun on Dessel and pressed it to the back of his head. Dessel roused. He knew what was happening. I could see it in his one good eye when he turned.

"Darby," he said quietly. "I always admired you. The whole time." He managed a bloody smile. "You always get your guy." He tried to shrug. Riley pulled the trigger and most of Dessel's head went away. Then he turned the shotgun on me and ratcheted in another round.

"I'll leave this film," he said. "If you survive the gutshot I'm about to dole out, it's life in prison with a colostomy bag. And I'll pay, too. To keep you alive in there. Because I'll pay every tormented pervert to make you suffer a thousand hells before you find a way to hang yourself. And I'll film it all. And when I'm done and you're dead and gone, years from now? Why, I think I'll show my masterpiece to Suzanne." He tossed his head at the screen. "This is just the trailer. Real movie won't be done for years."

The first shot rang out and my hands went to my stomach. I looked up. Riley's face twisted, and an expression of wonder filled his eyes. He tried to turn as Delia stepped out of the shadows. She pulled the trigger a second time and the bullet caught Riley high in the chest. In that last second, he turned back and pulled the trigger on the shotgun, but I was already gone. Delia's third round blew the back of his head off and he fell right on top of me. I'd grabbed the screwdriver and rolled in, but I never got to stab him.

I pushed his body off of me and rose. Delia lowered her gun and we stared at each other.

"I-I-I—" she stuttered.

"Holy shit," I breathed.

"I was at the shop." Her face was so white she glowed in the dark. The movie was still playing. "I was sure Dessel was hiding something. They left in a hurry and I followed them. Got this gun out of my station before I left. Then they came in here. I heard voices. I snuck in through the back window." She looked down at Riley's body. "He was setting us up, Darby. Both of us. I'm just collateral damage, but, but, I had to hear the whole thing. I had to go to jail to ensure that the Lucky died. He had to kill your luck, too."

"I, ah, I don't know—" I stopped. Delia dropped the gun.

"I feel so sick," she whispered.

Pressman moaned. Delia jerked at the sound like someone had touched her heart with a live wire. I rushed to him just as he raised his head.

"Bob!" I cradled his bloody face with my bloody hands. The movie was still playing, and something scarlet and gory was playing. The light of it on his face was terrible. "Bob!"

"Call 911," he whispered. "I know what happened but I'm bleeding out."

"Delia! 911!"

She jerked into action. Pressman whispered something. I leaned in to catch it.

"F-frame is in," he breathed. "G-g-get the video and r-r-run. Run, Darby. Take Delia and run f-for your lives." He gasped then and I pulled away. His eyes widened. "I'm so sorry." And then his head dropped. I felt his pulse. Weak and irregular.

"We gotta go!"

"What!?" Delia lowered the phone.

"We gotta run! Now! Or we go down! Get the tape!"

I searched Riley's body and found his phone, pocketed it. Then I turned to the projection screen and my heart went to ash. There was Hank, tied up and unconscious, the Dear John letter taped to his head. Riley had been following me again. The movie stopped and the room went black as Delia pulled the tape. I spun and looked, but she hadn't seen it because she'd been fixated on the controls. She shone the light from her phone over the projector and then the light came back on. The screen was empty.

"Ambulance is on the way," she said quietly. "Officer down, multiple shots fired."

I grabbed her hand and we ran for it.

Delia's car was parked three blocks down with a view of the Prius. We got in and she started the engine. The sirens were already coming in. Lots of them. I lit a cigarette and puffed. I was covered in blood and it wouldn't light all the way. She watched, her white face spattered with red on one side, her eyes wide.

"I'll call Gomez and have him meet us," I said. "We have to go underground now until, until, I dunno."

"Darby." Delia blinked. "Darby. I'm pregnant."

It was still raining at sunrise.

Gomez, Flaco, Chase, Santos, and Santiago stood in a loose circle around us. We were in the parking lot behind the old Tastee Freez on Powell. It had closed two years ago, and whatever kind of authentic bagel shop or artisan cheese joint was going in to replace it was behind schedule. Gomez handed me the keys to the little white minivan.

"Not much," he apologized. "But it will get you there."

"It isn't raining in Ruidoso," Flaco added. The old man looked older than ever, a scarecrow. He smiled, and even his gold teeth had lost their shine. He took his wallet out and opened it, took out all the bills. "Here. Gas money. Fifty-two bucks."

"You guys don't have to do this," I said as I took it. Beside me, Delia nodded.

"There's an APB out on us," she said. "This makes you accessories."

"We're all accessories to all kinds of shit already," Chase said. He gave her a hug and turned to me. "I got the shop for as long as it takes, homie." He passed me a fold of bills. "Almost two hundred there. All I had on me when the call came in. I'll find a way to get more to you. There's always a way."

We didn't have any bags. Delia was wearing a change of clothes Santos had brought for her, the trashy duds of his latest new girlfriend, still asleep at his apartment. She would wake to find that her clothes had been stolen in the night, so another easy relationship ending easily for him. Santos was fine with it. I was wearing Chase's yellow tracksuit. Our bloody clothes from the night had already been reduced to ashes.

"I'll see you there in three days," Santos said. "You got enough money to make it?"

"Almost three hundred dollars." I nodded toward the van. "It only goes sixty, so maybe three tanks to get us there. Who has my cats?"

"I'm taking them," Santiago said. "Your house is surrounded by police cars, Delia's too. But I think I can get the cats once they're taken to animal rescue." The big man took his wallet out and gave me two hundred. "You got an even five bills now. Maybe stop and get some jeans and a T-shirt. I'll give young Santos here as much as I can before he heads out. Won't be much, I'm afraid. We all have to stay below the radar for a while."

"Any word on Pressman?" Delia asked. Her face was scrubbed clean. In the rainy morning light, she looked like a porcelain doll before it got to the face paint part of the assembly line.

"Still in critical condition," Santiago reported. "He's in a coma. He makes it through surgery, it's gonna be a long haul."

If Pressman made it, we had a chance. If he didn't, Delia and I were gone for good. I took a deep breath. All of them looked sad, even Chase. I didn't know he could make his face do it. Delia put her arm through mine.

"I'm cold," she said.

I shook hands with them, one by one, except for Santiago, who gave me a huge hug before he hugged Delia. While the Mexican Conan whispered to her, Santos and I conferred.

"You sure about this detour?" Santos seemed skeptical.

"Yeah, man. Gotta be done. Don't forget the note. And don't let her see you."

Santos was taking a different route to Ruidoso, New Mexico, than we were. He was going to meet relatives he had never met before, a distant branch of the Familia who worked in immigration. But before he went, he had to drive to the Oregon coast, to a lonely hotel, to deliver flowers to the door of the only room with someone in it. The note read "Sorry." Meeting Suzanne at the airport was out, but there was a chance that she'd go there looking for me. If she got it, it would be the last in a long string of notes I'd sent. A single word. It was all I could think of.

"Okay then." Santos clapped me on the shoulder. "Okay."

Delia got in the passenger side and I closed the door for her. I walked around and got in, started the engine, and without any final nods or tearful expressions, we left. Traffic was mercifully light, and we hit I-5 south without a hitch. Neither of us said anything when we passed the sign that told us we were leaving the City of Portland. To the south, the forest and condo theme gave way to farming and industry, so the view opened wide. Delia turned on the radio and flipped through the stations, then eventually turned it off.

"You sent a letter to Suzanne?"

"Kinda," I replied. "I was supposed to meet her at the airport in about an hour. We were going to this hotel on the coast. That's where I sent Santos."

"I turned my phone off yesterday," she said. "Someone kept calling and calling, had to be Hank. Different number, but no one else calls every two minutes. But I was trailing Dessel"—her voice caught—"and Pressman. Then I was hiding in that warehouse. Now my phone is in a trashcan. I never even got to say goodbye."

Delia started crying then, at first the kind of sobs that happen when you're trying to hold it in, then the kind that came when you stop trying and let it out. I waited through it until she was done. Then we were both quiet. About forty minutes later I saw a Starbucks sign, so we went through the drive-through. Delia got a decaf soy latte. I got two triple espressos and a chocolate chip cookie. Then we went to the edge of a parking lot and got out so I could smoke. No one was around for as far as I could see in any direction. The wind picked up. Once I'd fired up my smoke, I took a single puff and shot it off into the tall grass. Then we hugged each other.

"We're gonna be okay, little woman," I said. It came out confident, and I realized I believed it. Delia pulled back a little and looked up into my eyes.

"I wonder what kind of mother I'm gonna be," she said. "Hiding out in a trailer in New Mexico."

I kissed her on the forehead.

"A fuckin' good one."

She squeezed me. "You dumbass."

I squeezed back.

"I guess Riley got his wish," she murmured into my chest, "even if he didn't get to see the final director's cut." She leaned back and searched my face. We'd thrown the tape in the river without watching the rest. The gun Delia shot Riley with was registered to her. She was wanted for a murder she actually committed. I smiled and brushed the tip of Delia's nose with the tip of my index finger.

"He most certainly did not," I said easily. "I get to be a daddy."

Delia gave me a long look then. I didn't flinch.

"We better get going," she said finally, still staring into my eyes.

"I guess we better."

As soon as were back on the freeway, she turned a little in her seat and regarded me.

"I always wanted to go on one of your road trips," she said. "See the world through your Dollar Store sunglasses. Eat different tacos at new holes in the wall."

"Dreams come real every day, baby. We cross the state line, well. I have a vision. Ross Dress for Less. Commando raid. I've been practicing. We go in, get new duds, pay, and leave in less than four minutes. You up for it, pregnant lady?"

"Try me." It came out fierce.

"Fuckin' good. I don't know how Santos charmed the dress off a bank teller, but that outfit of yours is—"

"Whatever, MC Hammer."

"We have to get into character," I continued. "Weirdos running from the law in other people's clothes is too obvious. Tell you what. I'm going to be Dan Smathers. Hear me out! Smathers is a janitor, digs model airplane glue. Fly fishing. Big fan of *Lonesome Dove*, secretly enjoys watching *Friends*. Going to Vegas to, to, to—"

"To drop off his step sister Fanny Jean Olson. Fanny is going to a three-day seminar on dental hygienics. Smathers wants to play the nickel slots."

"And?"

"Fanny dreams of becoming a baker. She's especially into cake decoration. At night, she likes to lie on her kitchen table and use a squirt frosting thing to—"

"Fanny. Back to earth."

"Fanny likes dogs, but she'd rather have a pony."

"What's she wear? What's she charging into Ross to get?"

Delia considered.

"No-nonsense tight-in-the-butt blue jeans. Underwear, because I'm not wearing any, cowgirl boots if they're less than thirty bucks, and a frumpy plaid shirt she can untuck and tie above the midriff for Karaoke Night down at the truck stop. Smathers?"

"Jeans. Long-sleeve phony Ross Polo shirt. Sandals. I already thought it out."

"Sandals! No one'll ever find us."

We were both quiet again after that, lost in our dreams of tomorrow. I'd never been to Ruidoso. Neither had Delia. Flaco and Gomez said it was in the mountains, and they both went on and on about a Hungarian restaurant they liked. The trailer that waited for us was an Airstream, used from time to time to shelter small illegal migrant worker families shuttling up to the Willamette Valley for fruit-picking season. It had some land. It had a woodstove. Eventually, Delia cleared her throat and looked up from her still flat stomach.

"Darby, tell me a story. Tell me the story of the day you got to Portland. Broke and starving and running from the animals. Tell me what you did."

She wanted to hear the story so she would have some idea what would happen when we got to Ruidoso. I flashed her a smile and hit the cruise control, settled back.

"That's a good story, baby." I searched for the feel behind the words and it came instantly. "I'd lost it all. The future was totally uncertain. I'd tried to find a life of some kind, but it was all fire and ashes and the law and a pack of monsters were right behind me." I smiled at the open road. "But I was free, Delia. There was nothing weighing me down but the sky itself. And it was a good feeling. Clean and clear. I could breathe, and every drop of water was sweet as sugar." I looked over at her. "You ready for the rest?"

"I already know how it goes. But tell me again anyway."

Jeff Johnson is a writer, filmmaker, and tattoo artist living in the Pacific Northwest. He is the author of a memoir, *Tattoo Machine*, and the novels *Everything Under the Moon*, *Knottspeed*, the Deadbomb Bingo Ray Books, the Darby Holland Crime Novel series, and numerous optioned screenplays.